Terence McAdams' books seek to educate with plot-twisting narratives interweaving science, technology and history. His writing focuses on positive role modelling through richly-drawn characters. His doctoral research focused on girls' computer programming, and he advocates for girls in STEAM. Terence also writes technical examination papers for the International Baccalaureate and publishes many articles on technology, data analysis and education. Terence seeks to enlighten and engage readers about scientific advancements through intrigue.

To the people of Jeju Island who have made us welcome these past 10 years.

Terence McAdams

BIOCODE – ENDEAVOUR

AUSTIN MACAULEY PUBLISHERS™

LONDON ∗ CAMBRIDGE ∗ NEW YORK ∗ SHARJAH

A CIP catalogue record for this title is available from the British Library.

ISBN 9781035818822 (Paperback)
ISBN 9781035818839 (ePub e-book)

www.austinmacauley.com

First Published 2023
Austin Macauley Publishers Ltd®
1 Canada Square
Canary Wharf
London
E14 5AA

A huge thanks to Chrystene Rae for designing the cover artwork.

Table of Contents

Chapter 1
Sanjung Academy

Ciara Alinac screamed, not from pain but from panic. She found herself sitting on a hard metal chair with her arms and legs strapped down and no idea how she got there. She felt a tug on her hair when she tried to look around. A dozen electrodes were attached to her head, and a nearby EEG machine emitted a low-frequency hum. Movement caught her eye, but it was only plastic wrapping wafting back and forth.

Trying to make sense of her surroundings, Ciara saw a wall of empty animal cages on one side of the room. The fluorescent light bounced off the metal, forcing her to squint. An fMRI scanner dominated the centre of the room, and just past it was a ridiculous-looking MEG machine. There were also several hospital beds neatly aligned. She hoped one of them was not reserved for her.

A wave of fear that began in the pit of her stomach, rose up. Her muscles tightened, and her foot started to cramp. Panicking, she desperately tried to break free of the straps pinning her arms. They were designed to withstand immense forces and were too strong to break. Her blood pressure increased as her heart pounded in her chest. Why wouldn't the straps break? She screamed. Her arms burst free, the tensile-resistant cotton fabric left in tatters.

Ripping the electrodes from her hair, Ciara leapt out of the chair like an animal released from a cage. She looked for somewhere to run and spotted an emergency door. Before she'd taken a step, the floor dissolved, pulling her down, and a weightless feeling arose from the pit of her stomach. Suddenly, Ciara's body convulsed, jerking her awake. With her heart still pounding, she looked rapidly around. Where was she?

Raw emotions faded as reality returned. Instead of a lab, Ciara realised she was in a classroom. Fifteen other students sat upright, focusing on the teacher but occasionally looking down to make notes on their iPads. Ciara felt her heartbeat slow as normality resumed.

Just four weeks ago, Ciara's life was good, perhaps great. She lived with her aunt Jean and uncle John in the Oxford suburbs in the only home she could remember. One night, her aunt announced that they were moving to South Korea. They'd taken a job at Sanjung Electronics. No discussion! Nothing! Ciara had to pack her belongings and move countries. This was her third week at Sanjung Academy on Jeju Island, a private boarding school for students with exceptional gifts.

Dr Sanjung Kim invested $2 million in the project. Small change for the CEO of Sanjung Electronics, the global biotech company whose mission is to improve the quality of life for those less fortunate. Their corporate message of technology for humanity is known worldwide. Inevitably, there were military applications for their inventions.

Dr Kim's only living family was his daughter, Hana Kim, who was practically royalty in South Korea. Hana was beautiful, moved with poise and spoke with an English accent. She embodied the princess persona with her appearance and actions. Hana was a voice for animal rights and, through her charities, dramatically reduced animal cruelty in Asia. In an interview on CNN, she casually dismissed comments about her looks and fame. Instead, Hana asked that she be judged by her actions. She sat a few seats away from Ciara.

Looking around, Ciara felt a little self-conscious. She was the only Western student in the classroom. On her right sat Zixin Yang, the only friend Ciara had made since she arrived in South Korea. The boarding mistress, Ms Hamilton, had placed them together because both were international students. Ciara was grateful because she found it difficult to make friends, and Zixin, with her supreme confidence, was easy to like. Even if she lost her temper too quickly.

The girls had similar interests and exercised together on most days. Although both were 16, Zixin was much more worldly. As the daughter of a diplomat, she had moved from country to country. Her parents finally decided that she needed stability and sent her to boarding school to finish her education. Sanjung Academy was ideal because Jeju was only a one-hour flight from their home in Shanghai.

Sensing some tension in the room, Ciara snapped out of her daze. The teacher was looking for someone to solve a problem on the board. She prayed he wouldn't ask her, so she slumped down in her chair. She didn't exactly blend in

12

with her tall, athletic frame and striking blonde hair. Ciara's desire to avoid attention had nothing to do with her ability because she was a good mathematician.

After several seconds that seemed like minutes, one of the girls was chosen and strode forward to solve the matrix factorisation question. Ciara breathed a mental sigh of relief. The rest of the lesson went by uneventfully, and before she knew it, they were dismissed. Since it was the last lesson of the day, the students would return to the boarding houses to get changed. Typically, they would head off to their after-school co-curricular activities. Today, however, was the house competition.

As Ciara walked through the doorway, she felt her Sanjung-One watch tap her left wrist. Pausing to glance down, she read the notification. It was a reminder to meet with the school counsellor in five minutes.

She was about to rush to the appointment, but Zixin slid her arm inside Ciara's, interlocking them and stopping her from leaving. "Come on, we have the relay house competition at 5:30, and we need to warm up."

Breaking Zixin's hold, Ciara stopped walking. "I have a meeting with the counsellor first. It won't take long. I'll meet you at the stadium."

"Just skip it. Counsellors are for people without friends, and you have me."

"I have to go, Zixin. I don't want to get into trouble."

"How many times do I have to tell you my name is Zee-shun."

Ciara felt a little crestfallen. "Sorry."

Zixin laughed. "Just messing with you. Your pronunciation's fine. But seriously, you must be at the stadium on time, so tell Fernley you only have twenty minutes. Don't let us down, Alinac. I don't want to lose to Halla again." And with that, Zixin ran to catch up with a couple of other girls.

Hoping that the sooner she got there, the sooner she could leave, Ciara hurried down the stairs to the second floor. On the ground were purple footsteps that led to the counsellor's office. She approached the large glass door and saw a small waiting area on the other side. Ciara entered and sat down on an uncomfortable wooden chair.

On the walls were several signs in the Korean language, Hangul.

The signs reminded Ciara of the sterile laboratory from her vision. It wasn't just the signs. The first extinguisher in the corner was identical to the one in the lab. Both had instructions on a red background with thick white letters that said 소화기 in Korean and FIRE EXTINGUISHER in English.

The visions only started a few months ago. But in them, Ciara was doing something courageous or living a life beyond her reach. In one, she was lying on a sun lounger in a bikini on board a superyacht. A handsome officer was flirting with her. Yeah right! As if that was going to happen. Maybe she needed counselling to address her desire to be special?

Trying to think about something else, she looked around the waiting room. It was mostly empty—three seats and a water dispenser. The walls were busier and plastered with motivational posters.

"May your choices reflect your hopes, not your fears," proclaimed a loudspeaker shaped like a heart.

"You must be the change you wish to see in the world," announced a world lifted by many multicultural arms.

"It takes courage to grow up and become who you really are," exclaimed a sunflower with multicoloured hands instead of petals.

She cringed a little at the obviousness of the posters. Students who needed emotional support didn't need slogans. They needed meaningful guidance, and these statements trivialised the real problem. She wondered what type of person would choose to put them up. She found out when the school counsellor opened his office door and beckoned her in.

Mr James Fernley was a tall thin man in his mid-thirties. He had pale, waxy skin and hollow cheeks. His suit was new but hung from him like a robe, suggesting he'd recently lost several kilos. He had a mop of curly ginger hair, and his thick unkempt beard needed a trim. Either he didn't care about his appearance, or Captain Redbeard was his hero. Ciara had to stifle a laugh when she noticed the silver earring in one ear. Definitely the pirate.

As Fernley sat down, he stared unblinkingly at her. His eyes, like two sapphires, shone the brightest blue. Ciara had never seen a redhead with blue eyes. Weren't they always brown or hazel? There was something not quite right, not quite human about him. He evoked the kind of unease you felt when a computer-generated character wasn't quite human.

Ciara couldn't put her finger on it, but there was something familiar about him. The thought tried to surface but dissolved like smoke when she tried to grasp it.

"Please sit down, Ciara. I'm sorry it has taken so long to meet with you. Beginning of the school year and all that…" his voice trailed off. He had an upper-middle-class London accent. Again, his manner of speaking didn't seem to fit his appearance. She'd expected a west country lilt or a Scottish twang, not the voice of a privately-educated schoolboy.

Ciara sat on the only free chair, facing a large dark wooden desk. On it was an open laptop and phone. Fernley sat opposite on the far side. An antiseptic smell wafted towards her, carried on the air currents by the air conditioner. It was the kind you applied to cuts and bruises, although he showed no outward injuries.

"You may be wondering why we're meeting today?"

Before she had time to answer, he said, "All overseas students meet with me in their first few weeks. We know how difficult it is to settle in, so we build relationships early. Does that make sense?"

The question was delivered as a statement, but Ciara nodded anyway. He picked up his smartphone and asked, "Do you mind if I record this brief chat, Ciara? I use voice-to-text software. Much faster than writing notes."

"Not at all, Sir."

Fernley activated the voice application, and his phone gave a loud ping. "It says in my notes that you didn't know you were coming to Korea until a week before the start of term."

Ciara nodded.

He placed his fingertips together as if in prayer and smiled. "It must all be a little bewildering. Perhaps I can fill in some of the gaps. Do you know much about Sanjung Academy?"

Ciara said she knew very little, so Fernley gave a well-practised speech. He explained that in 2010, the Korean Government decided to build an educational hub called the Global Education City or GEC, as the locals call it. The Jeju Province of Education chose the best educational institutions to construct international schools in Jeju. These schools would provide an alternative for parents who, in the past, sent their children overseas to be educated.

Dr Sanjung Kim, the wealthiest man in Asia, decided to build a school to rival and surpass the four international ones. A private institution for gifted and unique students. He discarded traditional curriculums and developed his own to promote creativity. A typical school week consists of two days of conventional lessons to acquire knowledge, two days of collaborative projects for problem-solving and two days of personalised learning.

Dr Kim bought 100 acres of the Gotjawal forest on the outskirts of the GEC and hired an award-winning architect to design a functional and beautiful school.

The state-of-the-art facilities included a sports stadium, an Olympic-sized swimming pool, an ice rink, and a theatre. An area in the middle of the forest was cleared, so the school could be surrounded by trees. With complete privacy, Sanjung Academy became something of a mystery. No website, no applications, and admission by invitation only.

Once his speech was completed, Fernley asked about Ciara's background. She explained that her father left when she was a baby. Shortly afterwards, her grief-stricken mother disappeared. She had no memory of her parents and had no interest in meeting them. Her aunt Jean and uncle John had taken her in. Since they had no children, Ciara grew up as an only child.

Every time she told her story, Ciara felt empty inside. What kind of person abandons their child, leaving a baby to fend for itself? If social services hadn't arrived, she would have starved to death. Like many people, when she was uncomfortable, she used humour to mask it. When Fernley asked about their house in Oxford, she joked that she slept in a broom cupboard under the stairs. He didn't seem particularly impressed.

Ciara's aunt and uncle were busy professionals who prioritised work, so they didn't do much as a family. Aunt Jean was a neuroscientist specialising in sleep research, while Uncle John taught software engineering. Both were professors at Oxford University before Sanjung Electronics headhunted them. Of course, they accepted. Their funding and salaries were doubled. They could focus entirely on research, with no graduate students to nurse through advanced degrees. Their niece's free scholarship at Sanjung Academy was the icing on the cake.

When Mr Fernley asked her how she was settling in, Ciara laughed. He looked at her quizzically, so she explained that she had burned pasta in the boarding house in her first week, and the alarm system had activated. A poorly translated recorded message blasted out in every building in the school.

"It felt like I was living in prison," said Ciara. "All of the doors automatically unlocked to release the students."

Ciara mimicked the emergency message, "The building was on fire. Take shelter in the emergency exit, orderly."

Mr Fernley laughed but then said in a more serious tone. "You do know that students aren't prisoners. They can lock and unlock their own doors. The automatic unlocking is for safety and speeds up the evacuation."

After ten more minutes of relaxed conversation, Ciara was allowed to leave. Fernley insisted that she book a follow-up appointment a week later. A sense of familiarity resurfaced, and she remembered what he reminded her of. An alien from an old science fiction film.

As soon as Ciara was out of earshot, Fernley dialled a number. "It's me." There was a slight pause while he listened, then replied, "Tall, athletic, pale skin, green eyes, and her hair is golden with a silver streak." He waited again, then said, "Yes, the sun and the moon." After almost a minute of silence, he ended the call.

The school campus contained five boarding houses. Four of them were named after Korean mountains—Halla, Jiri, Seorak, and Odae. The fifth was empty and referred to as the Ghost House. When Ciara first arrived at Seorak House, the house mistress had organised an icebreaker activity. Each girl had to say what their talents were. One girl had won a computer hacking contest, another was a world-class violinist, and a third was a Kendo Master. When they reached Zixin, she told them she was a black belt in three martial arts. Reluctantly, Ciara shared that she was the U17 Girls 100m UK champion. That was how she had ended up in Seorak's 4 × 100m relay team.

Tonight's event was one of many in the annual house competition. Every student took this contest seriously. It was more important than grades, which were everything to Korean students who would habitually stay up all night to revise. A trait that Ciara couldn't relate to.

The house competition leaderboard was proudly displayed in the school centre. The first event, capture the flag, took place in the first week of school. Halla beat Seorak in the final. A win tonight would move Seorak to the top of the leaderboard.

When Ciara jogged into the sports stadium, she was breathing deeply. It was a warm, muggy evening and nothing like the Autumnal weather she was used to in Oxford. Looking down at her watch, she noted that the race would start in 15 minutes.

As she crossed the brand-new track, she could feel the bounce in the polyurethane surface. Eventually, it would feel like running on concrete, but for now, it was perfect. Zixin waved, and spotting her, Ciara headed over to greet her and their teammates, Jimin and Sungho.

"We came third in the C race and second in the B race," said Zixin. "We have to win this race to win overall."

"Zixin thinks you should run the last leg," said Sungho. "She said you're the fastest runner in the UK. Is that right?" There was disbelief etched on his face.

In response to the accusation, for it was more than just a question, Ciara clarified that she was the fastest under-seventeen girl in the UK, not the fastest runner. Her time of 11.58, run into a headwind, was just 0.02 seconds slower than Jodie Williams' record, set in 2008. Ciara made no mention of this.

The house competition organiser was a PE teacher called Mike McGreggor. He was a short, thin Scottish man who never wore anything other than the school PE tracksuit. Despite his small stature, he had a deep resonating voice. "Relay teams come over here," he yelled. "Line up in the order you will run. The first-leg runner stands at the front. Anchor leg runners are at the back."

As they shuffled into the correct order, Ciara noticed Halla had three boys and one girl. She tapped Zixin on the shoulder, and when her friend turned around, she nodded at the Halla team.

Zixin's reaction was instantaneous. "What the hell are you doing with three boys?"

Halla's only girl, Hana Kim, said with a smirk. "Chan, here, identifies as she/her."

Outraged, Zixin advanced towards Chan but was beaten to it by Jimin, who shoved the Halla runner and hurled a stream of abuse in Korean. Ciara recognised one word only—씨발 (shi-bal).

Mr McGreggor pulled the two boys apart. "Calm down, Jimin. I realise this looks like a tactic to gain an advantage, but I checked with Seungchan's mother. She confirmed his, I mean her, wish to be recognised as she/her."

"Did you speak to her directly, or was it an email?" demanded Zixin, red-faced with rage. "She," pointing at Hana, "can get access to anything. All she has to do is ask her daddy."

Hana's response was to smile coolly, with the air of someone who knows they are untouchable. It made the situation all the more infuriating.

Speaking very calmly, McGregor said, "Be that as it may, young lady, it does not alter the fact that I have authorised Halla's team. Get back in line, or I will disqualify you."

Zixin swore in Mandarin and stomped back in front of Ciara. Then in a loud voice, McGregor called out, "All runners, go to your starting positions. You have three minutes to get ready."

As Ciara made her way to the yellow changeover line, she saw that Scottie Ngatai would be running against her. He was tall and handsome, with bronzed skin and a lovely smile. He hurried past her, then stopped and said over his shoulder, "Hey Ciara, I wanted to make sure you recognised me because you'll only see me from the back."

Ciara didn't respond. She'd competed against plenty of runners who'd tried to intimidate her. She chose to ignore him and focus on her routine. Ciara had spoken to Scottie once before. He mentioned playing on the wing in rugby. That meant he'd be quick. When she reached the yellow line, she saw that the other three runners were boys and smiled.

The gun sounded in the distance, and as Ciara watched the race unfold, she found it difficult to see who was winning. The mix of two girls and two boys led to extreme differences in each runner's speed. As the third-leg runners rounded the bend, Halla had a slight lead over Seorak. Scottie would receive the baton before her.

She started running when Sungho was ten metres away and hoped she had timed it right. Too soon, and he would never reach her. Too late, and they would waste valuable time on the changeover. She timed it perfectly and accelerated as soon as she felt Sungho place the baton in her palm.

She hit the straight after ten metres, but Scottie had pulled away. Ciara was still confident she'd catch him because only elite rugby players could hold top speed for more than fifty or sixty metres. Ciara pictured him tying up and going past him. Telling herself to focus on her running, she visualised the colour blue.

With her conscious mind busy, her subconscious controlled the rhythm. She could feel the tension fading and felt the extra speed that her body generated. Ciara became vaguely aware that, with each footfall, she was gaining. The crowd were roaring them on, but it was just white noise. With ten metres to go, Scottie's running had become disjointed. His rhythm had gone, and his stride had shortened. They crossed the line together, but Ciara finished faster, so it was hard to tell whether she'd passed him before or after the finish line.

The judges crowded over their video replays and awarded Seorak House the victory. Ciara's teammates jumped up and down, cheering joyfully. She glanced across at Scottie, who cut a forlorn figure. He must have sensed her gaze because he looked up and, with a wry smile, gave her a little wave. Was that humility? She wasn't sure. Then realising that she hadn't responded, she awkwardly waved back.

When they arrived back at the boarding house, they saw that Ms Hamilton had baked cupcakes. The party atmosphere didn't last long, though. There were two hours of study every night, and tonight would be no exception.

Ciara's uncle had taught her the basics of programming when she was younger, and she was keen to learn more. She had a machine-learning tutorial but struggled to install the necessary Python libraries. The online instructions for scikit-learn and NumPy were for an older operating system, so she kept getting an error message despite following the instructions perfectly.

Then Ciara remembered that SoYon Cho, or Sophie as she liked to be called, had won a hacking competition. It took five minutes for Sophie to install the libraries and fix the programming errors. Ciara was interested in the hacking competition Sophie had mentioned during the icebreaker activity, so she asked her about it.

"The challenge was to break into a locked mobile phone with a laptop. There were probably several ways to access the phone, but I went for the quickest. The laptop had a fingerprint scanner, so I extracted the fingerprint data and used that to open the phone."

Ciara was impressed. "You managed to do that under timed conditions?"

"Yes and no. Most movies depict hackers writing code to break into places. In reality, we write the programs in advance and then wait for an opportunity to use them. Some never use their programs. They sell them on the Dark Web. That's how they make their money. I wrote the program to extract the fingerprint data from the smartphone before the competition because I thought that might be one of the challenges. I put the software up for sale on the dark web, but it didn't sell very well. Smartphones changed from fingerprints to facial recognition because fingerprints are too easy to hack, so there wasn't a market."

Ciara and Sophie continued to talk for another hour or so. Like Ciara, Sophie was a loner, so it was nice to find a kindred spirit. They finally said goodnight and headed to their rooms. Ciara entered her bedroom. It felt like staying at a hotel. There was a single bed, a bedside table, and a writing desk. The only fixture was the empty box her Sanjung-One watch came in. Attached to the manila cardboard was a note from her aunt. She pulled it off and read through it again.

"Dearest Ciara.

Sanjung Electronics has been working on a new medical device. We thought that you were the perfect person to test it. It is called the 'Sanjung-One' at the moment. The name will probably change by the time it's released. The 'One' consists of a ring and a watch. You'll need to pair them with your phone.

It will record all of your vitals with a level of accuracy only available in medical-grade equipment. The batteries will last a week before they need recharging. The phone will automatically send your data to us, so please wear it night and day. Make sure you read the instructions thoroughly. It will take some time to learn all the features, but it will be worth it.

Best,
Aunt Jean."

There was nothing personal in the message. Aunt Jean was business as usual. After she'd first read the note, her excitement to test the new technology had gone. Ciara didn't like being a guinea pig.

She gazed admiringly at the watch on her wrist. The Sanjung One was beautiful with its brushed titanium alloy and small mountain symbol. The ring looked like one you would find in a high-end jeweller. It was impossible to tell that it contained electronics and sensors. All she did was install the app and open it. Pairing the devices had been automatic.

Picking up her phone, Ciara looked at her data. She'd burned 731 calories today. Spinning the dial to movement data showed that her top speed was 37 km/h in the relay. She continued to play with the app until she got too tired and went to sleep. She had the most unusual dream. Not only was it incredibly realistic, she saw everything through somebody else's eyes. A midshipman called William Hartley.

Chapter 2
The Transit of Venus

Tired from a long journey to Plymouth, 16-year-old William Hartley walked down Looe Street. The cobblestoned road was lined with timber-framed buildings crowding in on each side. He was looking for the Minerva Inn and spied the tavern halfway along. With hunger driving him forward, Hartley made his way to the small doorway. Ducking his head, he entered the public house for the first and the last time.

The room was dank and reeked of sweat and stale ale. Hartley's eyes slowly adjusted to the gloom to reveal thick timber beams crisscrossing the ceiling and a spiral staircase that probably led to private rooms. On one table sat a group of four drunken men. All were weatherworn and in their late thirties.

Hartley sat wearily at an empty table, and the innkeeper's daughter rushed over to serve him. She was pretty and looked two or three years younger than him. Hartley ordered a beer with some bread and cheese. The girl gave him a warm smile and promised to return quickly.

Hartley reached inside his jacket pocket and pulled out the naval letter he had received two weeks previously. He had been ordered to travel to Plymouth and report to First Lieutenant James Cook of the HMS Endeavour before the 1st of August 1768. Receiving a commission onboard a science expedition was a tremendous opportunity for a young officer. Despite his age, Hartley was determined to rise through the ranks quickly.

Not five minutes had passed before the door opened. Two naval officers strode in. Noticing the single epaulette on his shoulder, Hartley could see that the older one was a lieutenant. He was in deep conversation with his companion, a midshipman who looked around 19 years.

"Just this morning, 18 men ran off, so we are a tad short-handed. The captain will try to round up some men to complete our complement." A moment later, the lieutenant spotted Hartley. "I do not believe that we have had the pleasure."

Hartley's mouth was full of cheese and bread. He gulped it down without chewing and jumped to his feet, saluting. "Midshipman William Hartley, Sir."

"It is a pleasure, Mr Hartley. I seem to recall your name on the muster list. I am Lieutenant Zachary Hicks, and this is Midshipman John Bootie. We just arrived from the dockyard at Deptford."

"How goes the preparations, Sir?" asked Hartley.

"It's been hard going these past two months, but the Endeavour is now fully equipped. The captain has been most particular in the preparations. In addition to the usual provisions, we have loaded live sheep, ducks, chickens, a goat, a sow and piglets, and a boar."

Then Hicks added excitedly, "It will be an incredible adventure. I assume you have your orders with you?"

"Yes, Sir. They're here," said Hartley, pulling out an envelope again.

Hicks quickly read the orders and handed them back to Hartley. "Shall we sit, gentlemen?"

They promptly sat down. Hicks placed the paper bag he was carrying on the table. It gave a heavy chink of metal on metal. Bootie looked at the bag curiously but was too polite to ask. The lieutenant was genial and talked excitedly about the adventure ahead.

"We will set sail when the tides are favourable and reach Tahiti in Spring," said Hicks. He noticed Hartley eying the package on the table. "It's a bag of nails to take with me."

Puzzled, Hartley asked, "To what end, Mr Hicks."

Hicks did not answer the question directly, and a faraway look crossed his face. Instead, he described Tahiti with the love of a man returning home, despite having never been there.

"Tahiti is a paradise," he intoned. "Fruit hangs from trees in such abundance you could never go hungry. But that is not the best part. The island women are the loveliest in the world. They're slim with beautiful bronze skin, and love is their favourite activity. To gain favour takes very little courting. Nor do they have an interest in expensive jewels. Iron is enough to charm any woman."

To the relief of Hartley, the conversation proceeded pleasantly. These men would be his close companions for the next three years, and it was essential to get on well. And with that thought, he asked Hicks, "Do you know where we will journey once we leave Tahiti?"

"Alas," said Hicks. "Not even the captain knows the answer to that. His orders are sealed in an envelope with strict instructions not to open until after we depart Tahiti."

Before he could probe some more, a young girl's scream pierced the air. One of the rough-looking men had a tattooed arm around the innkeeper's daughter, pulling her onto his lap. His thick wrinkles and craggy skin were smoothed a little by the malevolent smile on his face.

Legs flailing and desperately trying to break free, the girl screamed, "Laissez-moi passer." Then followed it in English, "Let me go."

The landlord ran out of the kitchen, holding a cleaver, and looked around for the source of the commotion. He went as white as a sheet when he saw the man and his three companions, lowered the weapon, and then awkwardly tried to hide it behind his back.

"Mr Moody, Sir. How can I help you?"

Samuel Moody was a former seaman turned petty criminal. A drunkard with a violent temper and known to act on a vendetta. The last person to upset him was found in an alley with his throat cut.

The girl had stopped trying to escape Moody's grasp when she saw her father's reaction. Apart from her bottom lip quivering, she was frozen in fear.

"You're a damn Frog," spat Moody.

The hatred of the French had not lessened, despite Great Britain and Prussia's victory over France and Spain five years previous. A French man would not live long in an English seaport like Plymouth. Sailors had long memories, and many had suffered in the seven-year war.

The situation was about to turn ugly. Abruptly, Hartley stood up and strode across the room. He addressed Moody. "Let the girl go, or you will regret your lack of manners."

Moody went from astonishment to anger in a split second. He turned towards Hartley, a sneer etched on his weathered face. "Sit down, boy. Unless you're looking to die before you've reached puberty."

Hartley's voice quivered ever so slightly, but he was steadfast. He pulled a sword from his belt. "It is you who will do the dying."

The four cutthroats burst out laughing. But that only lasted a second. They leapt to their feet and pulled blades from their belts. The girl was released and scuttled off to hide behind her father. In response, Hicks and Bootie jumped to their feet to stand at Hartley's side.

"Our friends here need have no part in this," said Hartley. "You and I should step outside where one of us will die. But before then—" He stopped mid-sentence and turned abruptly to the landlord, "Bring everyone here a pot of beer. We should have one last drink before I kill this man."

Moody turned to his men, who nodded approval. Why risk their necks? Besides, they got free beer. "Very well, boy. You look like you need some courage," said Moody.

The landlord came rushing back with a beer-laden tray. Hartley took it from him and served Moody and his men. Taking one more pot from the landlord said, "Your health, gentlemen!" Then glanced at Moody and said, "Well, perhaps not yours."

They all gulped down the drink. Moody was the first to notice something at the bottom of his pewter pot. It was a round and metal shilling, with the bust of King George looking up at him.

"You four men have accepted the King's coin, and in his name, I enlist you to serve on the HMS Endeavour."

A gang of ten men exploded out of a hidden door in the spiral staircase. Moody and his cronies were quickly subdued. A tall, slim lieutenant strolled out after them. He was, perhaps, 40 years of age but still handsome with piercing brown eyes. He had a distinguished look affected by a long straight nose.

"That was clever thinking—dropping those shillings in each of their pots. I wondered how you were going to get out of your predicament."

"Thank you, Sir," said Hartley. I spotted a small hole in the staircase when I first came in. "I thought I saw an eye behind it and assumed it was the press-gang because Mr Hicks said we were a few men short."

"We were there for quite some time. I had hoped we might enlist a few more than these four. But, a bird in the hand…" His voice trailed off without finishing the idiom.

"I'm sorry, Sir."

"No matter." Then looking at his marines standing over the unconscious Moody and his friends, he said, "Take them to the ship. Lock them up until we set sail."

"Gentleman, would you care to join me? We are heading back to the ship. I suggest you stay there until we depart," said James Cook, first lieutenant and captain of the HMS Endeavour.

As soon as they exited the tavern, Hicks said, "Excuse me for a moment, Sir. I've left something inside."

Without missing a step, Cook said, "Leave your bag of nails, Mr Hicks. I expect you to set an example to the men."

As they headed to the harbour, Bootie whispered to Hartley. "You're a cool one. Did you really know the press gang was inside the staircase?"

Hartley paused before answering, "Let's just say I didn't want to see that poor girl abused."

When they reached the port, Hartley got his first sight of the vessel that would be his home for the foreseeable future. The main and foremast seemed to be the standard heights of 129 and 110 feet. Strangely, the mizzen mast was atypically short. She would be an uncommon sight in full sail when all three masts were fully rigged.

It was another two weeks before they completed the muster list. There were 68 sailors, 12 marines to keep order, and 14 civilians. In total, they numbered 94. Of the civilians, the most noteworthy was the 28-year-old botanist Joseph Banks. Having been appointed by the Royal Society, his role was to lead the scientific part of the expedition.

The tide was favourable in the early afternoon of the 25th of August 1768, so they weighed anchor and set sail. Leaving the seagulls' squawks behind them, they headed southeast across the English Channel. The journey to Tahiti would take months, with several stops en route.

The sea was stormy, and large waves buffeted the ship like clothes in a washing machine. Hartley suffered from seasickness in only mild weather, so, in this, he was permanently leaning over the side. He hadn't kept food in his stomach for a week and was so dehydrated that he kept hallucinating.

They reached the Portuguese island of Madeira after two weeks, and they'd already lost a man to the sea. In his no-nonsense manner, Cook shanghaied a replacement at the port. They provisioned the ship and purchased large quantities of wine. The vastness of the Pacific Ocean would mean months of travel under challenging conditions. Many more men would die before their journey was completed.

The shanghaied Moody and his three accomplices proved to be excellent sailors. Hartley was worried the first time he issued an order to Moody, but the man showed no malice. Despite this, Bootie warned his friend not to turn his back on the able seaman. He'd seen the cutthroat's eyes on Hartley, and they had the look of a man plotting murder. But there was nothing to be done, and Moody would not try anything while they were at sea.

The ship headed south towards its next stop at Rio de Janeiro. Hartley was introduced to a line crossing initiation rite when they crossed the equator. Any sailor who couldn't prove they had sailed the southern oceans had to donate a bottle of rum or be dunked in the sea. Cook willingly paid his ransom. So did Banks, whose penalty was three bottles, one for him and two for his dogs. Hartley, however, chose to be tied to a wooden chair and dropped into the sea.

Cook insisted his officers ate this fermented raw cabbage to ward off the disease, scurvy. He made this foul-tasting food available to the entire crew but allowed them to take it or leave it. When the seamen saw their superiors eating it at every meal, it became a delicacy. Bootie joked that he'd expire from sauerkraut poisoning if they didn't reach their destination soon.

The ship's bell chimed twice to signify it was 5 am. The second hour of the first watch was starting. Peter Briscoe spotted an uncharted flat island in the shape of a crescent. In the middle of this long thin land was a salt lagoon and on the east side were palm trees. The clouds of smoke that ascended to the sky were signals from the natives, who they spied through telescopes.

Cook named it Lagoon Island, but they did not stop. They continued to pass other small islands—Thrum Cap, Bow Island, Bird Island, and Chain Island. The unimaginative captain named each one for a particular trait.

It was the middle of April when the Endeavour fixed anchor in Paopao Bay, the three kilometre long inlet on the north coast of Moorea Island. A bank of thick early morning mist obscured the view of the land, so the crew weren't sure if they had been spotted. After securing the ship, the officers and gentlemen, accompanied by a party of armed marines, went ashore.

The natives greeted them by bowing low and gifting food. This behaviour was unsurprising, given that the crew of the HMS Dolphin had visited two years previously. However, Midshipman John Gore, who had been with the Dolphin, noticed several changes. The Tahitian numbers were far fewer, and many houses were levelled. He suggested that there might have been a revolution, and his assessment was indeed correct.

Two weeks after their arrival, the former ruler, Queen Purea, arrived with several young women. This noblewoman was in her late thirties but retained a youthful beauty. Clothed in white, she looked elegant with feathers adorning her raven hair. Cook invited her on board the ship and gave her gifts appropriate to her former position.

It was late when Hartley finished his shift. He headed towards the mess, where all but the highest rank ate and slept. As he walked along a passage, he saw Queen Purea slipping into Bank's cabin, the leader of the science expedition on her arm. A young and beautiful island girl waited outside. She was tall with blonde hair, nothing like any Tahitian woman he had seen. As he passed, Hartley could not help but stare. *She would not look out of place in the King's court,* he thought.

The girl stepped in front of him, placed a hand on his arm, and said in heavily accented English, "William, wait, please."

Hartley was astounded. Not that she spoke English, but that she knew his name. He quickly took off his hat and bowed, "Midshipman William Hartley. How may I be of service, miss?"

She laughed, then said, "We are not a miss. My name is Aimata. I am the daughter of Queen Purea."

"My apologies, your highness. How do you know me?"

"William, we know many things. We know that you will die if you eat fish for your supper. A seaman named Samuel Moody traded iron for ciguatera, a poison extracted from the liver of a coral fish, and will add it to your food tonight."

Hartley just stared at her. Unsure how to react and trying to comprehend what he'd heard. Aimata pulled out a sharp blade from her robe, cut a lock of her plaited hair and handed it to him. "Keep this hair, William. It will bind us together."

Hartley looked down at the lock of hair, but when he looked up again, she was gone, so he hurried to the mess to find John Bootie. When Hartley entered the living space, he saw the off-duty crew sleeping. Their hammocks hung down above the tables, the sailors swinging slightly with the motion of the sea. On the far side, he spied his friend. He was sitting on a wooden bench with three other men—Robert Molineux, the master; Sam Evans, the quartermaster; and Midshipman Johnathon Monkhouse, brother of the surgeon.

In front of the men was a table hanging down from the ceiling. On it was cooked chicken, yams, breadfruits and bananas. After months of stale biscuits, sauerkraut, and salted meat, this food was like a King's banquet.

"Join us, Will," called Bootie.

The four men were talking excitedly about an incident. A native had entered the fort constructed to house and protect the sailors on land and had stolen some critical equipment.

"I took the packing case to the fort this morning," said Evans. "It hadn't been opened since it came from Mr Bird, the maker. The quadrant must have been in there because the box was heavy."

"This afternoon, that astronomer fellow, Charles Green, went to check the supplies. He said the quadrant was missing," said Molineux.

"Armed guards were placed around the fort. Yet, somehow, a native sneaked in and took the one device needed to track the transit of Venus. The entire venture will be for nought without the quadrant," finished Bootie.

"How did the captain take the news?" asked Hartley.

"How do you think he took it?" said Monkhouse. "He took the native chiefs into custody and detained all of the large canoes. Told them they will not be released until the quadrant is returned."

The discussion continued for the next twenty minutes. One by one, the men went up to their hammocks, leaving Bootie and Hartley alone. They were about to retire when Matthews, the cook's servant, placed a large roasted red snapper on their table. Wafts of steam carried the incredible aroma to their nostrils.

"Some of the natives brought over some fish. They must be worried the captain is going to shoot the captives. Mr Thompson thought you might like one," said Matthews.

Mr Thompson was the ship's cook. He'd lost a hand in the seven-year war. Yet despite this disability, he and his team cooked breakfasts and midday dinners for the entire company for three years using a fire hearth. This colossal iron stove sat on a stone base surrounded by sand.

"Thank you, Matthews. Please send our gratitude to Mr Thompson," said Bootie.

The midshipman reached for the steaming white meat, but Hartley grabbed his wrist. "Don't, John. It's poisoned."

Hartley told his friend what Princess Aimata had said. His friend was sceptical. "Are you sure you didn't imagine this, Will? I saw Queen Purea arrive with her maidens. Very beautiful, they were too. But I don't recall seeing a tall blonde-haired native."

They argued for a while. Hartley made the point that the girl knew the name of the one man on the ship who wanted him dead. Bootie suggested that his friend had fallen asleep and dreamed the entire thing.

Hartley had finally given up trying to convince Bootie. "I shall not be eating the fish. You can do as you please." And with that, he left the midshipman at the table.

The following morning Hartley was awakened by an agitated Bootie. "I decided not to eat the fish. So, I left it for the cats."

"Let me guess. The cats died."

"Worse! One of the artists died after he ate the fish."

"Which one?"

"The one that looks like a dandy," said Bootie.

"Alexander Buchan?"

"Yes, Buchan. He left the mess with a fish and then collapsed later that night. The surgeon examined him, but it was too late."

Hartley said, "Maybe it wasn't the same fish. What did the surgeon say caused his death?"

"He said it was an epileptic fit. He didn't know about the poison, so I'm not sure."

The two midshipmen agreed to say nothing of their suspicions. Hartley was convinced Moody was out to kill him and decided to ask Princess Aimata when he next saw her.

The rest of their stay in Tahiti went by uneventfully. The quadrant was returned almost immediately, but it was severely damaged. By a stroke of luck, one of the civilians, Herman Sporting, was an expert watchmaker and had brought his tools. He managed to repair the irreplaceable device.

Cook ordered three observatory sites to be built in case clouds obstructed their view of the planet. The main observatory was constructed under Nevil Maskelyne, the Astronomer Royal. Hartley was delighted to assist with one of the lessor sites, his astronomy knowledge valuable.

The transit took place on the 3rd of June, 1769. The conditions were perfect, with not a cloud in the sky. The data was more precise than had ever been recorded. Cook and Maskelyne calculated the distances between the planets and approximated the solar system's size. Now, all of the Royal Navy captains could navigate with greater certainty.

The party stayed for two more months in Tahiti, but Hartley did not see Princess Aimata again. Queen Purea had returned to her home, and no doubt her daughter had left with her. He began to think Bootie might be right when he suggested he'd fallen asleep and that she wasn't real. Then, he remembered the lock of hair and pulled it from his pocket.

Determined to find out more, Hartley decided to talk to John Gore, the midshipman who'd voyaged with the Dolphin two years previous. Gore had not seen the golden-haired princess but said many of the islanders had blonde hair when he arrived on the HMS Dolphin.

William sought out one of the English-speaking Tahitians and asked him about the blonde-haired natives. The man was reluctant to talk about the people he called the Pleiades, named after the star cluster in the night sky. Talking about them was bad luck, and it took a bribe of three iron nails to convince him to say anything.

He said the Pleiades became sick shortly after the Dolphin arrived. The madness drove them to force the Tahitians to fight each other. Only after they were dead did peace return to the island. Queen Purea was banished because she had brought them to the island. When William asked how they had made the Tahitians fight each other, the man wouldn't say. Even an offer of more iron nails would not convince him to explain further. He was clearly haunted by the experience.

William could obtain no more information about Princess Aimata while on Tahiti. The Endeavour weighed anchor on the 13th of July, 1769, and the ship moved to deeper waters. A noble-born native called Tupaia in his long priest's robes accompanied them. Trailing behind was his servant, Tua, an unusual-looking youth with blonde hair and pale skin. Both had learned English from the crew of the Dolphin and would play a pivotal role in the expedition.

Chapter 3
The Patupaiarehe[1]

Ciara woke from her dream feeling exhausted. Her mouth tasted of—Oh no, she caught the acrid smell of vomit, making her eyes water. She must have retched without waking when Hartley was seasick. Thank goodness she didn't sleep on her back, or she might have choked to death.

Her hair was sticky and gross. She headed straight to the shower and felt much better after a thorough cleanse with scented soap. After disposing of her bedding, Ciara reached for her phone, tapped the One app, and waited a few seconds for her sleep data to transfer. An alert popped up. It read, 'Deep sleep: 0 minutes'.

Ciara clicked on the web browser icon and searched for deep sleep. The third link proved the most useful. When you sleep, your body goes through different stages. Deep sleep, also known as NREM Stage 3, provides the most recovery. A search for how much deep sleep is needed revealed that it should make up a third of the total in a teenager. She'd slept seven hours, so her deep sleep should be 2 hours and 20 minutes. Ciara was shocked to read, 'Insufficient deep sleep, for a sustained period, can permanently damage your immune system'.

As she lay in her bed, Ciara's mind raced. What was happening to her? The short visions she'd experienced for a few months had become vivid dreaming. It was like nothing she had ever experienced. In every way, she was William Hartley, a midshipman on board the HMS Endeavour. A thought occurred to her, but before she could act on it, there was a knock on the door. It was Zixin, reminding her to hurry up or they'd miss breakfast.

Today was a private study day, and Ciara had signed up for scuba diving. The instructor was a German man with a strong accent. He informed them they

---

[1] Pronounced Pat-too-pie-ara-hey

would take the NAUI open water examination in three weeks. Today's class was two hours of theory, followed by one hour in the swimming pool.

Ciara tried to persuade Zixin to join her, but her friend was already a master diver. Besides, she'd already signed up for Kendo lessons with Min, one of the Seorak House girls. Jimin, one of the relay team runners, had signed up for diving, so they sat together in the classroom. There were ten students in total, including Scottie and Chan, who were seated at a table near the front. As always, Scottie was wearing a t-shirt two sizes too small.

"Is that Scottie N-Gartie?" called Ciara.

Scottie turned around. "It's pronounced Nar-tie."

"I wasn't sure. I didn't recognise you from the back."

Scottie ignored the taunt and whispered something to Chan, who laughed.

Scuba diving was a lot more complicated than Ciara realised. The instructor gave them tables and dive computers you wore on your wrist. They calculated nitrogen levels and went through countless safety procedures. It was an hour before they learned to operate the equipment. Finally, they got to put on their wetsuits and dive in the swimming pool.

The diving instructor had given them one task to focus on. He said, "When you breathe in and out, your buoyancy fluctuates. So long as you are nearly neutral with a half-breath, you can fine-tune buoyancy adjustments by controlling your breathing. Never hold your breath, or your lungs may collapse." Yet it was easier to say than to do, and Ciara found it hard to control her buoyancy. She either sank or drifted up because she adjusted too little or too much.

The instructor called time, and Ciara surfaced. She took off her mask and looked up. Scottie was sitting on the pool edge with his wetsuit pulled down to his waist. The water on his naked muscular torso glistened in the lights. Chan sat alongside him but kept his wetsuit zipped up. Ciara got out, making sure that she didn't look at Scottie.

While she was rinsing off her wetsuit in the showers, fragments of her dream popped into her head. Ciara dried herself quickly and grabbed her phone. She searched for William Hartley and found an English physician who'd discovered how blood circulates the body. She'd wondered if the midshipman really existed because this was not the person she was looking for.

The rest of the day went by uneventfully until Zixin decided to cause trouble. She took a photograph of the leaderboard showing Seorak House at the top. Then she sent a group email to the Halla House students. That prompted an unpleasant encounter with Hana and Chan.

Ciara and Zixin arrived at the cafeteria just as Hana and Chan did. While they queued, Hana and Zixin got into an argument. Zixin called Hana a hypocrite, claiming that her father conducted cruel experiments on animals. Hana, in turn, said that Zixin's father was in the CCP. Then referring to a quote from the Chinese president asked, "When is your father going to smash any attempts of Taiwan independence?"

Zixin's temper got the better of her. She ran at Hana, but Chan stepped between them. With a smile on his face, he attempted to shove Zixin backwards. Nimbly, Zixin side-stepped and grabbed his wrist with both hands. One hand below his little finger, the other gripped under his thumb. She twisted his wrist to the back and side, forcing Chan to the floor.

With the speed of a master, Zixin had executed the Sankyo wrist lock. Chan was almost in tears. He was beaten, but no words passed his lips. Hana backed away to a safe distance, complete astonishment on her face.

Still holding Chan's wrist, Zixin said softly, "If you ever try to touch me again, I will break your wrist. Do you understand me?"

The pain evident in his face, Chan mumbled, "Yes. I understand you."

Everyone in the cafeteria stood motionless. Not a sound could be heard. Ciara couldn't tell whether the silence was a reaction to the violence or from the shock of a slim girl overpowering a larger opponent. As soon as Zixin released Chan, Ciara quickly pulled her friend away.

Shortly after they'd sat down to eat, Ciara heard someone with a thick New Zealand accent say, "Can I join you?"

Turning, she saw Scottie and felt a slight quickening of her pulse. Not trusting her voice, she nodded and slid the adjacent chair backwards. Scottie promptly sat down and placed his food tray on the table.

Glaring at the New Zealand boy, Zixin demanded, "What do you want?"

"To get to know Ciara better."

The line had clearly been rehearsed, but it was so unexpected that Ciara and Zixin burst out laughing.

"Really?" said Zixin. "Do lines like that work where you come from?"

"Nah! But it broke the tension," said Scottie smiling.

Scottie faced Zixin. "I'm guessing your superpower is hand-to-hand combat, judging by your little tête-à-tête with Chan." Then turning to Ciara, Scottie smiled and added, "And yours is running fast."

Ciara laughed. A girlish laugh that she wished she could take back. "Superpower! Is that what you call it?"

"Yeah! At least in Halla. Can you guess what Chan's superpower is?"

Having gotten over her initial hostility, Zixin chipped in with, "It certainly isn't fighting."

"Opera singing! On the second night, he sang Nessun Dorma in the atrium. The girls had tears in their eyes."

"What about you?" asked Ciara. "What's your superpower?"

Looking shocked, Scottie said, "Isn't it obvious?" He glanced back and forth at each of the girls as if surprised they didn't know. Finally, he said, "It's my good looks!"

Ciara groaned and rolled her eyes. Zixin put two fingers in her mouth, pretending to vomit.

"Seriously. Apart from bad jokes, what's your talent?" said Ciara.

"If you meet me after study hall tonight, I'll tell you," said Scottie, getting up from his chair and picking up a tray of untouched food.

Ciara thought for a moment, then said. "Okay. Come to Seorak House after prep. We can go for a walk then."

"Sweet," said Scottie. And with that, he left with a new swagger to his walk.

The rest of the day passed uneventfully. Zixin had tried to talk Ciara out of meeting Scottie, suggesting he was spying on Seorak House. Ciara thought this unlikely but promised not to give away their secrets. Not that they had any.

Just after 8 pm, Ciara put away her laptop and headed out of the boarding house. Scottie was already there, waiting. Dressed in jeans and a tight t-shirt, he looked great. "It's a bit cold to be wearing a t-shirt, isn't it?"

"Yeah—Nah. Still warmer than New Zealand."

Ciara strongly suspected that he was wearing a t-shirt to impress her. At least, she hoped he was. Without discussing where they were going, they started walking towards the lake. It was still light, but dusk was only twenty minutes away.

Not knowing how else to start the conversation, Ciara said, "This is where you tell me your superpower."

"Not everyone here is exceptional. Most are, but the connection to Dr Kim matters more. In my case, he wanted to buy land from our tribe."

Scottie stopped by a lava stone wall with a wooden bench pushed up against it. "Shall we sit while I tell you how I ended up here?"

Ciara nodded, and they sat down. They had a beautiful view of the lake and the surrounding forest. The sun was setting, and the sky glowed with a red hue. In the distance, Ciara could see two deer eating shrubbery. Every now and then, one paused and looked around nervously.

Scottie began his narrative, his Kiwi accent softening as if used to presenting.

"The Māori are the indigenous people of Aotearoa—what you would call New Zealand. The Kaumātua are our tribal elders, and my grandfather is one of them. He is deeply respected because he holds our knowledge, genealogy, and traditions. Since our language, te reo, was never written down, the Kaumātua pass on our history through songs and stories."

"Does that mean you will be Kaumātua when you're older?"

Scottie laughed. "No! Kaumātua are not kings. We choose the wisest people to be elders. You'll know how ridiculous that idea is when you get to know me better."

That sounded promising—getting to know each other better.

"Dr Kim visited us a few months ago and met with my grandfather," said Scottie. "Of particular interest to him was the Patupaiarehe, supernatural beings who lived in Aotearoa long before the Māoris. The Patupaiarehe were fair-skinned and had blonde or red hair. They were tall and slender with green or blue eyes."

"Some believe the Patupaiarehe were demons. My grandfather says that is wrong. He describes them as spirits with mana, meaning lifeforce energy. They could take physical form or be as mist. Then one day, they were never seen again. No one knows where they went. Some even doubt they existed."

"A 12-month archaeological dig unearthed skeletons and unusual artefacts. Then, for no apparent reason, the site was closed down. Everything they found was locked in a vault, with an order not to open before 2063."

"Who made that decision? Was it the New Zealand Government?"

"Well, they funded the dig, but the land belonged to the local iwi. I guess they both made the decision. Since then, no one has been allowed to return to the site."

"Why are journalists not investigating this? Surely, it's newsworthy."

Scottie just shrugged.

A small green bird with a white eye landed in a camellia tree a few metres away. It started chirping, and a second one joined it. Ciara had distractedly watched the two birds before asking, "But what has this got to do with you being here?"

"I'm getting to that."

"Our legends say the Patupaiarehe lived in Waikato, where I'm from. One of my ancestors was out hunting near the foot of Mount Pirongia and saw a beautiful golden-haired girl bathing in a pond. He moved silently to hide behind a clump of pampas grass, where he could watch her. She looked like an elf maiden, and his heart ached. It was a fleeting vision because she sensed his presence and vanished into thin air. He never saw her again."

"That night, he went to bed feeling an ache in his heart. He woke in the dead of night to find that he was high up in a tree. Music and singing drifted up from below. Yet, there was nobody there. He broke down and cried. His heart was broken because he knew he would never see the girl again. Eventually, my ancestor fell asleep."

"In the morning, he awoke and was back in his bed. When he arose, his mother asked him, 'My boy, where were you last night?' He replied that he was in bed dreaming of a beautiful girl. His mother told him, 'You were not here'. Patupaiarehe took you. Only those with a pure soul are returned. And she was proud that her son had a good heart."

When Scottie finished, he had a strange expression on his face. He looked at Ciara like he had seen her for the first time.

"That's a lovely story," said Ciara. "But you still haven't told me how you came to be here."

"I'm getting there," said Scottie.

"Dr Kim was very excited when he heard this story and wanted to buy our lands. He said he would find evidence of the Patupaiarehe by funding an archaeological dig. My grandfather agreed to sell as long as we were included in the excavation. While we couldn't afford the fund the dig, Dr Kim would spare no expense."

"So you were given a scholarship at Sanjung Academy as part of the deal."

"That's right!"

"Finally! You could have just said Dr Kim bought some land from my family and offered me a place at the school."

"Yeah—Nah. The story is what's important, not the outcome. Anyway, the dig hasn't started yet. I'll return home to assist after the Chuseok break." Then he paused before saying, "You could join me if you like?"

"Scottie, we've known each other for twenty minutes, and you want to take me home to meet your family?" said Ciara in a flirtatious tone.

"Oh yeah, I never thought of it like that. You could bring your friend, Zixin. Then it won't be so weird."

Ciara looked thoughtful before saying, "I'll think about it. I assume Hana will be going?"

"Yeah, but I expect she'll be less hands-on."

"Do you know why Dr Kim is so interested in the Patupaiarehe?"

Scottie shook his head. "No idea." Then added, "So you see. Not every student here has a superpower. But, every student is connected to Dr Kim."

The red sunset had become a faint pink as the night rolled in. "It's getting dark. We should head back," said Ciara.

They walked in silence until Ciara suddenly asked, "Why did you cheat in the relay competition?"

Scottie looked hurt. "We didn't cheat. We played within the rules."

"You believe that?"

"Well yeah, maybe, I guess. Hana said every house event is a problem to solve. It's the nature of competition. You use every tool you can."

"You lied, though. You found a technicality. That isn't in the spirit of the competition."

"I guess I should have refused to run. But it's pretty hard to say no to Hana."

Thinking back to Zixin's accusation, Ciara asked, "So did Hana send a fake email pretending to be Chan's mum?"

Scottie laughed. "Nah! She wouldn't do that. Chan told his mum that the school refused to allow a boy to identify as a girl. In protest, the boys asked their mums to tell Mr McGregor they identified as female. Hana confirmed the story, and Chan's mum agreed to support the protest."

"Wow! You have to hand it to Hana. She's a smart girl. Thank goodness their last leg runner can only sprint fifty metres before tying up."

Instead of playing along with the joke, Scottie looked puzzled. "Yeah, that was weird. I've never felt my legs go weak like that before."

When they reached Seorak House, Ciara stopped, and Scottie stood quite close to her. Lowering his voice, he said, "I enjoyed tonight."

Ciara laughed, "You've been watching too many movies. You're going to have to do better than that." Then she turned abruptly and headed to the door. Just before she walked inside, she looked back. He hadn't moved from where they had been standing.

She gave him a little wave. "Night, Scottie."

After signing in with her ID card, Ciara headed upstairs to the dormitory rooms. Five girls were eating ramen noodles and gossiping in Korean in the kitchen. No sign of Zixin. She walked along the corridor, past her room, to Zixin's door. She tapped lightly. No answer.

She guessed Zixin would be alone in the study room, so she headed downstairs. She heard muffled voices coming from outside. Holding her hand above her eyes to block out the light, she peered through the window. She saw Zixin and Hana talking intently under the streetlight. Not wanting to be seen, Ciara retreated quietly and decided to go to bed.

That night she dreamed about William Hartley again. But not like before. Thankfully, it was an ordinary dream and lacked the clarity of the previous one. Her Sanjung One app reported that her deep sleep was nearly three hours. Although she felt relieved, Ciara wanted to talk this over with someone. But who? Who did she know well enough to be a confidant?

She heard a light tap on her door, and Zixin's voice said, "Are you coming to breakfast?"

Ciara was dressed, so they headed to the cafeteria immediately. Sophie was sitting alone when they got there, so they joined her. They made small talk, but Sophie had already finished her breakfast, so she left. As expected, Zixin asked about her date with Scottie.

"I would not call a thirty-minute walk a date," said Ciara. "We walked, and Scottie told me about New Zealand. There's not a lot to tell. What about you? What did you do last night? I looked for you when I got back."

"You know what it's like here. I'm the only Chinese student, and nobody speaks English unless they have to. So I could study or watch TV on my own. I didn't fancy either, so I went to the gym to do some stretching."

Ciara considered mentioning that she saw Zixin with Hana but decided against it. Even though she liked her a lot, she'd only known her for two or three weeks. Better to talk to an adult. She would go and see Mr Fernley.

No electronics were allowed at breakfast, so Ciara headed to the electronics room as soon as they returned to the boarding house. This was where the students left their phones and computers on charge. Unlike the younger students, Grade 11s didn't need to hand their phones in at night. Ciara had been surprised to learn that many students had counterfeit electronics and handed those in. One girl even hid her cigarettes in her fake phone.

After collecting her phone, Ciara checked Fernley's electronic calendar. He was free now. Saying nothing to Zixin, she headed over to his office. The social counsellor had just arrived. When he saw Ciara, he said, "If you're looking for me, please come in and take a seat."

Fernley looked very different from the day before. His hair had been styled and his beard trimmed. He must have also visited a tailor because the suit fitted him perfectly.

Once Ciara had sat down, Fernley said, "Lovely to see you so soon." Then he realised that might not be the right thing to say and added, "I hope there is nothing wrong."

He was nothing like any social counsellor Ciara had ever met. But there was no one else, so she told him about her lack of deep sleep. Fernley suggested that her Sanjung One was faulty. After all, it was a prototype.

Ciara had expected him to say that. She considered that herself but knew the data was correct. Telling herself that he could only help her if he knew everything, she went into detail about the dream. He took it very seriously. Then asked her if she knew much about Cook's first voyage.

"I was vaguely aware of him, but I couldn't have told you where he went and why."

Fernley considered for a moment, then said, "It is unusual that you would be able to construct something you know nothing about. I assume that you aren't a fan of nautical adventures?"

"No. I know nothing about sailing. At least, I didn't know anything before the dream. Now I feel like an expert."

"Did you know it was a dream while you were asleep?"

"I think so. It was like real life. Not the vagueness that you feel in dreams. I could smell and sense everything around me. Even my emotions felt real."

"Have you heard of lucid dreaming?"

Ciara shook her head.

"Many lucid dreamers experience intense emotions while asleep. They are aware they're dreaming. Some can even take control of the dream narrative."

"Is that what I am experiencing?"

"No. What you are experiencing is far beyond lucid dreaming. Dream research is in its infancy. Advances have been made thanks to fMRI, MEG and EEG machines. I recently read a research paper on two-way communication with a lucid dreamer. It might be worth talking to a neurologist and doing some tests."

Ciara knew more about neuroscience than most girls her age. When she was younger, her aunt would take her to work and run tests on her.

"I could talk to my aunt. She's a neuroscientist and will be able to help."

"I wouldn't talk to her yet, Ciara."

"Why not?"

Fernley paused while he contemplated something. Having made a decision, he asked, "Do you remember that I told you every student in this school is exceptional in some way?"

She nodded, wondering where he was going with this.

"Do you know why you are exceptional?"

"Because I run fast."

Ciara thought he paused for dramatic effect, so she waited patiently. "The UK Government tests every baby born in a state hospital. When you were a baby, your DNA was tested. The results were interesting."

When this drew no response, he asked, "I assume you know what DNA is?"

"Yes, Sir. I took GCSE Biology."

It was like he hadn't heard her. "DNA is a molecule composed of two polynucleotide chains that coil around each other to form a double helix. It contains the genetic instructions for all organisms' growth, functioning, and reproduction."

Ciara started tuning out, wishing he'd get on with it.

"When you have an ancestry DNA test, it uses a computer algorithm to predict your ancestors' origins," continued Fernley. "You may have read that everyone has around 2% Neanderthal DNA. Asian populations have a small percentage of Denisovan DNA too. Most DNA tests return a fractional percentage of unknown DNA. New evidence suggests this is an extinct hominid species, unknown to science."

"What's a hominid?" asked Ciara. "I thought mammals could only breed with members of the same species."

"Hominid is the name given to all of the great ape species. Humans are just one subgroup. Typically, the amount of unknown DNA is minuscule. Something like 0.1%. You have twenty times that amount."

Ciara started to get suspicious. "What are you talking about? Just who are you?"

"I know this sounds unbelievable, Ciara, but—"

Interrupting him, Ciara yelled angrily, "Stop saying my name. You think it creates a connection between us. It doesn't."

There was a pause, and Ciara asked, "Tell me who you are, or I will scream."

Fernley reached into his back pocket and pulled out his wallet. Opening it, he pulled out an MoD identification card. "I work for the UK Government. Specifically, a secret intelligence division of the Ministry of Defence. I am here to keep you safe."

"By moonlighting as a social counsellor? I'm supposed to believe that?"

"You don't need to believe me, but I hope you will come to me if you need help."

It took Ciara a moment to process what Fernley had told her. "You have students confiding in you. Are you even qualified to help them?"

"I won't be here long enough to do any harm, and you need me."

"So, why am I in danger?"

Fernley smiled. "You're unique! A biotech billionaire has relocated you to the other side of the world. Something is happening. Something big, and it involves you."

Chapter 4
Trouble with the Natives

The rest of the day was a haze as Ciara tried to make sense of everything. She needed someone to talk to, but who could she trust? She was never close to her aunt, and Fernley advised against speaking to her. Her uncle had always been distant. Not that Aunt Jean was warm and loving. Far from it.

That left her friends. She'd only just met Scottie, so he was ruled out. She imagined telling him, 'By the way, I have an unknown ancestor that might be an extinct ape or an alien. Either way, I dream about someone who lived 250 years ago. Also, I'm in danger, so the UK Government has sent a special agent to protect me.' Eventually, she decided to talk to Zixin, but not yet.

Ciara had been subdued all day. Zixin had asked what was wrong on several occasions. Eventually, she told her friend she was coming down with something and needed to take it easy. Ciara went to bed early, hoping to get a good night's sleep. She was to be disappointed because her dream continued where it had left off.

As soon as the Endeavour was far out at sea, Cook was required to open the envelope containing the Admiralty's orders. Hartley was told to stand guard outside the captain's cabin and admit no one. While he waited, he wondered where they would be heading.

The following 30 minutes dragged by until, finally, the captain emerged and shouted instructions for all officers and civilians to come to his cabin. The assembly took only minutes to convene, everyone eager for news. Hicks had run a book, and several bets had been placed. Hartley had a shilling riding on the Americas.

In typical fashion, Cook took his time outlining the orders. "I wish to congratulate you all on a job well done. Our observations have enabled us to measure the size of the solar system. This information will be of immense benefit to future generations. For the transit of Venus will not happen again in our lifetimes, even if we were to reach one hundred."

He paused to sip from a glass, then continued. "We are now ten months into this expedition. I am sure that many of you wish we were heading back to England, but that will not be for some time. It is the wish of His Majesty that we head south into uncharted territories to find the legendary Terra Australis Incognita."

The existence of this unknown southern continent was based on the theory that landmasses in the northern and southern hemispheres should balance. For if they didn't, the earth would tilt.

Allowing no discussion, at least not with him, Cook immediately dismissed everyone and ordered the helmsman to set sail to the southwest. The Endeavour passed several uncharted islands. Huahine, Bora Bora, and Raiatea were visited and claimed for His Majesty King George III.

It was October before the Endeavour reached the land reported by Abel Tasman in 1642, known as New Zealand. Tasman had only briefly visited the islands and fled after Māori warriors killed several of his men. The region was largely uncharted, and Cook resolved to create detailed nautical maps. Banks, too, would be able to gather valuable samples of the unusual flora and fauna.

Upon reaching the northeast coast, they found a bay and dropped anchor. Half a dozen men took to the boats and headed for the shore, where they spied several natives whose muscular brown-skinned bodies were covered in tattoos. A native approached them, threatening with his spear. Unbidden, the coxswain shot him dead, causing the remaining natives to scatter. Cook ordered his party back to the Endeavour.

The next day, they spied several natives on the shore, so the landing party returned to speak to them. Around one hundred angry Māoris joined their kin, made war cries and flourished their weapons. They then performed an unusual war dance, hopping from one foot to another while pushing their tongues out.

The Tahitian noble, Tupaia, was able to talk to the Māori because their language was almost identical to his own. He negotiated a trade, provisions and water in exchange for iron. As they were about to make the exchange, a Māori snatched a sword from one of the civilians and ran off with it. Banks and the surgeon, William Monkhouse, promptly opened fire, killing the man.

The landing party returned to the ship and sailed south. After a short time, several fishing canoes came alongside. Tupaia negotiated an exchange of products, including Tahitian cloth for fish. The natives tried to cheat by bartering for one item and sending up something less valuable after receiving the goods. Tupaia's son, Tayeto, assisted with the trade, but he was grabbed and pulled into a canoe. The natives paddled away with their hostage, so the marines fired at the kidnappers, killing one. Tayeto escaped overboard during the confusion. Tua, Tupaia's servant, jumped into the sea and helped the boy back to the ship.

When Hartley managed to speak privately to Bootie, he asked, "What do you make of these natives?"

"They're savages. Much more aggressive than their cousins in Tahiti."

Hartley pondered, then said, "They are uncivilised, but I wonder whether we are the savages. In our encounters, we have killed three men."

"I am sure these natives would kill us all in our place. We only look to trade with them, but they cheat and threaten us," replied Bootie.

"Maybe," said Hartley. "Why do you think the natives grabbed Tayeto? Did they think he needed rescuing?"

"More likely, they wanted a hostage to exchange for weapons." Looking around to ensure no one was in earshot, Bootie said quietly, "You need to be careful not to express your opinions to anyone else. The captain might think your words are treasonous, and hanging is the only punishment for that crime."

Cook decided to turn the ship around and head north again. After a few hours, some Māori approached in their canoes and provided directions to a bay nearby. The relations between the explorers and the natives were cordial, and they traded without incident. Tupaia found the Māori willing to talk about their culture. One fact was shocking.

"The Māori believe that killing your enemy is not enough," said Tupaia. "If you chop them up and eat them, they become excrement. It is the greatest humiliation you can impose on those who oppose you."

The ship rounded the top part of New Zealand called the Bay of Islands, and headed south down the west coast. After several hours of searching, they found a suitable bay where they anchored. The tiller braces needed repairing, so Cook ordered the forge set up. These light repairs would take at least a day.

Natives came alongside and exchanged large mackerel for nails and cloth. Tupaia asked them about suitable softwood to replace some of the internal planks. The Māori pointed to the large kauri trees that towered over the forest.

Cook organised a group of men to fell one of the kauris. He ordered Hartley, Hicks, and Bootie to form three groups to find fresh water and meat. The empty casks were brought to shore, and when water was found, they would return to collect them. Each search party consisted of an officer and three marines for protection. Each man carried a Brown Bess musket, a .75 calibre flint-locked weapon capable of firing three or four shots per minute.

The Brown Bess was made for a particular purpose. To shoot at a mass of enemies. It weighed 10 pounds and could be fitted with a bayonet. After shooting two or three people, you could use it like a spear in close-quarter combat. It was highly inaccurate over anything more than 20 metres.

As the senior officer, Hicks organised the direction each group would take. He planned to ensure they were close to each other if they encountered hostile natives. Hartley's party was ordered to head northeast, Bootie's east, and Hick's chose to go southeast. As Hartley headed into the bush, the naturalist, Herman Sporing, called after them, "Running water is most likely found in low points such as a valley or ravine. So, if you feel the ground sloping down, head in that direction."

Hartley pushed his way between thin trees covered in moss and leafy ferns. Trees, larger than oaks, towered over them and blotted out the sun. The ground was moist underfoot, and the vegetation dense. Strange birdcalls filled the air. After thirty minutes of battling nature, they reached an open area devoid of plants. The forest had been burnt out.

To the north of the clearing was what could only be a fort built on top of a hill. Each plateau was lined with stakes and wicker barriers.

Hartley stopped dead in his tracks. He raised his right arm with an open palm. The universal gesture to halt. They backed into the forest as quietly as they could.

Almost immediately, he heard a cry of pain, then several shots. Hartley ordered his three marines to move towards the sound. "Hold fire until I give the order. I don't want any of our own being shot," called Hartley. After ten minutes, which seemed much longer, they found Bootie's party. Two of the marines were lying motionless on the ground. Blood leaked from head wounds caused by heavy blunt weapons. There was no sign of Bootie or the third marine.

Musket fire rang out in the distance. "That will be Hicks' party," Hartley called. "Head over towards them. Muskets ready. Do not fire unless I give the order." They heard more shots, enabling them to locate the others. Hartley called out repeatedly to prevent Hicks from firing at them.

"Mr Hartley, hurry. Over here, now." Hicks quickly explained that ten natives had burst through the bush carrying Bootie and a marine. They had fired on them, wounding one, and killing another. They had fled to the east and away from the shore.

"We have to go after them, Mr Hicks. If we delay, John will be lost for good."

"Agreed, Mr Hartley." Then turning to one of the marines, he said, "Head back to camp and tell the captain what has happened. We are going to follow them to rescue poor Mr Bootie. I will send another man back with our location if we have not caught them within an hour."

And with that, the marine dashed off west. There was no point running blindly to the east. Instead, they examined the trail left by the Māori. It went east and then curved to the north.

"I think they are heading towards a fortified settlement we saw before we heard the shots," said Hartley.

"How big was it? Did you see how many of the savages there were?"

"I have no idea, Mr Hicks. We left as soon as we heard the muskets fired. But it looked well-fortified, and being on a hill would make it nearly impossible to assault."

They headed north. The Māori had passed this way. Broken branches and trampled ferns made that clear. When they arrived at the clearing, they realised it had been burned to prevent a sneak attack.

"The natives must be at war," said Hicks. "Why else would they destroy the forests around their settlements and build fortifications to protect their village."

They saw no sign of Bootie or the marine that had been carried off. The only way to see beyond the wicker barriers was to get up high, so Hartley climbed one of the kauri trees. The lowest branches were 100 feet in the air, and the trunk circumference was 50 feet.

The kauri had several burr knots on its trunk, helpful handholds for climbing. Their scarcity meant Hartley had to plan his route carefully. The climb was painfully slow. All the while, he worried about his shipmates. If Tupaia was right, the Māori would likely kill and eat the two hostages. A wave of nausea washed over him. He nearly vomited, but the shock of almost falling brought him back.

It took thirty minutes before Hartley climbed between two thick branches and could stand. It was worth the effort. He could see directly over the wicker fences and into the Māori village. There must have been 200 Māori. What struck him as odd was how few women there were. He wondered if the natives practised infanticide, killing female babies. He must ask Tupaia about that.

Then he saw Thomas Dunster, the marine who was with Bootie. He was being dragged from a pit by three Māori warriors and struck on the head with a wooden flat-bladed club. Hartley had to look away as they butchered the marine like a pig.

It took Hartley 10 minutes of careful foot placements to climb down. He told Hicks what he had seen. The two officers sat, formulating a plan. Hicks suggested that Hartley approach from the far side, shoot two or three Māori, and then run to draw them away from the pit where Bootie was held.

The plan failed because Hartley was too far from his target. He missed his first shot, then his second. The Brown Bess musket was not an accurate weapon, and the loud noise had no effect on the enemy. The Māori ran towards him, and his rising panic meant the third shot was wide of its mark. He turned and ran.

Only five Māori ran after him. The distraction had not worked. Hicks and the marines were spotted and attacked from behind. They had no chance and were killed or beaten senseless. They didn't even fire a shot. Hicks survived and was thrown into the pit with Bootie.

Now on his own, Hartley could do little. He ran as fast as he could away from the natives. Tall fern leaves slashed at his face and obscured his vision. He leapt over a small stream—the freshwater he had been sent to find. Hartley stopped in the dense forest and looked left and right, desperately trying to find somewhere to hide.

The sound of the Māori crashing their way through the forest became louder. Hartley was breathing heavily, but he pushed on. He heard a loud scream, turned his head to look, and ran straight into a tree trunk. He reeled away, but the loss in momentum had closed the gap.

Hartley burst through the trees and into a sheer rock face. Could he climb it? No, there wasn't time. The Māori warriors would spear him before he reached the top. He resolved not to be captured, not to be a prisoner for the cookpot. Better to die here and now.

"William, come this way," called a female voice just behind him.

Then he noticed that there was a thin gap in the rock face. It was practically impossible to see but might be wide enough to squeeze through.

The voice called again, "Hurry."

He ran for the gap and forced his way between the rocks, badly scraping his body. At one point, he thought it was too narrow. Panic started rising. Then two strong hands grabbed his arm and pulled him, ripping his coat. He was inside the rock. He could hear Māoris' angry voices. They tried to climb through the gap, but their large muscular torsos were too big.

"This way, William," said a tall blonde-haired girl who held his hand and pulled him inside the cave.

At first, Hartley thought it was Princess Aimata. She was almost identical. The unknown girl led him down several narrow but high passages. He could see the cave ceiling high above them. It was covered with colonies of bioluminescent fungus gnats and glow-worms. It was like looking at the milky way when at sea.

Every time they reached a junction, there was a totem, roughly the width of a man but much taller. The carvings included faces and body parts but were somewhat abstract. They looked to be elaborately engraved from one piece of wood. He wanted to stop and study them, but the girl would pull him down another passage. Her selection seemed random. He had no idea how she memorised the route.

As they travelled deeper into the mountain, the air became colder. The path descended until eventually it reached a large open area. Hartley thought they must be in the heart of a hollow mountain. He could hear a low-frequency hum, which sounded like a cat purring. He could make out a large dark shape in the strange luminescent light. They headed towards it. The girl was still holding his hand and pulling him in the direction she wanted.

The dark shape split open, and the vast cavern was bathed in bright light. Several human figures emerged from the dark object. There were 11 in total. Six boys and five girls. They were all tall, slim, and had blonde hair. They walked towards William and the girl he was with.

One of the boys spoke. "You will need to go back and save your friends."

When William Hartley woke up, he was high up in a tree. He was disoriented and unsure of what was real. But, the heaviness in his heart told him that his friends had been killed. Despite expecting to receive a flogging when he returned, he made his way to the camp. It was dark by the time he got there. Cook said it would be folly to attack a fort in the dark, so they returned to the ship and waited until first light.

In the morning, Hartley directed Cook and fifty men to the fort. It was deserted. The Māori had taken everything they could carry and fled. They saw the steep pit where Bootie and Dunster were held, waiting to be killed and eaten. Cook was furious. He ordered the marines to arrest Hartley and take him back to the ship in irons.

Hartley was dragged in front of the officers, where Cook demoted him to Able Seaman and ordered him to be flogged. There would be no coming back from this disgrace. Even if he survived the lashes, his career was in ruins.

Floggings were administered with the cat-o'nine-tails, 9 lengths of cord, each with three knots designed to rip into a victim's skin. Hartley had been forced to watch Able Seaman John Marra lashed a dozen times with this diabolical instrument of torture.

The man had been marched through the silent ship's company, stripped and spread-eagled across the grating. The force of the cat-o'nine-tails drove the air from the lunges, and Marra didn't have the breath to scream when each blow landed.

After six lashes, Marra's back was a bloody mess. After eight, his head slumped, a sign he had passed out. A bucket of ice-cold seawater was thrown over him. Hartley could only imagine the pain of salt in the open wounds. After the twelfth strike, Marra was cut down and carried to the surgeon.

When Cook ordered 24 lashes, Hartley nearly fainted. Twice the usual amount and a punishment that few men lived through. The Master, Molyneux, took Hartley below deck, where his shirt was ripped off to expose his back. His arms were raised like a crucifix and tied to iron loops. Even if he collapsed, his body would stay in place, and the flogging could continue.

Hartley's mouth went dry, and his throat constricted. He waited for the first blow. When it came, the pain was excruciating, worse than any he'd ever experienced. It coursed through his body like an electric shock. As he tensed, ready for the second blow, Ciara woke up.

Her heart was pounding, and she was panting. It was 3 am. Much too early to get up. *Damn it*, she thought. If only William Hartley hadn't panicked. They might have rescued their shipmates. She remembered what Fernley had said about lucid dreamers. They can take control of the dream narrative.

After tossing and turning for 20 minutes, Ciara fell asleep. Instead of the dream continuing, it returned to when Hartley and his three marines headed into the bush. The naturalist, Herman Sporing, called after them, "Running water is most likely found in low points such as a valley or ravine. So if you feel the ground sloping down, head in that direction."

Hartley was aware that he had been here before. He knew what would happen if they separated. His first reaction was to speak to Hicks and tell him they should stick together. He knew where fresh water could be found. Then he realised that this would make him sound insane. Even if he proved correct, his shipmates would consider that knowledge the devil's work.

Hartley needed to think. He could stay close enough to Bootie to prevent the Māori from capturing him. It would be easy to approach their hiding place without being seen. If he did that, he would be asked why he ignored Hicks' order to head to the northeast. Disobeying an order would be 12 lashes and a permanent blot on his record.

After all, Hicks' plan was a good one. He had to let things happen as they did before. Do everything the same, except he could not afford to miss with his musket. The diversion would work.

When the time came for Hartley to sneak up and fire at the Māori, he did so with far more confidence. He ran to within 20 metres of the Māori camp and fired the first shot. A man went down dead. It took him eight seconds to reload the musket. By that time, several Māoris were running at him. He fired again, and a second Māori dropped to the ground.

Hartley turned and ran, throwing his coat to the ground. He hoped the valuable material would cause several natives to stop. It didn't! He ran faster than before, knowing the terrain and direction. He headed straight for the thin gap when he reached the sheer rock face. The Māori were much closer, and he barely made it inside.

One of the thinner Māori warriors managed to squeeze through the gap and ran at Hartley, brandishing a greenstone mere, a short broad-bladed weapon. The midshipman raised his musket to block the blow, but before the native got close, he pitched forward and fell flat on his face. The mere flew out of his hand and landed between Hartley's legs. It shone bright green in the luminescent light.

"Welcome back. The others are waiting for us," said a voice nearby.

Hartley turned to see Princess Aimata's clone. "What happened to the Māori? Why did he collapse?"

"Only we can enter this mountain. Now hurry. There is much to discuss."

As they followed the route back to the heart of the mountain, Hartley asked how she knew which way to go.

"The pouwhenua directs me. When the eyes are made from pāua shells, go left. When a tongue points to the right, go right. When the tā moko is a different colour to the face, go straight."

Hartley had no idea what the tā moko was but didn't ask. What would be the correct direction when the pouwhenua had all three signs? Perhaps the signals never contradicted each other? He decided to say nothing and simply let her lead him. When they entered the large cavern, the dark shape was in the same place. Once again, it split open up, and the vast cavern was bathed in light. The girl had let go of his hand and joined the other nine Pleiades.

"Welcome back. We have much to tell you," said one of the boys.

Chapter 5
Escape Room

Ciara woke early and checked her sleep data, knowing it would say, 'Deep sleep: 0 minutes'. It did, but she wasn't concerned. She was excited about controlling the dream and wanted to talk to Fernley, but his schedule was full. So, she booked an appointment for the following morning.

Ciara needed to talk to someone today, so it was time to get over her trust issues. She walked to Zixin's room and tapped on the door. She must have woken her friend because she groggily called out, "Who is it?"

Ciara pushed open the door to find Zixin still in bed. "Get up! I need to talk to you. Come to my room when you're dressed."

It was 15 minutes before Zixin knocked on Ciara's door and let herself in. Her hair was still wet, but she was more awake.

"What has got into you this morning?" asked Zixin.

"Remember that you asked me about Scottie at breakfast yesterday."

"Yes, and you brushed me off."

"I said that Scottie talked about New Zealand, which was true. He told me about an extinct race of tall, blonde, pale-skinned people who lived in New Zealand before the Māori arrived."

Zixin looked scornful. "That's his idea of a date? Let's go for a walk and discuss ancient civilisations."

Ciara said impatiently, "I asked him how he ended up here. He said they sold land to Dr Kim, who is organising an archaeological dig there. Scottie's going to help with the excavation during the holidays."

"And he asked you to go to New Zealand with him. And when you said that was a bit weird, he said you could invite me."

Ciara was astonished. "That is what happened. Except I was funnier. I said he wanted to introduce me to his family after one date." Then she added, "How do you know he invited us both?"

"While you were out with your lover boy, I saw Hana at the gym. She wanted to de-escalate the rivalry. She still wants to win but not at all costs. Then as something of a peace offering, she told me about the archaeological dig and invited us."

"I think we should go," said Ciara.

"Of course you do. Tall, dark, and handsome invited you." Zixin paused briefly, then laughingly said, "Although I did get invited by a gorgeous and rich celebrity."

"Can you be serious? I have an important reason," said Ciara.

"I have an important reason," echoed Zixin dramatically. Then added, "Okay, okay. Tell me, already."

"I have been dreaming about an alien race who lived where they are excavating."

"I'm not going to lie to you," said Zixin. "I did not expect you to say that."

Ciara spent the next 20 minutes telling Zixin every detail of her dreams. She carefully watched Zixin's face for a reaction, but she was impossible to read. When Ciara finished talking, her friend said she would be back in a minute and dashed out of the room. Ciara sat on her bed, feeling deflated. Did Zixin think she was insane?

After 10 minutes, Zixin came back with her laptop open. She had found several websites about Cook's first voyage to New Zealand, including the captain's journal.

"Nearly everything you told me is supported here. All of the names are the same, too," said Zixin. "There is nothing about the UFO in the mountain or aliens, but there wouldn't be unless William Hartley wrote a journal."

"You mean there was a Midshipman called William Hartley?" asked Ciara. "When I searched for his name, all I found was a physician."

"Oh yes, he was real alright. Except that he was born William Dubois of French descent. His father changed their name to Hartley to avoid discrimination."

"Maybe that's why he protected the French girl in the tavern," said Ciara.

Zixin rotated her laptop to show Ciara. "It says here that he went on all three of Cook's voyages and eventually became a captain. There was nothing about the incident in the Minerva Inn, but the tavern exists. It opened in 1540 and has been there ever since. And even more remarkable is that press gangs hid in a secret room under a spiral staircase."

She clicked on a link, and a photo of the Minerva Inn appeared on the screen.

"Oh my God. That is the inn in my dream."

"I can't find anything about the Māori taking Bootie and the marine. What did you say his name was?"

"Thomas Dunster."

Zixin turned the laptop back towards her. "He is only mentioned twice. Once in Cook's journal, where he was flogged for refusing to take fresh beef. What does 'take fresh beef' mean? Take it from where?"

"I think it means to eat fresh beef. I can't imagine Dunster was a vegetarian," said Ciara.

"The second time Dunster is mentioned is in Banks' journal, and he wrote, one more of the people died today. That person was Thomas Dunster, a marine."

"So a man who gave his life serving his country doesn't get a mention in the captain's diary on the day he died," said Ciara. "It was more important to record that he was flogged for not eating beef."

Both girls sat in silence. Ciara was trying to make sense of everything. She looked at her friend and tried to imagine how she would react if Zixin was in her place.

Finally, she said, "What do I do, Zixin? What is happening to me?"

"I don't know. None of this makes any sense. But I agree that we should go to New Zealand. The Pleiades in your dreams must be the mythical beings Scottie told you about."

"There is one more thing, though," said Ciara hesitantly.

Zixin said nothing and looked at her friend expectantly.

"This is going to sound really weird. I have a high percentage of unknown DNA. I might be descended from them."

That statement prompted many questions from Zixin. Ciara did her best to explain what Fernley had told her but did not disclose her source.

Eventually, Zixin asked, "Apart from these dreams, have you noticed any special abilities?" She held up her hand to stop Ciara from interrupting. "I am deadly serious. You might be descended from this alien race. If that is the case, who knows what you can do."

Reluctantly Ciara said, "All my life, I've had fragments of dreams. Some of them are places I have never been to and include things I have never experienced. Most of the time, they don't mean anything."

"Like these dreams of William Hartley?"

"Never so long. Normally, the visions last a few seconds or minutes. But yes, as vivid as those dreams."

Ciara felt better, having opened up to her friend. For the first time in her life, she had shared her secrets with someone. She knew that there would be at least one more dream. The Pleiades had said they had much to tell her.

When the afternoon arrived, the students went to the theatre, where they waited. The third event of the house competition was an Escape Room. Dr Kim had personally designed some of the problems, basing them on challenges his employees were trying to solve. There were cameras in the room so the non-participants could watch the game unfold.

The rules of the competition were simple. A team of five students would enter a locked room. Several puzzles needed to be solved to escape the room. The event was timed, and the house that exited first would win. Some puzzles were linear, so they needed to be tackled in order. Additional puzzles could be solved for time bonuses. The main challenges had several solutions to make the game fairer.

If a team failed to exit in 45 minutes or put themselves at risk, the game would be stopped. The order of houses was their reverse position on the leaderboard. Odae went first, and their five members entered the room. After 35 minutes, the judges stopped them. Apparently, they had tried mixing chemicals to make an explosive device.

Jiri went second and exited the room after 40 minutes. They had solved a 10-minute bonus problem, so their final time was 30 minutes. Halla went third and escaped in 32 minutes. They were arguing when they exited. Chan wanted to stay to solve the bonus time puzzles, but Hana had overruled him.

"Chan, I am only going to say this one more time. You don't need to win every battle to win the war," said Hana.

Chan was waving his arms around in protest. "Yes, but we could have spent eight minutes on the 10-minute bonus challenge. If we'd solved it, we would have beaten Jiri."

"It doesn't matter if Jiri were quicker," said Hana. "We only need to beat Seorak to go top."

After a 15-minute wait for the room to be set up again, it was Seorak's turn. Their team included Ciara, Zixin, Sophie, Jimin, and Sungho. They entered the large room and looked around. There were desks, tables, cupboards, chairs, boxes, posters, a piano, and many other items. An apothecary cabinet housed many tiny bottles of liquids.

Jimin laughed when he saw the room had a piano. "Would you like me to play while you're solving the puzzles? It's good for your concentration." He sat down on the piano stool and started playing Mozart's Lacrimosa.

Zixin snapped, "Jimin, stop wasting time. Familiarise yourself with everything in the room."

The beautiful music stopped with a low tuneless note. Sulkily, Jimin started examining the sides and back of the piano.

Ciara stared at a poster of a cartoon pig wearing a Roman toga and standing in an animal enclosure. It was shouting, "Ista quidem vis est!"

"Why is the pig shouting in Latin?" asked Ciara. Then a moment later answered her own question. "Pig Latin."

Sophie walked over to Ciara and looked at the poster. She said, "It might have more than one purpose. This Roman pig is inside a pen, and Pigpen is a cypher. The pig is also supposed to be Julius Caesar, and there is a cypher named after him."

"Why is the pig Julius Caesar?" asked Zixin, who had also walked over to look at the poster.

"Ista quidem vis est! Caesar's last words, according to the historian Suetonius," answered Sophie.

"I thought Caesar's last words were, 'Et tu Brute'?" said Jimin.

"They are in the Shakespeare play, but historians disagree. I suspect that part was made up," said Sophie.

"How do you know all this?" asked Sungho. All five students formed a semi-circle around the poster.

"When I was nine, I studied cryptography. Caesar's cypher was the first one I learned to program, so I read about his life. He was incredible. At one point, he was taken hostage by pirates and—"

"Sophie, I think we have more pressing matters than a history lesson," said Zixin.

"Oh, sorry. Anyway, I think 3006 is the code to that box," said Sophie pointing to an ornately carved wooden box with a four-digit combination lock.

"Explain why it's 3006 while I try it," said Zixin.

"The Ides, or fifteenth of March, is when Caesar was killed. That gives us 1503 or 0315. Then Sophie pointed to the small symbols in the corner of the poster."

This message is in Pigpen, and the symbols translate to 'ultiplymay ybay otway', which is pig Latin for multiply by two. The original numbers multiplied by two are either 3006 or 0630. I thought it would start with a three and not a zero.

"I think we should sit back and watch Sophie solve everything," said Jimin. To prove his point, he sat down on a chair, put his feet on a small table, and leaned back with his hands on his head.

The others ignored him. Zixin had already opened the box and pulled out a laptop. They could gain access using facial recognition or entering a username and password.

"We'll look around for a username and password," said Sungho.

"Don't bother," said Sophie.

She rebooted the laptop. While reloading the operating system, she held down a combination of keys. When the operating system was ready, it was in recovery mode. Sophie opened an application and typed 'reset password', which allowed her to reset the password. She restarted the laptop to log in. On the desktop was a folder. Inside were several files.

Sophie and Ciara continued to work on the laptop while the others explored in more detail.

Sungho found a piece of cardboard with a circular maze printed on it. This kind of puzzle was easy but time-consuming. He picked up a pen and traced the route. Every time he passed through a letter, he wrote it down on the cardboard. By the time he reached the end, he had the letters: FRIVOPOKE.

Sophie watched Jimin complete the maze and then shouted, "PROKOFIEV."

Jimin sat down at the piano and played Prokofiev's most famous symphony—Romeo and Juliet, Dance of the Knights. The haunting melody filled the room, and a tiny door to a hidden compartment sprang open. Inside was a key.

Jimin picked it up and said, "I guess this will open the cabinet lock."

But it didn't. The key was far too tiny for any of the locks. Perhaps it was a red herring?

They continued to look for other clues. The clock was ticking. Eventually, Sungho turned over the maze they had solved. "There's another maze on the back."

It took less than 30 seconds to trace the letters and solve the anagram. "BEETHOVEN," he called out.

Jimin sat back down, and the familiar sounds of Beethoven's Fifth filled the room. Like before, a door to a hidden compartment popped open. Inside an aluminium box about six inches long, four inches wide, and two inches deep.

Zixin picked it up and rotated it. "There's a hole here. I wonder what that's for?"

Zixin opened the box to reveal two distinct sections. On one side were tiny metal pins that could be depressed to form a shape. On the other side was a semi-solid gel. Zixin pressed down on the metal pins. The outline of her finger was mirrored in the gel but twice the size.

"These must be tiny sensors. What do you think this device is for?" asked Zixin.

Sungho picked up the key and placed it in the left-hand section. As he pressed the key down, the outline appeared on the right, except twice the size. The top of the box also had tiny pins, so a complete key would be formed when the case was closed.

"If we had something to pour into that mould, we could create a larger key," said Jimin. "A key that fits the cabinet lock."

Sungho started looking through the bottles in the apothecary cabinet. Ciara helped him with the search and, spotting a couple of sodium bicarbonate tablets, pocketed them.

Sungho frowned and momentarily stopped looking. "Why are you taking them? Aren't you too young to suffer from heartburn?"

"I'm going to prank Zixin. Make her think I'm having a seizure."

Sungho shrugged, clearly not impressed and carried on looking. After a moment, he held up a small bottle containing a liquid, "a-cyclodextrin. If we can only find 4-methylpyridine. Help us look, Jimin."

"4-methyl what?" said Jimin, moving over to join Sungho and Ciara.

"4-methylpyridine," said Sungho, enunciating each syllable.

Almost immediately, Jimin found the solution. He opened the bottle and sniffed. "This stuff stinks."

Sungho took the small bottle from him, "When we combine 4-methylpyridine, water, a-cyclodextrin, and heat them, we get a solid. One strong enough to use as a key."

"Heat? Don't you freeze liquids to make them harden?" asked Zixin.

"Not these two solutions. They require heat to form a solid," said Sungho.

"Ahhh! So we pour the liquids into the box," said Jimin. "But how do we heat it?"

"I suspect the device heats the solution for us," said Sungho. "If not, we can heat it a little, extract the formed key, then heat it again to harden it further."

Jimin picked up the box and looked closely at it. "There is a power button here. I think you're right."

"Hurry up! Less talk, more action." Zixin had grabbed the bottles from Sungho and passed them to Jimin.

He poured in the liquids and pressed the button. The box went warm, then hot. After a couple of minutes, it switched off. Sungho opened the box and took out the large key. When he tried it in the cabinet, it fitted perfectly. He turned the key, and the mechanism gave a resounding click. The door opened to reveal a mobile phone. As expected, it was locked.

"I thought a mobile phone would turn up," said Sophie to Ciara. "Remember I told you about my fingerprint hacking software?"

Ciara nodded.

"I updated it to bypass facial recognition software. Once I've extracted the face data, it will generate an image of their face. Not a photograph but a 3D image that mimics a real face. If the person who locked the laptop also locked the phone, we can access it."

It took about three minutes to render the distorted 3D image of the person who'd locked the laptop. Even though it looked nothing like a photograph, Dr Kim's impassive face stared at them. Proof that he did design some of the challenges. Sophie moved the phone in front of the image. It unlocked.

The others gathered around to look at the image. There were two files on the phone. The first was a note containing six digits—probably the code for the door. The second was a jpeg, which Sophie opened. They saw a series of strange symbols that looked a little like Pigpen.

"Ignore the photo," said Zixin. "We only took 30 minutes to get the code. We don't have to solve it to win."

"The sun and the moon sounded for the key," said Ciara.

"How did you get that from the symbols?" asked Sophie.

"I have no idea. I just know what it means."

Sophie gave Ciara a quizzical look while Zixin grabbed the phone and said, "You might not want to win this competition, but I do."

They bundled out of the room in 27 minutes. They also received a 10-minute bonus for translating the alien pictograph.

The students in Seorak house celebrated another victory that night. Ms Hamilton joked that it took longer to bake victory cakes than to win events. Ciara went to bed early in the hope that her dream would continue. But she awoke to a feeling of disappointment. She hadn't dreamed about anything.

As she lay in her bed, a thought occurred to her. Ciara grabbed her phone and searched for the muster list for Cook's first voyage. The crew were listed with their dates of birth and dates of death. Tears filled her eyes, and she started shaking. John Bootie and Zachary Hicks had both died during the voyage.

Next to John Bootie's name was his rank, and the words died of dysentery in February 1771, just before his 21st birthday. Hicks died of tuberculosis in June 1771, at the age of 34. They were her brothers, and they were gone. Ciara dropped her phone and sobbed into her pillow.

Zixin tapped on the door and let herself in. She looked at Ciara, whose eyes were red and swollen, and asked, "What's happened?"

"Bootie and Hicks are dead." She paused for a brief moment. "Obviously, I know they are dead. They lived 250 years ago. But they died a year after they left New Zealand. I thought I had saved them."

"Bootie and Hicks were killed by the Māori the first time. You did save them." Ciara stifled her sobs.

"Sorry, I know that doesn't help," said Zixin.

"But it begs the question, did you change time?" said Zixin.

Ciara looked at her. "If only I had checked what happened during Cook's voyage before my second dream. Would history have recorded their deaths in 1769?"

"I think it would make sense to read everything about the rest of the expedition," said Zixin. "Then, if you change events in any future dreams, you'll know you're changing time."

"This is getting weirder with every passing day. What are we going to find when we go to New Zealand?"

"That's weeks away. I want to know who or what the Pleiades are now."

"Me too. But there's nothing to be done while I'm awake," said Ciara. "Let's go for breakfast."

After her morning repast, Ciara headed over to Fernley's office. He offered her a cup of tea, which Ciara declined, and then asked how she was doing. She told him about her dream and how she had taken control the second time.

Fernley seemed excited and interrupted Ciara. "You remembered what I told you about lucid dreamers altering their dreams. This opens up so many more questions. But I stopped you before you finished your story. Please carry on."

Ciara told him that she and Zixin had checked nearly everything on the Internet. Just about everything that happened was either verified or plausible. All except William Hartley's encounter with the Pleiades. The Māori name of Patupaiarehe was too tricky to pronounce, so she didn't even try.

"Perhaps it was a good idea to confide in your friend. Two heads and all that. Did you tell her about me?"

"I told her I'd spoken to you about my first dream. Nothing about you working for the UK Government."

"I think that was wise. You have a good head on your shoulders, Ciara."

"So what do you think, Sir? Why am I dreaming about things I know nothing about?"

Fernley looked thoughtful for a while, then said, "Despite great advances in neuroscience, we know remarkably little about the human brain. Every time we make progress, there is a case that disproves everything. A few years ago, a man woke up from a coma and could speak fluent French, a language he couldn't speak before."

"The situation most similar to yours was in a newspaper. A two-year-old boy had repeated nightmares about being shot down by the Japanese in a fighter plane during the second world war. Doctors questioned him about the event, and he knew details that a two-year-old wouldn't know. He stated the name of the American aircraft carrier, the first and last name of a friend on the ship with him, and the location where his Corsair was shot down."

"These two examples are not isolated cases," said Fernley. "There are many more. None, however, are quite as detailed as yours. Head trauma tends to be the cause. I do not believe that is something you have suffered from?"

"No, Sir."

"Hmmm!" said Fernley thoughtfully. "We must first assume that what you dreamed happened. As you say, most of it is verifiable, and the rest is plausible. Details get lost over time, and the records leave out the unsavoury aspects."

"There are several possibilities as to how your dreams have come about. All of them are highly improbable. The Pleiades could still be alive and communicating with you. You may have some of their abilities if you are descended from them. Your dreams might be a manifestation of those abilities."

"That sounds very unlikely. What are the other possibilities, Sir?"

"That someone else is transmitting the dreams into your subconscious. There is research doing exactly that, but it is not very advanced. At least, I don't think it is. It requires an electrical device that transmits suggestions to your brain. We could search your room, but the equipment would require physical contact with your body."

"Like this prototype device from Sanjung Electronics," said Ciara, holding up the watch.

"Exactly like that. Do you wear it at night?"

"Yes, Sir. My aunt's note said to wear it at all times."

"You are making assumptions. Perhaps the note didn't come from your aunt?"

"It was handwritten, and I recognised her writing."

"Computer algorithms can replicate handwriting if they have a sample," said Fernley. "But, let's not get ahead of ourselves. The device may be what they claim it is. I am not sure what I'm suggesting is possible. If anyone could do it, Sanjung Electronics would be the one. In 2017, they hired neuroscientists from the Advanced Telecommunications Research Institute in Japan. And, they were leading the world in dream research."

Fernley was thinking aloud but said, "Let's assume they have this technology. What else would they need?"

"Details of William Hartley's personal experiences on the Endeavour," said Ciara. "Most of the officers wrote diaries. Perhaps he did too?"

"True. We don't really have enough information to go on. I suspect that we will learn more the next time you dream. Which means you should continue to wear your watch."

"And ring. They work together."

Fernley seemed not to have heard. "You have given me much to contemplate, Ciara. Is there anything else I should know?"

"Just one more thing, Sir. Zixin and I have been invited to join Dr Kim's archaeological excavation in New Zealand. He is researching a Māori myth about a supernatural race who lived there. The description of the people in the legends match the Pleiades, and the location is where William Hartley met them."

"It seems that there is more going on here than we realised. I thought that Dr Kim had brought you here to experiment on you. Now it seems that your role is a little different. They need you for something. If you don't mind my asking, who invited you?"

"Scott Ngatai invited me. His grandfather sold the land to Dr Kim, so he is part of the project. And Hana Kim invited Zixin but said I could go with her."

"Interesting. Thank you for telling me. If you think of anything else, please come and see me."

Chapter 6
Forbidden Island

The Chuseok break finally arrived. Rather than stay in Jeju, Ciara suggested she visit her aunt and uncle at their home on Geumdo. That way, they could continue to work but still see her. In reality, she wanted to know more about their research on the Sanjung One prototype without arousing suspicion.

Ciara had woken up late and missed breakfast. The driver arrived early in a large white range rover. The journey to Moseulpo harbour took 20 minutes. All the cars they passed were white, grey, or black. Koreans must not like brightly coloured vehicles.

The small boat was waiting for them, but Ciara needed to eat something. She pointed to a row of restaurants. "식사 먼저 합시다 (sigsa meonjeo habsida)," one of the few phrases she learned. "Let's eat first."

The driver nodded. "네 (ne)," which sounds like no but means yes.

As they walked along the road, Ciara saw several large tanks full of fish or squid. Even though she ate meat, she still felt a pang of guilt. An old lady came out of the restaurant and saw her looking at the tank. She said something in Korean, which Ciara didn't understand.

A pretty Korean girl about 11 years old stopped. "She said the yellowtail fish is a great delicacy and only available at this time of year. She suggests you go inside to try it."

Turning to the old lady, Ciara said, "아니야, 괜찮아 (aniya, gwaenchanh-a)." Then added, "감사합니다 (gamsahabnida)." She hoped she had said, "No, it's fine, thank you." She looked at the Korean girl, who smiled approvingly. *Nailed it,* thought Ciara.

The girl put out her hand. "Hi, I'm Ellie!"

Ciara smiled at the formality but shook her hand. "Nice to meet you, Ellie. Your English is amazing."

"My dad is Canadian, so it's kind of my first language."

"Well, in that case, your Korean is amazing."

"My mum is Korean, so it's kind of—"

"Your first language?"

"No! I didn't learn Korean until I came to Jeju six years ago. But having a Korean mum helps."

Ciara nodded.

"So, do you go to Branksome?" asked Ellie.

Branksome Hall Asia was the Canadian school in the GEC. "No—"

"Of course, you're English," Ellie interrupted. "You must go to NLCS."

Ciara could hear the North American lilt now that she knew the girl was Canadian. "No, I go to Sanjung Academy."

All colour drained from Ellie's face. She muttered, "I have to go," and half-ran down the street. When she was far enough, she looked back over her shoulder.

What a strange reaction. Ciara looked at the driver to see his response, but he was impassive. They continued walking, and when they reached Glagla Hawaii, she sat at a table out the front. One of the teachers said they served fish and chips better than those in England. Ciara couldn't wait to try them.

The driver indicated he was going to eat elsewhere. It would have been awkward to sit together and be unable to communicate, so Ciara was relieved. The waitress took her order, and 10 minutes later, she had her meal—John Dory and chunky chips and a mango coconut smoothie.

As Ciara sat eating a chip, she watched the gently splashing waves hitting the harbour wall. A fish, probably a mullet, leapt out of the water. Its underbelly glinted white in the sun for a brief moment before it returned with a tiny splash.

A large white heron flew down and landed on a large rock. He fancied fish for lunch too. This was the life promised to her when back in England. She was finally experiencing Jeju outside of the school bubble.

When the driver returned, she could smell soju on his breath. Sophie had told her that many Korean men drink soju with every meal. She hoped that he'd only had a small amount.

"I need to pay," said Ciara, taking money out of her pocket to show the driver what she meant.

He replied in Korean and pointed at the small boat anchored alongside the jetty. He walked off, so Ciara went inside to pay. It was very busy at the counter, so she left what she owed, plus a 3000 KRW tip, on the countertop. "That was delicious, thank you. Here is what I owe you," she called.

She made her way towards the jetty. A woman was shouting behind her, so Ciara turned to look. The waitress, puffing from exertion, handed her 3000 KRW. "No tip!"

When Ciara reached the boat, it looked unlike those on either side. They were rusty and didn't look seaworthy. She stepped into the vessel, and the driver started the engine, which roared into life at the first pull of the cord. They slowly drifted out of the small inlet towards the vast ocean. Once there, the driver turned up the engine, and they bounced over the choppy waves, heading for a tiny island five miles south of Jeju.

The Sanjung research and development lab was built underground inside a dormant volcanic island called Geumdo. The island's name translates into English as Forbidden Island. Ciara had laughed when she read that. She teased her aunt about being an evil scientist. The kind in a spy novel. The truth was a little more mundane. The Seoul lab had burned to the ground in a fire started in an adjacent building.

Dr Kim decided he needed to move out of Seoul and somewhere private. Many of their innovations were highly classified. An island was the perfect solution, and after looking at several, he purchased Geumdo. Ninety people lived on the island, so he offered them jobs as labourers, cleaners, and other domestic roles. Those that refused, he moved to Jeju, giving them a generous relocation package.

Geumdo was designated as a nature reserve due to its subtropical marine life. As part of the agreement with the Korean Government, Dr Kim could not build on the island. The island provided a unique habitat for animals and birds with its exceptionally rocky coastline. The volcanic region produced many natural caverns and lava tunnels inside the island. These had been converted into a spacious laboratory built entirely underground.

As they approached the island, Ciara could see a gigantic grid of solar photovoltaic panels dominating the skyline. The small boat manoeuvred around an outcrop of rocks. Spray kicked up into Ciara's face. It refreshed her after the warmth of the sun on her skin. The helmsman handled the board expertly, making the journey all the more exhilarating.

He pointed to a large dark outline on the cliff face. "그것이 우리가 가는 곳이다 (geugeos-i uliga ganeun gos-ida)."

It took a moment for Ciara to realise it was the cave entrance. She smiled at him and nodded, understanding the meaning, if not the actual words.

Barely slowing down, the boat entered the cavernous entrance. Green algae covered the volcanic stone walls and then transitioned to red algae as they floated further into the cave. Lights hung down on both sides, creating shadows, and making the place seem eerie. It reminded Ciara of a movie set.

The vessel drifted slowly to the jetty, and Ciara clambered up the slippery wooden staircase embedded in the rock. A man in a pale blue uniform reached a hand down to help her up. She didn't want to appear rude, but she refused to be treated like a helpless girl. She was a world-class athlete, physically strong, fast, and flexible. She pretended she hadn't seen his hand and leapt up the last step. The man seemed unconcerned and beckoned her to follow him.

They approached a door set in the rock. Above it was a camera, its domed face looking down at them. The door opened automatically. *Probably facial recognition*, she thought, scanning everything like a burglar casing the joint.

On the other side of the door was a brightly-lit corridor, with no way to tell they were underground. They passed several doors, each one with a sign in Korean. Each room had a glass window, but when Ciara tried to look through them, the tinted glass showed her reflection rather than the inside. She put her face to the glass and cupped her hands around her eyes. She could just make out an office.

"그만 (geuman)," barked her guide.

She guessed he wanted her to keep walking. Eventually, they reached the end of the corridor. The doors slid open. On the other side was a large room with an art deco carpet on the floor. Several of Monet's water lily artworks adorned the walls. Having been to Monet's Garden in Giverny, Ciara knew that the artist had created 250 different water lily paintings. Were these real? Surely, they must be copies?

The sound of the water fountain in the centre of the room added to the ambience. Several large leafy plants completed the setting. Ciara briefly wondered how they survived with no natural light. Then she turned her head, and her jaw dropped. Instead of a wall, a large glass window provided a gateway to the outside. Since they were underground, that outside was the ocean. Fish, unaware of her presence, swam between rocks and nibbled seaweed.

The guide indicated that Ciara should sit down, but she was in no hurry. The room was incredible, and she would happily stay there for hours. All too soon, a door opened, and Aunt Jean and Uncle John walked into the atrium. Ciara got up and gave them both a quick hug. They walked through a maze of corridors to their serviced apartment. It had an open-plan kitchen living area and three large bedrooms.

"These two rooms are identical, so pick either," said Uncle John.

Ciara walked into the first. Her suitcase was already in the room. "Looks like this one has already been chosen for me. I'll unpack later."

The three of them stood facing each other, and an uncomfortable silence ensued. Aunt Jean broke the spell and said, "We need to finish some work. Perhaps you should unpack now?"

The last thing Ciara wanted was to stay locked up in a room for the afternoon. "I could come to your lab while you work. I'll be quiet. When I was little, you used to take me with you to your lab in Oxford."

Aunt Jean looked stern before the frown lines around her eyes softened. "Fine. Bring your laptop to entertain yourself."

"I nearly forgot. Dr Kim would like to meet you," said Uncle John. "He has invited us to dine with him tonight at 6 pm. Wear something elegant. Those jeans you're wearing are ripped. You should throw them out."

Ciara's aunt had told her to bring a dress because they would be dining together. It had never occurred to her that she would meet Dr Kim. The most powerful man in Korea and possibly Asia. It was pretty intimidating.

Ciara grabbed her laptop and followed her aunt through the labyrinthian building. It would be easy to get lost. As they walked, she visualised a chessboard to remember the route. Her starting point was e4 in case they backtracked. She also counted doors on her right.

They set out along a corridor, e4 to e5, passing three doors on her right. Ciara visualised the move on the chessboard and substituted the number 3 for a tree. Then they moved to e6 and passed five doors. She pictured a beehive in the tree because five rhymes with hive. This went on for several minutes until they reached Aunt Jean's lab.

The facial recognition software recognised Aunt Jean, and the doors opened automatically. They walked in. Ciara half expected it to look like the laboratory in her nightmare. It was similar in style but much smaller. Ciara was relieved that there were no animal cages. She didn't like the idea of animal trials.

After killing time for an hour, Ciara plucked up the courage to interrupt her aunt's work. "I am impressed with the Sanjung One, Aunt Jean."

Aunt Jean stopped what she was doing and turned to face Ciara. "I thought that you would like it. What aspects do you find the most interesting?"

"I love that it tells me my running speed, recovery, and sleep data. The amount of REM, deep sleep, and all those things." Ciara looked up to gauge her aunt's reaction. "How accurate is the sleep data?"

Aunt Jean looked thoughtful. "It won't be as accurate as this equipment." She gestured with her arm to several machines. "We use an EEG to measure the brain's electrical activity, an EMG to detect muscle tone, and an EOG to identify ocular movement. The Sanjung One estimates your sleep phase based on your heart rate and its variability. The technology was developed in a different department, so I haven't tested it myself."

"So, did you pull a few strings to get me one?"

"Actually, no. Dr Kim suggested that you might like to use the prototype. He seems very pleased with the data he is getting from it."

Ciara hadn't realised she had been holding her breath. She breathed out, helping her muscles to relax. There was no guilt or deception in her aunt's body language. She wasn't involved, even if the Sanjung One influenced her dreams. This, however, made it more difficult. She had intended to hack into her aunt's laptop to see what data they held on her. Now she knew there would be nothing.

Ciara left her aunt working and headed back to their apartment. The door automatically opened when she walked up to it. Somebody had updated the facial recognition to include her. The question was how to get past the facial recognition security system on other doors.

She sent Sophie a message on the Kakao app that most Koreans use. "Can you send me your facial recognition hacking program? Will explain later."

When they sat down for dinner, it was in a room similar to the atrium. Instead of Monet, the oils were by Renoir. Ciara recognised the painting, 'Luncheon of the Boating Party', which she thought was apt for dinner under the sea. Like the Monet room, one wall was glass and provided a view of a reef. The seaweed that swayed in the undercurrents had a hypnotic quality.

They had arrived five minutes early. At exactly 18:00, Dr Kim strode purposefully into the room. He was in his mid-40s, about 5'6" tall, and weighed about the same as Ciara. There was nothing particularly remarkable about him. Ciara tended to judge people by the intensity in their eyes, but Dr Kim's round, slightly tinted glasses hid his.

Walking behind him was Hana Kim. Towering next to her was the athletic frame of Scottie Ngatai. There was a sharpness in Ciara's breath. Was Scottie dating Hana Kim? Her anger was irrational. He had expressed an interest in her. *I'm not going to New Zealand with them,* she thought, but she knew she was kidding herself.

Aunt Jean and Uncle John stood up, but Ciara was too stunned to move. Her aunt nudged her with her foot, and Ciara got slowly to her feet.

"Please sit down," said Dr Kim. "No need to stand up on my account."

Once they had all sat at the table, Dr Kim continued. "John, Jean. This is my daughter Hana and her friend, Scott."

Dr Kim gave a slight nod in Ciara's direction. "It is a pleasure to finally meet you, Ciara Alinac. I have heard much about you."

Dr Kim was charm personified. The food was more delicious than anything Ciara had ever eaten. The conversation was relaxed and light, like old friends catching up. Dr Kim asked Ciara what she thought of the underground complex.

"It's incredible," said Ciara. "And I love your choice of artwork, Dr Kim. Are these real Renoirs?"

"These are copies," he said. "I own the originals, but they are too fragile to be on display in such a humid environment."

"Whoever you got to paint these copies is an incredible artist," said Ciara.

"These were 3D printed using specialist technology. Infra-red reflectography allowed us to record the exact depth of the paint and every brushstroke. These paintings are exact reproductions of the originals."

Then he smiled and said, "And do you know what we found on some of the paintings?"

"Another painting underneath," said Ciara. "Renoir reused the canvas."

Dr Kim's face contorted in anger. "Don't ever read my mind again!"

There was an intake of breath around the room. Aunt Jean actually jerked back in her chair. Ciara gave a nervous laugh. "I—" She wasn't sure how to respond. Finally, she said, "I read that many artists reused canvases because they were too poor to buy new ones."

Dr Kim did not look pacified. Uncle John tried to de-escalate the situation. "I imagine that Dr Kim is the only person who knows which Renoirs have paintings underneath."

After a brief moment, Dr Kim said, "Yes, I suppose I am!"

The conversation stopped, and they ate for a while. Dr Kim broke the silence. "Next month, we are travelling to New Zealand for an archaeological excavation of an ancient civilisation that predates the Māori."

"I didn't know you were interested in archaeology, Dr Kim," said Aunt Jean.

"Ordinarily, I'm not, but this situation is unusual. These people had extraordinary abilities." Dr Kim looked directly at Ciara when he said the word extraordinary.

The waiter moved unobtrusively around the table, topping up the drinks. Dr Kim ushered him away impatiently.

"Extraordinary abilities! What kind of things could they do?" asked Uncle John.

"They could communicate telepathically across great distances and bend others to their will."

"Sounds like he's talking about himself," thought Ciara sulkily.

Dr Kim carried on talking. "I would like to know how they managed these incredible feats. Was it an innate ability, or did they use advanced technology?"

"Advanced technology from nearly a thousand years ago! Is that likely?" asked Uncle John.

"It depends on whether they were from this planet or not," said Dr Kim.

Aunt Jean and Uncle John both looked sceptical but, wisely, said nothing. Ciara had never seen them this agreeable before. They were used to being the most intelligent people in a room, and with that knowledge came a degree of arrogance. With Dr Kim present, their air of superiority had vanished.

Dr Kim asked Scottie to tell some of the Patupaiarehe mythology. Which he did. Then Dr Kim spoke to Ciara. "Hana tells me you and your friend would like to join our little adventure. Is that right?"

"Yes, Sir. Zixin and I would love to be part of the excavation team."

Aunt Jean turned to Ciara. "Really? Since when have you been interested in archaeology?"

"Just in the last few weeks."

"I don't mind you going to New Zealand. What do you think, John?" said Aunt Jean.

Before John could answer, Dr Kim spoke. "Then it's settled. You can join us on my private jet. So don't book tickets or arrange accommodation. My assistant will organise everything."

When they got back to their apartment, Aunt Jean said, "Dr Kim's daughter didn't say much tonight. Is she usually like that?"

"No, but then I've never seen her with her father."

Aunt Jean looked earnestly at Ciara. "Are you sure you want to go with them to New Zealand? You don't have to go."

"I know," said Ciara.

"Okay, dear. I am off to bed now. Don't stay up too late."

Ciara waited 30 minutes, then took her aunt's laptop out of her bag. She booted it up in safe mode and reset the password. Exactly like Sophie had done in the escape room. She opened her email and saw that Sophie had sent the file as requested. After 10 minutes, a distorted 3D image of her aunt's face appeared on the screen.

Ciara took off her Sanjung One to charge it. At midnight she exited the apartment. Tiptoeing along the corridor, Ciara retraced the route to her aunt's lab. When she approached the door, she held the laptop in front of her face. The door slid open. Even though she didn't suspect her aunt of anything, she thoroughly searched the room. Where should she go now?

Ciara heard male voices from outside the room, so she quickly hid behind the counter and held her breath. Thankfully, the door didn't open, and the voices continued down the corridor.

The interruption had made the decision for her. Grabbing a white lab coat from a peg, she hurried out. Keeping a safe distance, she followed the two men. They walked up to a door that automatically opened for them. Once the men were inside, Ciara ran to the window and peered through.

The glass was tinted, and she could barely see through it. There was no movement, so she opened the laptop and displayed the 3D image of her aunt to the camera. The door slid open. Ciara waited by the side of the door for a brief moment. When she heard no sounds, she ducked inside before the doors closed.

The room was some form of office. There were cubicles with grey fabric partitioning the different sections. A nameplate with a photo was attached to each office space. Ciara looked inside cupboards and drawers for anything that might be of interest. Nothing was.

73

There was only one place the men could have gone, through a door on the far side of the room. Ciara held up the 3D image as she had done before. Nothing happened. Ciara swore quietly. Then she had an idea. Despite the late hour, she sent a kakao message to Sophie, who immediately replied.

Ciara hid in one of the cubicles, opened her aunt's laptop and logged into her email. Before she could check it, there was the hiss from the doors sliding open. She slammed the laptop shut to extinguish its light.

The two men walked towards the exit door. One of them stopped suddenly and turned around. He was looking at Ciara's cubicle. He said something in Korean. Ciara interpreted the tone of his voice to mean, "Did you hear something?" The second man mumbled something, but Ciara couldn't catch it.

Ciara held her breath. Her heart was pounding in her chest. The tension drained from her when one of the men said, "가자 (Gaja)," and walked out of the room. A moment later, the first man followed him. Ciara breathed a sigh of relief.

She opened up the laptop again. There it was, a distorted 3D rendering of Dr Kim's face. Sophie had made a copy of it. Typical hacker thinking—this might be helpful one day. Ciara walked up to the door with the laptop pointing at the camera. The door slid open, and she walked through it.

Ciara made her way along a corridor. Whenever she encountered a door, there was also a window. They were spaced out evenly, suggesting that the rooms were all the same size. The last room had two windows. Ciara headed for the door, which slid open thanks to Dr Kim's face.

Ciara's head spun as soon as she walked inside. It was a vast new laboratory. On one side of the room, she could see a wall of empty animal cages. The room was littered with medical equipment—an fMRI, an EEG, and an EMG. The hospital beds with restraining straps were identical to her vision. This was the room she was trapped in.

Ciara backed out, practically running down the corridor. Before she knew it, she had reached the last room. A silver plaque engraved with 'Dr Kim, CEO' was on the wall.

She lifted the laptop to the camera, and the door slid open. The light came on to reveal an ordinary-looking room. Ciara had expected a luxurious space but quickly realised it was the annexe. This was where the personal assistant worked.

She walked across the room to the far door, which slid open. The room was everything Ciara had imagined. Apart from the entry wall, the others were glass.

A massage chair, which looked vaguely like a pilot's seat in a spaceship, was sitting in one corner. Whoever sat there would have a panoramic view of the world beneath the sea.

Ciara headed towards a large wooden desk. On it was a thick manilla folder. She almost laughed. One of the world's wealthiest technology billionaires kept paper files. Her amusement soon faded when she saw her photo and name on the cover. Ciara opened the folder and tipped the contents onto the desk.

Her entire life spread out before her. A copy of her birth certificate, the DNA test Fernley had told her about, and even her GCSE results. She stopped suddenly! A coldness crept through her body, and her hands started shaking. There was a complete transcript of everything she had said since arriving in Korea.

The Sanjung One device was recording everything. Her conversations with Zixin about her dreams were typed out. That meant they knew the Pleiades' location and the route there. No wonder they wanted her to be part of the excavation.

All of her search histories were listed and underlined, suggesting that the electronic version of this document had hyperlinks to the pages she had visited. They knew everything. Perhaps not everything—none of her Kakao messages or emails were included. There was a summary page at the end of the file.

Ciara Alinac is probably descended from an alien race and has visions of the future and past events. She may have telepathic capabilities. The subject requires additional study.

Ciara closed the file. She sat for a moment and watched the underwater world around her. Dr Kim was a ruthless man, willing to exploit a teenage girl to access alien technology. She was not going to be manipulated anymore.

Chapter 7
The Taser Incident

When Ciara returned to Sanjung Academy, Zixin was waiting for her at the entrance. They had texted but decided talking face to face was safer.

"Do you know how long I've waited for you to get back?" said Zixin.

"Long enough to get irritated," said Ciara. "So, I am guessing ten minutes?"

"Five hours!" Zixin held up five fingers in front of Ciara's face. "You said you'd be back in the afternoon."

"It is the afternoon."

"Only just. Just tell me what you've found out."

Ciara pointed silently to her Sanjung One watch and then put her finger to her lips in the universal way of telling someone not to say anything. "Just give me a couple of minutes to drop off my stuff."

After Ciara had left the Sanjung One in her room, she explained that it was a recording device. Then she told Zixin about Dr Kim's strange accusation at dinner, how she'd bypassed security and found the manilla file on the desk.

"So, what do you think?" asked Ciara.

"I think it's outrageous. A violation of human decency. I can't believe Hana Kim was using me to get to you."

"Seriously!" said Ciara. "The most powerful man in Asia thinks I'm reading his mind, has a dossier on me, and suspects I'm an alien with superpowers. And you focus on Hana using you to get to me."

"It is pretty disappointing," said Zixin. "I had visions of us appearing on TV together."

"They were listening to every conversation we had."

"No, they were listening to every conversation you had. I was fine when you weren't around."

"Argggh, you're unbearable when you are like this."

Zixin simply smiled at Ciara, who knew her friend was trying to help her by making light of the situation. "So, what now?" asked Ciara.

"Has anything really changed?" said Zixin. "It was obvious Hana's invitation was a way to invite you. She was trying to sound casual but not doing it very well."

"You could have told me that."

"What? And let it go to your head," said Zixin. "If you didn't realise that you are the centre of everything happening…"

Zixin tailed off. Then she said quietly. "Causally turn around so that you are facing the trees behind you. I think someone is spying on us."

Ciara looked. "I can't see anyone."

"Let's walk casually towards the trees," said Zixin.

"Don't you mean away from the trees—in the opposite direction?"

"Where's the fun in that? Besides, we have security at the entrance and high fences with barbed wire all around the campus. No one is in here that isn't supposed to be."

The two girls walked towards the trees but saw nothing nor heard any unusual sounds. The faint sound of a diesel engine was gradually getting louder. The school bus pulled up about 30 metres away. Students started getting off. Ciara could make out Hana, Scottie, and Chan.

As if sensing he was being watched, Scottie looked up and waved. He said something to Hana, who nodded. The three students started walking towards Ciara and Zixin.

"They're coming over to—" said Ciara. A strong tug threw her off-balance and interrupted her sentence. Zixin dragged her towards the trees.

"And we won't be here because we'll be looking for the man I saw," said Zixin.

As soon as they entered the forest, two men burst out of it, running past them. Both were Asian, slightly shorter than Ciara and not much heavier. Running after them was Fernley, who shouted. "Ngatai, get Hana Kim somewhere safe."

Ciara looked at Zixin, undecided about what to do. After a brief pause, she exclaimed, "They're not after Hana. They're after Fernley."

Ciara turned and ran after the social counsellor, who was slowly closing in on the two men. With their cover blown, the intruders seemed focused on escaping. They sprinted along the path and towards the lake.

Zixin swore to herself and then set off in pursuit.

Scottie turned to Chan, "Take Hana into the main building. Send security this way. Hurry!" Then he ran after the two girls.

Ciara was rapidly closing the gap on Fernley. "Mr Fernley! It's a trap," she shouted. "They don't want Hana. They want you."

It was too late. The men ran into the forest on the far side, and as Fernley followed them, they waited. One of them fired a taser. Two prongs with wires attached delivered 50,000 volts of electricity into Fernley, who collapsed on the floor in apparent agony. The second man had a needle containing the general anaesthetic, propofol. He bent over Fernley, grabbed his hand and lined up the syringe to inject the drug into his vein.

Ciara saw what he was doing and accelerated. She hit the man at around 9 m/s. At 65 kg, the force generated was nearly 600 kg m/s. She had lowered her shoulder so that its bony point rammed straight into the man's face. Because the man was stationary, Ciara's velocity after the collision was just over 4.5 m/s. She ran through the man, knocking him out cold.

The other man fumbled with the firing cartridge and tried to reload his weapon. Ciara didn't think she would have time to reach him before he could fire again, but she had to try. She ran at the man as he raised the reloaded taser. A foot flew through the air kicking it from the man's hand.

"你会后悔的，小女孩," said the man who raised his arms in a boxer's pose and walked towards Zixin.

He threw a swinging right hand, somewhere between a straight right and a hook. It was a mistake going for a big punch because Zixin ducked below it without difficulty. Simultaneously, pushing off her right leg to propel herself forward, she threw a short jab to the throat. The blow, which had her entire body weight behind it, landed flush on the man's larynx. He staggered back, clutching at his neck and struggling to breathe. Before he had time to recover, Ciara shot him with 50,000 volts of electricity. He collapsed to the floor, convulsing in agony. The whole incident lasted only a few seconds.

"Really, Alinac," said Zixin. "I was just about to have some fun."

Scottie ran into the trees and stopped dead in his tracks. "What the hell—"

Fernley, who had struggled to his feet, interrupted him. "We need to go before round 2 starts."

"But they'll escape," said Zixin.

"Are you going to keep knocking them down until the police arrive?" asked Fernley. "My first priority is to keep you three safe."

"I think you have that backwards. We were keeping you safe," said Zixin.

"They could have guns," said Fernley. "Did you search for them?"

Zixin and Ciara just looked at each other.

"Exactly, so stop arguing and let's go. Quickly!"

They encountered four security guards on their way to the school buildings. The men asked Fernley where the intruders were last seen. He pointed to the trees behind them, and they headed in that direction.

"They're about as useful as a chocolate teapot," said Zixin.

"You know something Zixin," said Ciara. "You are the strangest girl I have ever met."

"Back at you, Alienac."

Dr Lockley, the school principal, met them in the main building. She was a tall, blonde-haired Canadian woman in her early fifties. An intelligent gleam in her eye suggested nothing happened without her knowledge. She insisted they go to the medical centre for a check-up. Under no circumstance were they to leave until the police interviewed them.

Fernley had no ill effects from the electric shock, but Ciara's shoulder was painful. The nurse moved her arm around to check mobility and said it would be fine in a few days. She gave Ciara some painkillers and put her arm in a sling.

When the police arrived at the medical centre, Fernley did most of the talking. It took a great deal of time because they needed a translator. Every question was translated into English, and every answer, back into Korean.

Fernley explained that he had seen two men skulking in the woods. He had followed them to see what they were up to. When Ciara and Zixin entered the woods, the men saw them and ran. He gave chase, and the students foolishly ran after him. He caught up with the two men, but one tasered him, allowing them to escape.

Zixin started to protest. "Miss Yang, please do not interrupt me," said Fernley. "It is important that I explain what happened." He emphasised the word 'I'.

Zixin bit her tongue but looked on the verge of saying something else.

Fernley continued, "Rather than pursue them, I took the students to safety. I suspect it was an attempted kidnapping of Hana Kim, the daughter of Dr Sanjung Kim. She was by the trees when the men ran out."

The police then asked Ciara, Zixin, and Scottie for their statements. They all confirmed Fernley's lies. Zixin added one crucial point—one of the men spoke

Mandarin, although she couldn't make out what they said. Quietly to Ciara, she whispered, "He said you'll regret that little girl—but he's the one with regrets. His larynx will be bruised for a week."

When the interviews were concluded, the police told Ciara, Zixin, and Scottie that they were foolish to run after their teacher. It was brave, but they should have gone with the other students to the security office. The police told them that a fence had been cut by wire clippers. There was an old walking trail that used to go through the school grounds. The attempted kidnappers had used that route to reach the fence.

When the police had gone, Fernley asked to speak to Ciara and Zixin. Scottie said he'd meet them in the cafeteria afterwards. Fernley looked grave. "Thank you for saving me. I can't believe I needed rescuing by two 16-year-old girls."

"I don't think Hana was the target!" said Ciara.

"I think you were the target," said Fernley. "Perhaps another intelligence agency is interested in you?"

"I don't think it was me they were after either," said Ciara. "I think it was you."

"Why would anyone want to kidnap the school counsellor?" asked Zixin.

Ciara looked at Fernley. "Zixin knows everything else. She should know this too."

Fernley sighed, "Very well. I work for the UK Government. Specifically, a secret intelligence division of the Ministry of Defence. I am here to protect Ciara."

"You don't really look like a secret agent," said Zixin. "But if it was you they were after, your cover is blown."

"Which means those men were working for Dr Kim," said Ciara.

Zixin caught on. "Of course, Dr Kim has recorded all of your conversations. I am guessing Mr Fernley told you he worked for the UK Government."

"Dr Kim planted a bug on you?" asked Fernley.

"Yes, he did," said Ciara. "But why didn't he get the principal to sack you? Kidnapping seems a little extreme."

"Sacking me would raise too many questions. Besides, it wouldn't get rid of me. Better to make me disappear and question me to find out what I know."

"So, what will you do now?" asked Ciara. "Will the Government replace you with someone else?"

"No! My real job hasn't changed. I will stay in Korea, but I doubt it will be as a social counsellor."

"There is something neither of you has asked," said Zixin.

They both looked at her. "Why were the kidnappers Chinese? If they worked for Dr Kim, they would be Korean."

"Hmmm! That is a good point, Zixin. I will ask London. Perhaps they have intel that we don't."

Then Fernley smiled. "Thank you both. Ciara, would you mind meeting me tomorrow morning before your classes start. I would like to know about your trip to Geumdo Island."

The cafeteria was abuzz with excitement when Ciara and Zixin went for lunch. Everyone knew that there were intruders on campus. Scottie had told everyone he had found the two girls standing over two prone men. One was out cold, while the other was incapacitated. The girls were inundated with questions, so they added more details. They stuck to Fernley's story, though. When Hana Kim entered the room, everything went quiet. She came over to Zixin and Ciara and hugged them both.

Ciara made the decision to leave the Sanjung One in her bedroom. It was time to stop pretending that she didn't know it was recording her. If her aunt asked her why she wasn't wearing it anymore, she would tell her the truth.

Ciara headed to Fernley's office the following morning. She half expected him to have gone into hiding, but he was waiting for her. More than that, he had made them both a cup of tea.

"Earl Grey," he said. "Impossible to get this brand here, so I had it imported."

Ciara hated black tea. Its smell turned her stomach. The thought of drinking it brought a wave of nausea. The other food she hated was prunes. Slimy and sticky—awful things. Why did she think of prunes every time she was given tea? The thought of them made the tea even more unpalatable.

"Thank you for the tea, Sir. You shouldn't have," said Ciara.

"No problem, Ciara. So, how is the shoulder?"

"A little sore, but fine. I imagine the intruder's head will hurt more than my shoulder."

"Indeed. Did you find any evidence in Dr Kim's institute that they are behind the dreams you have been having?"

"No evidence at all, but my aunt is definitely not involved. It was Dr Kim who suggested I try the Sanjung One. It must have a microphone embedded because he had transcripts of all my conversations. That's how he knew you worked for the UK Government."

"Where did you see the transcripts?"

"I broke into Dr Kim's office and found a dossier on me. The transcripts were just part of it. Dr Kim thinks I might be descended from an alien race."

Fernley looked down and shook his head slowly. "I should have guessed he'd planted a bug on you." When he looked up, he was chewing his lip as if in thought. "You don't think they are manipulating your dreams?"

"I saw no evidence of it. I suspect it would have been in my dossier if Dr Kim was behind it."

"Is there anything else, no matter how small, that you haven't told me?"

"A week ago, I fell asleep in Maths class and had a vision about being trapped in a lab. I saw that room when I was inside Dr Kim's research institute. It was identical in every detail, including the empty animal cages along one wall."

"Was this your aunt's lab or one she uses?"

"No, her facial ID wasn't registered, so she's probably never been there. I had to use Dr Kim's to get access."

"Very ingenious. I won't ask how you managed that."

Fernley looked at Ciara's tea. His was nearly finished, and hers was untouched. She picked it up and swallowed a mouthful, trying not to taste it.

"I am not sure what it all means, Ciara, but we will know more in time. London wants me to leave the school, but I will stay close by at all times."

He gave her his business card with his phone number on it. "Contact me anytime, night or day, if you are concerned about anything."

"Thank you, Mr—" Ciara paused. "Is Fernley your real name?"

"That's what my passport says."

Fernley looked uncomfortable. "One last thing. When I told my boss about Zixin disarming one of the attackers, he had a file on her. Apparently, her dad is a high-ranking Chinese intelligence agent who poses as a diplomat. He was posted to the London Embassy a few years ago. Zixin spent 12 months at a private school in the UK." Ciara was shocked and left Fernley's office with more questions than answers.

The trip to New Zealand was delayed a day because of the police investigation. The excitement of the intruders quickly died down. Mr Fernley resigned, and it barely caused a ripple. No one was surprised, given he was tasered at work. Who would want to stay in a place where they didn't feel safe.

The principal, Dr Lockley, had given Hana, Scottie, Chan, Zixin, and Ciara permission to join the excavation in New Zealand. Not that she had much choice in the matter. They were due to leave the following morning, so Ciara and Zixin packed for their trip.

When Ciara finished packing, she went to see Zixin, who was still in her pyjamas.

"Why aren't you ready?" asked Ciara. "We have to be downstairs in five minutes."

"They'll wait. I just need to shower before I get dressed."

"What? You don't have time to shower. Just put your clothes on now."

Zixin walked into the bathroom carrying her clothes. She swung the door over but not completely shut.

Ciara heard the shower start and called out in an exasperated tone, "Zixin."

There was no answer. Ciara called again, even louder. After a minute, the shower turned off. Ciara had given up trying to hurry her friend. She walked up to the bathroom door and called through the gap, "Can I ask you something personal?"

Zixin pulled open the door and stepped into the bedroom. "Here it comes."

"Here what comes?"

Using a sarcastic voice, Zixin said, "I don't know anything about you. How is it that you're trained to fight like you are? Tell me your story."

Ciara snapped back. "Oh, so you won't share anything about yourself when you know everything about me." She emphasised the word everything.

Zixin's shoulders lowered, and her facial muscles relaxed. "Okaaaay! What were you going to ask?"

Ciara thought for a moment, then decided to be brutally honest. "Mr Fernley told me that your father is an intelligence agent who poses as a diplomat. Is that true?"

Zixin started the hairdryer and started blow-drying her hair. After 30 seconds, she turned it off and turned to face Ciara.

"Of course he is. That's what Chinese diplomats are. Why do you think I am trained in self-defence and other stuff."

"What other stuff? What else can you do?"

"I started firearms training at 14. I've taken courses on psychology, first aid, languages, lock picking, ballroom dancing—"

"Ballroom dancing? That I have to see."

"Diplomats attend functions and have to socialise with dignitaries. It isn't all about combat."

"How come you were allowed to use firearms at such a young age?"

"Have a look in that drawer over there," said Zixin pointing to the standard bedside cabinet.

Ciara went over and opened the drawer. She rifled through some papers, a book on weapons training, red lipstick, and a stopwatch. Finding nothing, she asked, "What am I looking for, Zixin?"

Zixin muttered something under her breath and came over. She delved into the bottom of the draw. Eventually, she pulled out an identification card. It had a large gold and red emblem with a silver sword. There was disbelief in Ciara's voice. "It's a Ministry of State Security ID card with your photo and name. Surely, you're too young to be a member?"

"Of course I am. But my father got me an ID card so he could send me on MSS courses. He wasn't going to wait until I was 18."

Ciara felt genuine awe. "Imagine if one of the house events was espionage. We'd win easily."

Both girls laughed. Then Zixin's expression changed. "The truth is my dad wanted a son to train as an intelligence agent. I wanted to study medicine and become a doctor. I persuaded my mum to talk to him and convinced him that two years here would improve my cover. I needed to get away from him and the MSS."

"So, who exactly is the Ministry of State Security? Are they the same as MI6 or the CIA?"

"More like the CIA and FBI combined into one agency."

"So, if you weren't a spy and didn't study medicine, what else would you want to do?"

Zixin laughed. "I have no idea. All I have ever done is prepare to be an intelligence agent."

Ciara suddenly looked serious. "Have you…have you ever killed anyone?"

"I'm 16 years of age. Of course, I haven't killed anyone." Then Zixin paused for dramatic effect and added, "Yet."

They both laughed again. Ciara gave her friend a hug. "Well, I'm happy that my friend is a lethal weapon. I need all the help I can get."

Zixin picked up her luggage and walked to the door. "Hurry up, Ciara. We'll be late. They walked to the lift, and Zixin pressed the down button."

"Seriously! I have one more question, though, and you won't like it."

The lift doors opened. They got in.

"Get it over with," said Zixin.

"Is your dad working with Dr Kim?"

"I don't know. I have been asking myself the same question since I heard the intruder speak Mandarin."

"There must be some connection," said Ciara. "Scottie said everyone here has ties to Dr Kim."

"I never considered how I got a place here," said Zixin. "I assumed my dad pulled some strings, but I never considered that Dr Kim might be working with the Chinese Government."

"It might also explain Hana's comments about your dad working for the CCP."

"She was just spreading rumours. Although, now that I think about it, there could be a connection."

The lift stopped. The doors slid open. As they walked towards the main entrance, Ciara asked, "What about your comment about Dr Kim testing on animals? Is that true?"

"I'll tell you later."

Just outside, a minibus was waiting for them. The driver grabbed the bags and put them inside the luggage hold. The two girls clambered up the steps. They saw Scottie, Hana, and Chan were already on board. A range rover was parked in front of the minibus and a second behind it. Ciara guessed they were a personal protection detail. Clearly, they were taking no chances after the kidnapping incident.

When they arrived at Jeju International Airport, they still had to go through security. That only took a few minutes. The airport staff opened a new lane for Dr Kim and his party. Airport staff ran ahead of them, opening doors and ushering them through. When they reached the tarmac, a limousine took them to Dr Kim's Gulfstream jet.

The Gulfstream G650ER is an American-made luxury jet preferred by Elon Musk, Bill Gates, and Jeff Bezos. The aircraft powered by its Rolls-Royce engines can reach Mach .925, over 700 mph. Ciara walked up the steps to the 46-foot cabin area, which was divided into three living spaces. The scent of jasmine wafted through the air as Ciara was welcomed by the staff.

The luxury aircraft seated thirteen passengers. The five students sat in the main cabin, which housed seven fully reclinable, cream leather seats and had a large flat-screen TV. Dr Kim, his personal assistant and bodyguard, took the stateroom so that he wasn't bothered by the students.

A cabin attendant served drinks as the pilot started the engines. The plane moved slowly to the runway. From arriving at the airport to taxiing had taken just 20 minutes.

"Just to warn you. When we take off, the g-forces are much greater on this plane compared to commercial aircraft," said Hana.

"Have you ever been on a commercial aircraft?" asked Zixin.

Hana looked a little embarrassed. "No, but it doesn't mean it isn't true."

It was true. The acceleration pushed Ciara back into her seat, and she felt the crushing pressure on her chest. It didn't last long, though. They were cruising at 50,000 feet, high above the commercial jets ten minutes later.

After a few hours of watching films, eating food, and chatting about what they would do in New Zealand, the cabin lights dimmed. Despite the adventure to come, Ciara went straight to sleep. When she woke, it was still dark. She could see the light emitted from a laptop further down the cabin. Ciara walked to the service area and past Scottie, who was watching a film.

A range of snacks was left in wicker baskets, so Ciara picked up an apple and made herself herbal tea. Scottie brushed past the curtain and into the service area.

"How's it going?" he asked.

"Fine, thanks. Just getting some snacks, then heading back."

"And your shoulder?"

"Much better, thanks."

Scottie grabbed a chocolate bar and a can of cola. The silence continued for a few moments before Ciara broke it. "So you and Hana are a couple."

"Yeah—I guess. We met in New Zealand when her dad was visiting my grandfather. There was nothing to do, so I gave her a tour. We went to Hobbiton—"

"Hobbiton? As in Lord of the Rings?"

In that instant, the plane hit turbulence, and Ciara fell forward into Scottie. He instinctively grabbed her to stop them both from falling. She wouldn't fall into his arms like a damsel in distress. She thrust out an arm and pushed him away.

Realising that he might be offended, she quickly said, "You were talking about Hobbiton."

"Oh yeah. It's pretty cool. Peter Jackson had the set built for The Hobbit movie, but they left it as a tourist attraction. Anyway, that's when we realised we liked each other."

"So, what was the 'to get to know Ciara better' line about?"

Scottie looked like he wished he was somewhere else. Looking down at his feet, he said, "The flirting was a bit much. I do like you. I guess I got a little carried away. I'm sorry!"

"Did Hana ask you to invite me to be part of the dig?"

"I wanted you to come anyway, but yeah. Hana said it would be a good way to defuse the tension after what happened between Zixin and Chan."

"Well, at least we know how things stand," said Ciara. And she abruptly turned around, walked back to her seat and fell asleep without touching her snacks.

Chapter 8
The Pleiades

The dream continued where it left off, with William standing in front of twelve Pleiades, six boys and six girls.

"Welcome back. We have much to tell you," said one of the male Pleiades.

William looked startled, "Who exactly are you?"

"We call ourselves the Pleiades and have travelled 442 light-years from a planet within this galaxy," said another boy.

"Our planet was dying, so we looked for other planets that could support life," said one of the girls. "We found yours but did not know it had a species nearly identical to our own."

"Your evolutionary path must have been similar," said a different boy. "Like us, your brain development and social nature enabled you to become the dominant life form on your planet."

"It makes you wonder if there is a creator," said the first speaker. "It is unlikely that two nearly identical species followed the same evolution on different planets."

William found the switching from one Pleiades to another unsettling. He wished they would choose one spokesperson. He would look at a speaker, and then a different person would speak. It was like watching a tennis match.

"Our evolution is around 300 years in advance of your own," said the first boy. "In that time, we learned to manipulate our genome."

"Genome?" said a confused William.

"A genome is the complete set of genetic information for an organism. In essence, it is the instructions that create us. The human genome is mostly the same for all people, with only tiny differences between individuals. We learned to rewrite our genome. We age ten times slower than humans once we reach physical maturity."

"And we gave ourselves the ability to read each other's thoughts," said another.

"This accelerated our understanding because when one person learns, we all do," said the first speaker. "Eventually, our thoughts merged into one mind."

This was a lot for William to take in. He got the feeling the message was meant for someone with far more knowledge than he had. Wishing to change the subject, he pointed to their ship and asked, "Did you come here in that?"

"Yes," said one of the girls. "This vessel is a prototype with only two in existence."

This was more within William's understanding. He started walking towards the ship. "May I look inside?"

One of the Pleiades continued talking. "We think the other ship crashed into central New Zealand causing a volcanic eruption that left a huge crater. Critical technology was lost to us."

The interior of the craft seemed much larger than the outside. There were two seats and a panel with lights at the far end. William could see a wall of vertical coffin-like shapes, the size and shape humanoid but much larger than the Pleiades.

The thought that the Pleiades had been here for many years popped into his head. His brow furrowed. "Your people arrived a long time ago?"

"Yes."

"So, are you descended from the original survivors?"

"We are the original survivors. We age more slowly than you and have technology that allows us to sleep without ageing."

"Why are you still here?"

"When we arrived, this place was uninhabited, and we had no means of leaving this land. This wasn't the only ship. One landed in Tahiti, where the natives fed and housed us."

It was different here. When the Māori arrived in New Zealand, they were aggressive. We manipulated their minds so that they could not see us.

"You can manipulate other people's minds. Is that why the Māori following me collapsed?"

"Yes! He is unharmed," said one of the boys. "If he is left, he will die of dehydration. Any animal that comes within the confines of the mountain falls asleep."

William's mouth was dry, and he felt uncomfortable in the vessel. But he wanted to know more. "How did you know the Pleiades interacted with the Tahitians?"

"We have told you that we communicate telepathically. When Princess Aimata talked to you in Tahiti, we were all aware of your conversation."

"Everything is shared with everyone else?" said William. "None of you have any privacy?"

"You are still thinking of us as separate beings. We are physically separate but not mentally. Why would you want privacy from yourself?"

"What happened to the other Pleiades in Tahiti?"

"They died!" said one of the girls without displaying emotion. "When the HMS Dolphin arrived from England in 1967, they brought diseases, and we had no immunity. Within two weeks, all died. Princess Aimata was away, so she survived."

"I'm sorry!" said William awkwardly.

"If we had a sample of what caused the disease, we could prevent it from harming us," said the girl. "Alas, we did not know we were infected until it was too late."

One of the boys took over the narrative. "Their deaths were painful. The diseases were terrible, but the isolation was worse."

"The isolation?"

"They became disconnected from our minds. The loneliness they experienced must have been unbearable."

This was the first time William had sensed any emotion in this alien race. The thought of being disconnected from each other scared them. "If the danger was so great, why did Princess Aimata board the Endeavour?" asked William.

"It was the only way to ensure you survived. We knew that without you, our species would become extinct."

"Me?" said William. "I think you must have made a mistake. How can I save you?"

"We do not make mistakes. You do not need to worry about how you will help us."

William looked doubtful but decided not to press the issue. Instead, he asked, "What happened to Princess Aimata?"

"She died! She contracted tuberculosis shortly after speaking to you."

William's eyes widened. "Did…did I give it to her? Will we all die?"

"No, and no! Every generation, one of us can see glimpses of the future. They are slightly different to the rest of us. He had a vision of you coming here and living a long life."

William wasn't sure what to say. This didn't seem real. The Pleiades were an alien race that could see the future, control minds, and communicate telepathically. This must not be real. Were these hallucinations? Was he delirious with tuberculosis or some other disease?

"What do you want with me?"

"We will show you," said the first speaker.

William collapsed to the ground like a marionette with its strings cut. Ciara woke up, confused. Had William passed out, or had she simply woken from her dream? She looked around, then remembered where she was. The cabin lights were on, and the others were eating.

"Hey, sleepyhead," said Zixin. "Come and have some breakfast. We'll be landing soon."

No sooner had she said that than the Gulfstream descended towards Auckland airport. It had been less than 10 hours since take-off. Far faster than a commercial airline. Ciara moved her seat to the upright position and strapped herself in. She would have to go without breakfast.

While waiting for their luggage to be inspected, Ciara whispered to Zixin, "I had another dream."

"Really?" exclaimed Zixin. The others, who stood a little ahead of the two girls, didn't notice.

"Shhhh," whispered Ciara. "Not so loud."

"Tell me!"

Ciara told Zixin the main points of her dream as quickly as possible. "So, we need to get samples of the viruses that caused eighteenth-century diseases. They said they need a sample to protect themselves."

"Good point," said Zixin. "Let me look!" She pulled out her phone and opened the web browser. "Smallpox, diphtheria, tuberculosis, measles, yellow fever, cholera—"

"Okay. Okay. I get the idea. But how are we going to get the viruses?"

"I guess we'll have to tell Dr Kim what we know."

Ciara frowned. "I dislike helping that man get what he wants, but, you're right, I can't see any other solution."

When they walked out of Auckland airport, the sun was shining, and the sky was a deep rich blue. Ciara had to squint because it was so bright. After her eyes adjusted, she found that everything was sharper than usual. It was like looking at the world in 4K HDR. She assumed it was the lack of pollution but had read that the hole in the ozone was above New Zealand. Did that make a difference?

The students bundled into one of the two limousines waiting near the entrance. The cars headed south along State Highway 1 towards Hamilton, a destination 90 minutes from the airport.

Ciara was astonished by the open spaces everywhere. You could tell only five million people lived here.

"Is anyone hungry? Hamilton Central has loads of great restaurants, especially those alongside the Waikato River," said Scottie.

They agreed to eat before heading to the excavation site. Scottie spoke to the driver, and he radioed the other limo. Dr Kim obviously agreed because the car turned off the highway onto Norton road. After a few minutes, the driver found two empty bays on the roadside. They parked just opposite an orange building that was a Vietnamese restaurant.

"I love Vietnamese food," said Hana. "Shall we eat here?"

"We can if you want, but it might be nice to walk along the river first," said Scottie. "There are better restaurants there."

Hana glared at Scottie. "Fine. We'll do what you want for a change."

"I was only…" Scottie's voice trailed off, and his shoulders slumped.

Zixin whispered in Ciara's ear, "She's got him whipped."

Dr Kim chose the place to eat, or more accurately, his driver made a recommendation. The restaurant had an incredibly high ceiling that gave a sense of space. Three giant walls made of glass panes were set inside an elaborate framework. Trees and bushes practically touched the glass outside, and the river winded its way past.

The students sat on their own and ordered canapes and tapas to share. The canapes were dressed with sundried tomatoes, mozzarella and basil pesto. The tapas were filled with salmon sashimi, toasted sesame seeds, wasabi mayo, and wakame salad. They say hunger is the best sauce, and Ciara, who had missed breakfast, thought the food was incredible.

Their relaxed lunch was interrupted by the scream of a girl around their own age. "Scottie! You're back!" A girl with brown hair, a fuller figure, and who was sort of pretty came running over and threw her arms around Scottie, then sat down on his lap.

Ciara felt a little uncomfortable with the commotion that Liv's entrance caused. Glancing around, she saw other diners returning to their conversations. All except three Asia men, who sat at a table by the far wall. They wore dark suits and sunglasses and continued to watch them.

Scottie stood up and untangled her arms. Looking very uncomfortable, he said, "Hey, Liv. Good to see ya. Let me introduce everyone here."

Liv finally noticed everyone else. "This is my girlfriend, Hana," said Scottie gesturing at the Clearly unhappy billionaire's daughter.

"Great to meet you. Don't mind me. We go back years—nothing to worry about."

Hana stood up and regally extended an arm. "The pleasure is mine. I am always happy to meet one of Scottie's friends," she said through clenched teeth.

Scottie introduced everyone else at the table. The entire time, Hana was giving both Scottie and Liv daggers. After a few minutes, Scottie managed to persuade Liv to leave. She was oblivious to the disruption caused by her arrival.

Dr Kim paid the bill, and they headed out of the restaurant. They hadn't walked far when Chan said, "I've left my phone on the table." And he rushed back inside.

The others waited for five minutes, but he didn't appear.

"I'll go and see where he is," said Scottie.

Hana let out a big sigh. "We might as well all go."

They walked back into the restaurant. Zixin whispered to Ciara, "Hana's keeping an eye on Scottie."

Chan was over by the far wall talking to the three Asian men in suits and sunglasses. He bowed and walked briskly back to the others. Hana said, "What were you doing talking to those men?"

"Oh…um…they said they saw someone take something from our table," said Chan.

Hana frowned. "Why were you even talking to them?"

"I went around all of the tables asking if anyone had seen my phone."

"Shall I go and ask the manager?" asked Scottie.

"Oh…no…it's okay. I found my phone in my pocket," said Chan. "It was there all the time."

Dr Kim did not look very impressed when the four students arrived back at the limos. He called Hana over. Ciara couldn't see what was said, but Hana was looking at her feet, and Dr Kim's finger was wagging up and down at her. The remaining journey was only thirty minutes, but nobody spoke. The atmosphere was so bad that Ciara put on her headphones and listened to music.

It was a relief when they arrived at the purpose-built cabins. Each was a self-contained apartment with a kitchen, laundry room, bathroom, two bedrooms, and a living area. The bedrooms had twin beds, so Ciara and Zixin shared one bedroom while the boys the other. Hana stayed in a different building with her father.

Ciara unpacked her suitcase, which consisted of some clothes and a few essentials. She picked up her toiletry bag and carried it over to the bathroom. She pulled out her toothbrush and noticed a small glass perfume bottle with a clear liquid inside. Tied around the head of a bottle was a tag. It said, Visionade—drink before sleep. It was signed 'JF'.

JF must be James Fernley. He obviously had a strange sense of humour, calling it Visionade. She'd dreamed about William Hartley on the flight, so she probably didn't need this concoction. She wasn't sure whether she should drink anything that might invoke a vision. She decided to leave it on the bedside table and then went to the bathroom to clean her teeth.

The rest of the day was spent settling in, but they were called to a meeting to discuss the excavation. Some skeletons have been found in a cave on Mount Pirongia, and equipment had to be carried over. An experienced archaeologist called Mathew Walker had flown over from the UK. He was standing over a 3D map of Mount Pirongia. By his side were two local archaeologists.

The effectiveness of the Terrestrial Laser Scanning (TLS) instruments was mixed. In some areas, the level of detail was incredible, but in others, it was useless. Water levels, temperatures, and different rock densities affected the accuracy of the scans.

Pointing to some areas on the map, Walker said, "We will need personnel to enter, here, here, and here. If they all carry a hand scanner, it will fill in the blanks."

One of the assistant archaeologists, Bill McGraw, called over to one of the workers. "Tana, organise three teams of five men and give them all a laser scanner." He indicated a pile of boxes with Leica BLK2GO Handheld Imaging Laser Scanner written on the side.

Hana had not joined them since she left with her father, so Ciara, Zixin, Scottie and Chan stood around wondering what they would be doing. "You four," said McGraw indicating the four friends, "go with Tana. He'll put you on one of the teams."

They followed Tana, and he gave each of them a box and some safety clothing. "Don't lose or damage these scanners. Wear these clothes and report back here tomorrow at 7 am. Don't forget your hard hat."

There was nothing left to do, so they headed back to the cabin. The friends sat on the sofa chatting before Ciara said she was ready for bed.

It was 05:30 when Ciara woke. Someone was shaking her gently. It could only be Zixin. Unless it was Scottie. He was in the next room. But no, that was ridiculous. Determined not to wake up, Ciara slurred, "What do you want?"

"Who do you think I want?" said a voice in a fake New Zealand accent.

Despite her sleepiness, Ciara knew it was Zixin but played along, "Are you the maid? Do you want to make up the bed?"

There was no reply, so she sat up! Zixin was standing by her bed wearing an army camouflage uniform and carrying a spare set. Zixin handed her the bundle. "Type 07s. Put them on and leave your electronics in the cabin. We don't want anyone tracking us."

Without arguing, Ciara took the clothing and got dressed quickly. "Where did you get these from?"

"I bought them online. We have army surplus stores in China too."

Then the two of them silently left the cabin. It surprised Ciara that they were sleeping in comfort and not in a tent on the excavation site. Apparently, contractors had been sued for health and safety violations, so all areas were closed down at night.

Once they were clear of the hotel, Zixin put her hand on Ciara's arm, and they stopped. "Do you think you can find the entrance to the mountain?"

"I'm not sure. It's not going to be easy in the dark."

"We have an hour before sunrise," said Zixin. "I have been studying the area, and there are some caves in the mountain. They're called the Kaniwhaniwha Caves. Perhaps the entrance is near there?"

"You're getting pretty good with Māori names."

"I asked one of the local Māori. He said the most important difference is that wh is pronounced as an f."

Ciara thought it was unlikely the entrance would be a known caving spot, but what did they have to lose. Mount Pirongia might only be 959 metres above sea

95

level, but it had 13,500 hectares of bush-covered slopes. They had to start somewhere.

All of the volunteers had been given an electric quad bike to travel to and from the site. The two girls did not want to disturb anyone, so they pushed their quadbikes a short distance along the trail. Although they were quiet, the high-pitched whirring sound might alert someone. They started the engines and headed off to the Kaniwhaniwha Caves. They didn't spot a dark figure following them on an identical machine.

As soon as they got to the caves, Ciara knew it was the wrong place. "This is on the north part of the mountain. William Hartley didn't travel around the mountain. The entrance has to be on the left side, near the sea."

"You could have told me that before we set out."

"We only arrived yesterday. I didn't have time to think. Should we carry on around the mountain or not?"

"If we do, they'll know we've gone," said Zixin.

"We still have 30 minutes before it gets light. We can make up some excuse if we're not too long," said Ciara.

Zixin beamed. "I think I am becoming a bad influence on you."

The quad bikes whined that high-pitched sound of all-electric vehicles, and they followed the trail west. Eventually, the trail headed up and in the wrong direction. Ciara stopped her bike, "We either leave the bikes here or proceed on foot. What do you think?"

"What's the worst that can happen? They start looking in the wrong place without us," said Zixin.

Ciara hesitated a moment. "We could phone Scottie and say…What could we say?"

"Nothing! Let's go," And Zixin headed off to the southwest.

"Where are you going? It's me that's been here before. Remember?"

Zixin stopped walking and stood with her hands on her hips. "No, you haven't. You dreamed about it, and that wasn't even here. I thought we should head down to sea level and then head south alongside the mountain. You might recognise the cliff face."

"Hmmm! Good idea. I'll follow you and keep my eyes peeled." They set off fighting their way through the bush. Now that there wasn't a trail to follow, it was hard going.

Shortly after Ciara and Zixin left the trail, a quad bike stopped next to the other two. A figure wearing a balaclava and a mask climbed off. They held a pair of thermal-imaging binoculars to their face. Then they proceeded to head in the same direction as the girls.

After the sun had risen, it became easier to push through the bush. They had been walking for at least two hours. Ciara was starting to get disheartened. She was famished and knew they would be in trouble when they got back. "Maybe we should head back?"

"Seriously? You're giving up already," said Zixin. "What did you think would happen? We'd walk for 30 minutes and then happen upon the cliff face with the vertical entrance?" said Zixin.

That was pretty much what she thought would happen. She'd recognise something that would lead them to the entrance. Stupid, really—it wouldn't look the same after 250 years.

"Maybe we should call Scottie and tell him we're safe?"

"There is no signal here," said Zixin. "Fine! Let's stop and have a snack."

"You brought food," said Ciara excitedly.

"You are wearing Chinese military combats," said Zixin. "Do you think I would bring them and not other supplies?"

The girls sat down on a large volcanic rock. Zixin opened up the rucksack and took out two small cartons of coconut water, two packets of crisps, and two energy bars.

They heard the loud snap of a broken branch about 50 metres back.

"Somebody's following us," whispered Zixin.

It was the urgency in Zixin's behaviour that caused Ciara to tense. The neocortex section of her brain—the thinking component—believed it must be a deer or another animal. The reptilian and limbic parts of her brain thought otherwise.

Ciara instinctively crouched down. "What should we do?"

Zixin nodded to a section of the cliff face that jutted out. "Let's head over there as quietly as possible. They might walk past if there's enough room behind that jutting rock."

They moved as quietly as possible. Ciara could not hear a single sound from Zixin. Her footsteps and breathing were silent. She was sure that she sounded like a wounded animal crashing through the bush. Her heart was pounding, and the blood was pulsing in her ears. Eventually, they reached the jutting rock and moved behind it.

"Zixin. This is it!"

"Shhhhh. You're giving our location away."

Ciara grabbed Zixin's arm and pulled. Her friend turned around irritably. "Stop it." Her face changed from a scowl to wonderment, and she immediately followed Ciara through the tall thin gap. Trying to peer out, they could only see a thin sliver of the forest. They heard the footsteps of someone and pulled their heads back. The sounds got louder, then quieter, then louder again. Whoever it was had lost them and was trying to find them again.

"I think they must have had thermal binoculars to have tracked us in such a dense forest. The rocks block our heat signatures," whispered Zixin. "As long as we stay in the cave and he doesn't find the entrance, we'll be fine."

Keeping her voice as quiet as possible, Ciara said, "How do you know it's a man?"

"The movements sounded like a man, but I suppose it might not be," said Zixin. Then in a slightly louder voice, she said, "I think they've gone now."

They moved back from the entrance, and Ciara turned around. Lying on the floor by her feet was a human skeleton. She jumped backwards in shock and tripped over something on the floor. She fell flat on her back, knocking the air from her lungs. Gasping, she sat up. "What the…"

Her voice trailed off. The object she had tripped over was Zixin. Ciara crawled over to her and shook her inert form. There was no reaction, so she put her ear to Zixin's mouth. "Thank God!" she said out loud. Ciara was in a dilemma. Should she leave Zixin here and try to find her way to the Pleiades in the centre of the mountain? Should she drag Zixin outside and risk being caught by whoever was stalking them?

She finally decided to ask Zixin. She dragged her friend to the entrance, only two metres away. Zixin's eyes opened, and she moved her arm to the back of her head. "Why is the back of my head sore?"

"You passed out as soon as you moved inside the cave," said Ciara. "It looks like I am the only one who can go further in."

"Noooooo! That is so unfair. I've come all this way, and I have to wait here. Damn you, Alinac."

"It's not all bad," said Ciara. "We found the entrance."

"Easy for you to say. You get to go on ahead and make first contact."

Ciara left a sulking Zixin at the entrance to the cave. She was relieved that the passages extended to a high ceiling. As a child, she suffered from claustrophobia, a fear of confined spaces. Had any of the tunnels been narrow, she wasn't sure she would get through.

The trail was identical to the one in her dream. It was lit by bioluminescent fungus glow-worms, like tiny candle wicks burning in the sky. The glowing blue light was not only beautiful but calming. Why weren't they affected by the sleep spell? Perhaps they lived above its effects?

After a couple of hundred metres, she came to a junction. An ornate wooden totem stared at her. Ciara tried to remember the rule. "When the eyes are made out of pāua shells, go left. When a tongue points to the right, go right. When the tā moko is a different colour to the face, go straight."

Ciara still had no idea what the tā moko was. She hadn't thought to look it up and forgot to ask Scottie. She had also left her electronics back at the base camp though she doubted there would be a signal inside the mountain.

The first totem was easy. There was no tongue, and the eyes were a rainbow of colours found only on sea snails and mollusc shells. In Korea, pāua was called abalone. It was served regularly in the cafeteria, and Ciara was violently sick after trying it. Even now, the thought of the chewy, salty food brought back vivid memories of kneeling over the toilet bowl.

After passing a couple more totems, she reached a junction with three passages. She headed down the left passage and picked up her pace. She couldn't leave Zixin stranded at the cave entrance. What if the stalker came back? The totem's eyes were wooden slits, so definitely not left. The tongue poked out of the left side of a yawning gash that was its mouth.

The face glared at her menacingly. The tattoo spirals stood out against the rest of the wooden facade. Somehow it made the totem all the more frightening. If she took the wrong path, she could be wandering around for miles and miles. She might never find her way out again.

It must be straight. Then it dawned on her. Tā moko must be the tattoos. The other totems had them, but these markings were dark blue. Feeling better, she headed straight on. Eventually, she came to the central cavern and could make out the dark shape of the Pleiades' ship.

Chapter 9
The Sun and the Moon

Ciara slowly made her way towards the craft. As she got nearer, she saw it was silver in colour. There were no windows or any way to see inside. She half expected it to split open and light up the cavern, but nothing happened. She placed her hand on the metal. It was warm to the touch.

"Hello," she called. Her voice echoed lightly around the cavern.

Then a little louder, shouted, "Anybody there?"

Ciara spent the next 15 minutes running her hands over the craft. It was completely smooth with no gaps. Then she wrapped her knuckles firmly on the metal. Nothing happened. So she tried again but harder. Ciara looked around for something, picked up a large rock and threw it against the ship. There was a loud clang.

Not sure what to do, Ciara sat down on a large rock. She racked her brains, and after five minutes, gave up and headed back the way she had come. When she reached Zixin, she outlined her plan. The two girls headed back to the quad bikes. There was no sign of the stalker. By the time they reached the excavation site, it was 11 am.

"Where the hell have you been?" shouted the red-faced archaeologist, Bruce Adams. Spittle was flying from his mouth and sticking to his beard. "You were in my team, and you buggered off all morning."

Ciara said slowly, "We need to see Dr Kim. We've found what he is looking for."

"I'll be the one speaking to Dr Kim," yelled Adams. "As far as I am concerned, you two and your friend are out." And he stormed off.

"That went well," said Zixin.

Ciara frowned. "What friend was he talking about?"

"Yeah, that was a bit odd. What else has happened?"

"Let's try and find someone and find out," said Ciara. "It's unfortunate he spotted us arriving."

Eventually, they found Scottie. He'd stopped off to have lunch. "Adams is furious with you two and Chan. Where did you go?"

"Chan's been gone too?" said Ciara. "You don't think he—"

"No, I don't," said Zixin firmly.

"Are you going to tell me anything?" asked Scottie. His voice had become an octave higher.

"We need to find Dr Kim," said Ciara. "Come with us if you like."

They knocked on Dr Kim's cabin door, and his assistant, Yuna, answered. Ciara could see the hulking shape of Dr Kim's bodyguard, Dongwoo, behind her.

"We need to see Dr Kim immediately," said Ciara.

A voice called from inside the cabin. "Let them in, Yuna."

Dr Kim and Hana were sat at a dining table eating. The food looked incredible—prosciutto, salami, olives, grapes, sun-dried tomatoes, and other delicacies.

"Dr Kim," said Ciara excitedly. "We've found—"

"Please calm down," said Dr Kim, interrupting Ciara. "There is nothing worse than the whine of a hysterical child."

"Hysterical?" shouted Ciara, and then she composed herself. "I can think of many worse things—like a person planting a listening device on a minor."

Dr Kim's eyes narrowed. "Unfortunately, pre-production prototypes often malfunction. If you don't want your visa revoked, I suggest you calmly tell me what you have found," said Dr Kim, a definite chill in his voice.

Ciara glared at him but sat down and popped a grape into her mouth. Dr Kim looked like he was about to yell at her, so she quickly said, "We found the spaceship."

"Show me where the entrance is on the map," demanded Dr Kim. He got up and walked over to a large map of Mount Pirongia.

Ciara followed him and pointed to the location. Dr Kim pulled out a pen from his breast pocket and carefully marked the spot.

"An actual spacecraft," he said thoughtfully. "You must have had another vision. Tell me about it." It was a command, not a request.

Ciara told Dr Kim about her dream. "So, unless we can provide a sample of the eighteenth-century viruses, I don't think they will leave their ship."

"You think they are still alive?" asked Hana incredulously.

101

"입 다물어 (ib damul-eo)," shouted Dr Kim.

Hana's head dropped, and she stared at her feet. Dr Kim turned back to Ciara, and as if nothing had happened, he said, "I can have the samples here within the hour. Then you and I will go directly there."

Ciara, Zixin, and Scottie left Dr Kim and headed to their cabin. A voice called after them. "Wait for me." It was Hana.

"I'm surprised he let you join us," said Scottie.

"I told him I would keep an eye on you and report back to him," said Hana.

"So you'll spy on us for him?" said Zixin.

"Not a chance in hell," spat Hana. "I hate him."

They entered the cabin. Someone had tidied and left a buffet on the dining table. The students grabbed a plate each and loaded it with food.

Ciara bit into a cracker covered in pate. "Oh my God! This food is so good." Then addressing Hana, she said, "It must be amazing being you."

"I need the bathroom." Hana, who looked like she was fighting back the tears, dashed off.

Ciara looked around at the others. "What did I say?"

"Don't worry about it," said Scottie sadly. "Hana lives under a microscope— her father, the press, everyone. She claims to hate her father, but she is desperate for his approval. No matter how well she does, he always finds fault. But she'll be right!"

"I had no idea," said Ciara.

"Do you know how you will get inside the spaceship?" asked Zixin.

"Perhaps they'll open up when they see you have the samples," suggested Scottie.

"Yeah. I was hoping that too," said Ciara.

Hana came back from the bathroom and seemed her usual composed self. "Has anyone had an idea while I was away?"

"Why don't we call Sophie and ask her?" said Zixin.

So they did. Ciara spent 20 minutes telling Sophie everything that had happened so far. Most people would ask a million questions, but Sophie took it in her stride.

"The Pleiades want Ciara to free them, so there must be a way to open the spaceship," said Sophie.

"How did you work that one out?" said Ciara.

"Remember when you translated the message the sun and the moon sounded for the key," said Sophie. "None of us could translate the alien script, yet you could read it. You are the sun and the moon with your blonde hair and silver streaks. Plus, your visions. Ergo, you are the key to some destiny."

"Why didn't you say Ciara was the sun and the moon?" asked Zixin.

"The reference was obvious," said Sophie. "I assumed you knew."

"Sounded for the key," said Ciara repeating the phrase. "Do you think that a sound frequency opens the spacecraft?"

"Hmmm! Sound frequencies make some sense," said Sophie, her nose wrinkling in contemplation. "In the search for extra-terrestrial life, we used sounds. Drake and Sagan created the Arecibo message by modulating frequencies. The voyager's golden records were—"

"So that's a yes, is it Sophie?" said Zixin interrupting Sophie.

"You could try different sound frequencies, but it's not likely to work. We're missing some critical information," said Sophie.

"Like who put the alien code in the escape room?" said Zixin.

"I assumed it was Dr Kim," said Zixin. "But maybe he wouldn't be that hands-on."

"My brain hurts," groaned Scottie. "Hana and I are only just catching up, and it's a lot to take in."

Hana turned to her boyfriend. "I knew most of this already. My father asked me to keep an eye on Ciara." A guilty look crossed her face, and she said, "Sorry."

"It's fine! What else could you do?"

Hana brightened. "We need a plan. As Sophie said, we don't have enough information. Ciara needs to go back to the spacecraft with the virus samples. If the aliens come out, fine. If not, she needs to walk around the craft and record everything. If you take one of the LED flashlights, it will light up the entire cavern."

"After you record the video, please phone me back," said Sophie. "I might be able to help." She ended the video call.

"Do I have to sing at different frequencies to see if it does anything?" asked Ciara.

"Yes, and that reminds me. I would like to know where Chan is," said Zixin. "Someone followed us to the cavern entrance, and I wonder if it was him."

"He talked to those three Asian men and acted very suspiciously in the restaurant," said Scottie. "Did anyone believe he'd lost his wallet?"

"He's your friend," said Zixin looking at Scottie and Hana. "Are you sure he hasn't sold us out?"

Hana looked uncomfortable. "I can't be sure. Chan's parents are from Heilongjiang, China, on the border of North Korea. They are Chinese citizens but ethnically Korean. Maybe he has links to the Triads."

"He's from China, so he must be involved with the Triads," snapped Zixin. "Is that what you're saying?"

Hana looked horrified and quickly raised both hands in a pacifying gesture. "No! Of course not. It's just that the intruders at the school were Chinese. So were the men in the restaurant. I didn't mean anything by it."

"How can you tell they were Chinese?" asked Scottie.

"I can't be certain, but they looked Chinese," said Hana. "Sometimes the facial features give it away, but usually body language gives you a better indication."

Zixin's hands were on her hips, and she scowled at Hana.

"Do you think we should ring Chan's mother?" said Hana. "What if something has happened to him?"

"There's no point worrying her," said Scottie. "He's only been gone for a few hours."

There was a knock on the door. It was Yuna, Dr Kim's assistant. "The samples have arrived, so it's time to go."

Seven of them set off on the quad bikes—Dr Kim, Dongwoo, Yuna, and the four students. Zixin found it hilarious that Dr Kim rode in his tailormade Savile Row suit. Dr Kim insisted his assistant go inside with Ciara to check whether she would sleep. She immediately collapsed, but Ciara caught her to prevent any injuries.

It took Yuna's fainting to convince Dr Kim that only Ciara could enter the cave. He held out the case containing the samples. As Ciara grasped the handle, Dr Kim refused to let go.

"The doctor who gave me this said it would provide immunisation for measles, influenza, tuberculosis, typhoid fever, and cholera," he said. "These were the most common diseases of the eighteenth century. It was impossible to get the smallpox virus. That won't matter because the disease died out in 1980."

Dr Kim suddenly released the case handle, and Ciara staggered backwards. No wonder Hana hated him.

Ciara headed into the cavern and followed the route to the spacecraft. She took out the 100,000 lumens flashlight and turned it on. Light flooded the cavern, and Ciara saw that the silver ship had a bluish hue.

She pressed the record video button on her phone, walked up to the vessel, and started narrating. "The craft in front of me is an unidentified flying object from the Pleiades star cluster. The material is a silver-blue metal that feels warm to the touch. The object is ellipsoid in shape and does not appear to have a door."

Ciara spent 10 minutes banging on the metal and shouting for the Pleiades to come out. Nothing happened. "Okay," she called. "I can see you're shy. I'll leave the virus samples for you. They're what killed your people in Tahiti."

When Ciara returned, they watched the video at least a dozen times. Dr Kim became angry. "I bring you here at great expense, and you can't get the ship to open. What use are you?"

Zixin reacted angrily. "She did find a UFO, which is more than you would have done without her."

"Get them out of my sight," shouted Dr Kim to his bodyguard, Dongwoo.

The hulking man stepped forward and said quietly, "It might be better if you leave."

So the four students left Dr Kim with his bodyguard and assistant. They could hear him shouting as they walked away. When they returned to the cabin, Chan was inside, stuffing his face with food.

"Where have you been," demanded Hana.

"Sorry about that," said Chan looking sheepish. "I had a meeting in Hamilton with an agent today. I didn't want to tell you, just in case I jinxed it."

"An agent?" said Zixin. "Are you going to be Korea's top model?"

"Haha," said Chan sarcastically. "No! Opera Australia wants me to perform at the Sydney Opera house in January next year. I had to do an audition today, and they accepted me."

Hana looked genuinely pleased. "That is amazing, Chan, but you should have told us. We've been worried sick."

Ciara was surprised. It was the first act of selflessness she had seen from the billionaire's daughter.

"I'm sorry, but I was a bag of nerves, and I didn't want the extra pressure."

"That's amazing, Chan," said Scottie. "Who would have thought my friend would be an international opera star."

"Congratulations," echoed Ciara and Zixin.

Chan was beaming. "We should go out and celebrate later."

"I have a better idea," said Scottie. "Why don't we join my family for a Hāngī? They have them once a month and tonight is the night."

"What's a Hāngi?" asked Chan.

Scottie was already on the phone, so it was Hana who answered. "A traditional method of slow-cooking food using hot stones buried in the ground."

When Scottie got off the phone, he said, "A car will be here in 30 minutes to collect us." He must have heard Hana's response because he added, "A Hāngi is more than a meal. It is a spiritual ritual that must stay true to our beliefs. We believe the food is spoiled if someone walks on the earth covering the oven. A failed Hāngi is a bad omen."

They changed quickly, and then Ciara remembered Sophie. She sent the video footage to her friend. Five minutes later, her phone rang.

"I got your video—you weren't kidding about the UFO," said Sophie. "I can never be sure when people are serious or making fun of me."

"Of course, we were serious," said Ciara. "I would never make fun of you. We're friends, Sophie."

"Oh! That's good. I don't think you will get into the spaceship."

"Try not to sugar coat it, Sophie," said Zixin. "Tell us straight."

Sophie frowned. "I thought I had, but never mind. You'll need a key to open it."

"Really? What—" began Zixin.

Ciara elbowed her friend, which cut her off mid-sentence. "Please explain what you mean, Sophie?"

"I realised after you had gone. The clue was that the sun and the moon sounded for the key. A sound is a body of water between two landmasses. Sound is also a verb that means to plunge headfirst into a body of water. So the sun and the moon sounded for the key means—"

"I have to dive into some water, where I will find the key to open the ship," said Ciara excitedly.

"But where does Ciara have to dive?" asked Hana.

They all looked at Sophie expectantly. She simply looked back at them. "Well?" asked Zixin.

"I have no idea," said Sophie. "I assumed Ciara would have a vision and know where to go."

"They just happen. I don't choose when to have a vision," said Ciara.

"Maybe you just need to try," said Sophie.

Dr Kim had not returned, so Hana left him a note. It was a 30-minute drive to the Māori Village. When they got out of the car, they walked across a wooden bridge. Ciara could see a group of young children in shorts playing in the river. A boy nearest the bank climbed out and ran up to them. He was shivering, his skinny body dripping water on the floor.

"Hey, Miss," said the boy. "You want me to dive for $2?" When he spoke, it sounded like he had a mouthful of marbles. Ciara could see a bulge, like a giant gobstopper, pushing out one cheek.

Ciara was unsure how to react and looked at Scottie for guidance. Her friend, however, swung a kick at the boy and told him to bugger off. The kid moved out of range but was persistent. "Throw a $2 coin into the river, Miss."

"These aren't tourists, Huatare," said Scottie. "They're guests, so leave them alone."

"It's okay, Scottie," said Ciara. "He's not bothering us."

"Will he dive from this bridge to find the coin?" asked Zixin.

"Yes," said Hana. "I saw him do it for some tourists last time I was here."

The boy had already climbed over the wooden railing, ready to jump into the water. Zixin threw a $2 coin over the fence and into the river. In a blink of an eye, the boy was after it. There was a large splash, and thirty seconds later, he resurfaced, holding his prize high for them to see. Then he shoved it into the side of his mouth.

Another boy had already climbed over the railing. "Throw another coin, miss."

This time Zixin dropped a coin from the bridge, and he was after it in a flash. Like his friend, he surfaced, holding the $2 piece in the air before shoving it into the side of his mouth.

"Let's go before they come back up," said Scottie. "They'll do this all night if you encourage them."

Hana delved into her purse and pulled out a handful of $2 coins that she threw into the river. The children reacted in a frenzy, pushing each other out of the way to get to the coins. It was like feeding time in an aquarium. Ciara couldn't imagine throwing $20 or $30 away like that, but it was a drop in the ocean for Hana.

Scottie led them to a fenced-in complex of ornate wooden buildings with the largest resembling a human body in its structure. The carvings reminded Ciara of the totems in the cavern. Scottie took on the role of a tour guide, something he probably did in the past.

"Welcome to our marae," he said, waving his arm to indicate everything behind him. "My grandfather has organised a traditional Māori welcome ceremony called a pōwhiri. Its purpose is to unite the Tangata Whenua, the people of this land, with their visitors."

Scottie whispered to Ciara. "You're being honoured because you're Patupaiarehe. You'll be the youngest person ever to receive this welcome."

An oratory summons by a female elder rang out. Scottie replied to this call with one of his own, then said, "Walk towards the wharenui[2], our meeting house, then stop 20 metres in front."

A man blew into a large conch shell creating a trumpet-like sound. Four topless warriors wearing short grass skirts and two women adorned in flax cloaks exited the wharenui. A warrior carrying a wooden spear spun it aggressively while siding his back leg across the ground. Suddenly, he ran towards them with a loud cry. As he got closer, Ciara noticed a fern tucked into his waistband.

A tall, slim figure with blonde hair walked across the grass and into the meeting house. Nobody reacted to his presence. Was he real, or was it an echo from the past? Ciara glanced at Scottie, but his attention was on the Māori warrior, who had moved much closer. She desperately wanted to go after the strange man, but breaking this ceremony would not only be an insult, it might get her killed.

The warrior was close now, cheeks puffing in and out while brandishing the weapon. He started to move towards them slowly, his spear extended. Ciara's mind flashed back to William Hartley, facing the Māori warriors running at him. She felt a surge of adrenaline—her heart pounded, and her hands shook slightly. She noticed Scottie looking at her, with concern etched into his handsome face.

Bending down carefully while still making eye contact, the warrior placed the fern on the ground. He backed away, making loud barks and threatening gestures with his spear. Scottie whispered to Ciara, "Walk forward and pick up the fern but never take your eyes off him."

Ciara collected the fern and backed away slowly. She was desperate to go after the blonde man. Her attention was brought back by the Māori warrior who stalked her, spinning his spear and making war cries. He stopped suddenly,

_____

[2] wharenui is pronounced far-ae-nu-ee

poked out his tongue, and gave a loud bellow. Then he lunged forward and made sweeping movements with the spear. When he stood up, one of the Māori women started singing. The warrior turned around and walked away, pausing to encourage them to follow.

The Māori performed the haka, their voices calling out eerily into the evening. An older man, who Ciara presumed was Scottie's grandfather, welcomed the visitors. Ciara caught the word Patupaiarehe among the Māori greeting. Several songs followed, and Chan performed Schubert's Ava Maria. Ciara had never heard anything so beautiful. The final part of the ceremony was the hongi and harirū, where the two parties pressed noses and shook hands.

Then the spell ended, and everyone relaxed. Ciara turned to her friends and said, "Did you see the tall blonde man enter the meeting house during the ceremony?"

None of them had. "Are you sure you didn't imagine it, Ciara?" said Scottie. "One of the warriors would have reacted if someone had strolled past them."

Ciara started to doubt whether the man was real or not. She headed across the grass to the meeting house to check for herself. Now that she could see the designs more closely, she marvelled at their beauty. It was more detailed and cleaner than the totems in the cave.

Slipping off her shoes, Ciara entered the building. It was empty, with no sign of the blonde man and no other doors. The older man who had welcomed them during the ceremony entered the room. Ciara could see a family resemblance to Scottie.

"Ciara," he called, "pleased to meet you."

"Kaumātua, I am honoured," said Ciara.

"I see that my grandson has taught you some Māori te reo…badly," said the elder.

It took Ciara a moment to register the insult. Her face must have shown shock because Scottie's grandfather started laughing.

"Don't let an old man's jokes bother you. You did very well, and I appreciate the gesture."

Not sure how to react, Ciara focused on her reason for entering the building. "Kaumātua, did you see a tall blonde man walk in here during the ceremony?"

"No. But it's not uncommon to see visions during the pōwhiri. If the Patupaiarehe have returned, it's because you are here."

He smiled, and Ciara noticed that his facial tattoos curved around his mouth. "I would like to show you something. Would you join me?"

They walked outside to the edge of the marae. "Do you see the silver poupou facing inwards?"

Ciara nodded. The small silver totem was pointing in the opposite direction to the others.

"There are four of these, one in each corner. If the poupou faced outwards, they would be sentries looking out for an enemy. But facing inwards, they become the caretakers for the marae."

They continued to walk, and the Kaumātua took her to a smaller building. He opened the door for her to enter. "I have one more thing to show you."

Ciara walked inside and on the wall was an oil painting of a tree-lined lake with a rocky cliff and a waterfall. Elegantly stepping out of the lake was a naked girl, her blonde hair wet, and in the foreground was a Māori boy hiding behind a clump of pampas grass. It was the story Scottie had told her.

"The girl looks just like me," said Ciara, stunned. "The artist is a genius to have captured the scene so perfectly."

"I thought you might be upset at being painted," said a younger voice. "I'm glad you like it."

Ciara turned to look at Scottie, who was standing in the doorway.

"At least now, I know your superpower," said Ciara.

When it was finally time to eat, two locals went over to the hāngī and dug into the ground. When they reached a cream sheet, they pulled it to one side to reveal trays of steaming food. Delicious smells wafted from the chicken, pork, lamb, sweet potatoes and other root vegetables. Saliva formed in Ciara's mouth, and her stomach rumbled. Slightly embarrassed, she pressed her belly to stop it.

Scottie smiled at her. "The smell gets me every time too."

The men placed the food on a long table alongside salad, sauces and homemade bread. Scottie's grandfather said a blessing for the food, and they lined up to fill their plates. Ciara sat chatting, all thoughts of the Pleiades gone from her mind. Then she saw the tall, slim figure again. He was standing on his own, a short distance away.

Was it an—? No, it couldn't be. Then realisation dawned. It was Mr Fernley. His beard was gone, and his hair was no longer ginger, but it was him. She nudged Zixin and pointed to where he had been. But he was gone.

"It was him," said Ciara. "A tall blonde-haired person stands out here."

"You certainly do," replied Zixin.

"Arrrgg," groaned Ciara. "Be serious, for once in your life."

They looked, but there was no sign of anyone tall, slim and blonde. Although Zixin kept joking, I see one now, referring to Ciara. They asked several people there, but no one had seen Mr Fernley.

The evening ended, and the four friends headed back to the site. Hana was not looking forward to facing her father.

When Ciara went to bed that night, she decided to run through the events of her last dream. She hoped it would continue exactly where it finished but couldn't fall asleep. Hours went by with no sign of sleep. Maybe her visions only went as far as finding the Pleiades?

Trying not to disturb Zixin, Ciara got out of bed to read in the other room. She stopped mid-step, noticing the small bottle of liquid from Mr Fernley. Ciara opened it, sniffed the contents, and downed it in one gulp. She got back into bed and was asleep in minutes.

Chapter 10
Run Aground

When William Hartley awoke, he was lying on a warm metal table. An arm reached down and clasped his hand. It heaved, pulling him upright.

"What happened?" asked William.

"It is time for you to return to your ship," said the girl who had helped him stand. She handed him his musket, which he took, feeling slightly confused.

Why had he collapsed? Did they do something to him? He was relieved they were encouraging him to leave. The sooner he left, the happier he would be. It was then that he noticed a thin metal band around his wrist. He held it up. "What's this?"

"A gift," said one of the female Pleiades. "It will save your life, so do not try to remove it."

He set off on the long journey through the tunnels. One of the girls, possibly the one he had met at the entrance, guided him. When they reached the cave entrance, she said, "Goodbye, William," and abruptly turned around.

The unconscious Māori was lying where he fell. The greenstone mere lay a few feet from the outstretched hand. William picked it up before squeezing through the gap and stepping out into the bright spring day. The sunshine was blinding after the gloom of the cave, and he instinctively raised his right arm to shield his eyes. The bracelet glinted. It reminded him of a prisoner's manacle. He desperately tried to pull it off, but it was too tight to fit over his hand and too strong to break.

Giving up, Hartley headed towards the bay and his shipmates. When he got within sight of the camp, a loud cheer rang out from the crew. Bootie and Hicks rushed over to greet him with slaps on the back. Captain Cook called, "Three cheers for Mr Hartley," and the crew sang, "hip hip hoorah" three times. Cook then asked Hartley to recount what had happened when he created the diversion.

A story about aliens would see him locked up, so he said, "I moved silently to within 20 metres of the blighters and shot one of them dead. Ten or more of them ran at me, but I held my ground and reloaded. I shot a second one, but that didn't slow them down. They were too close to fire a third time, so I turned and fled. One of them grabbed me from behind, throwing me off balance. I thought I was a goner, but I slipped out of my coat. I hoped whoever took it would stop chasing me. They didn't!"

Bootie handed Hartley a pot of beer. "You've earned this, my friend."

Hartley took a swig and continued. "I ran south for at least a mile with the savages hot on my trail. When I reached a sheer rock face, I was trapped, so I resolved to stand and fight. Then I saw a narrow entrance to a cave and squeezed inside. One of the Māori warriors followed me in, so I killed him and took his weapon."

Hartley removed the mere from his belt and lifted it above his head. The greenstone reflected in the sunlight, and the crew let out an 'Oooo'. "The remaining Māori were too large to fit through the gap and camped outside. I waited until they fell asleep, then sneaked past them."

A loud cheer rang out when the story finished, followed by another call of 'three cheers for William Hartley'.

The Endeavour headed south, and winds blew them east to a body of water between the North Island and South Island. They passed many small islands and anchored in the cove at Motuara Island. Joseph Banks named this region the Cook Strait.

Almost immediately, two dozen Māori approached in their canoes and hurled stones at the sailors. Rather than shoot the natives, Tupaia spoke to them and invited their leaders on board the ship. After several gifts of cloth, the natives left, and the sailors could go ashore to fill the casks with fresh water. The men caught 300 lbs of fish from trawling the nets.

Bootie noticed the metal band on Hartley's wrist and asked him about it. Unsure how to explain it, he told the truth. "I fell asleep in the cave where I hid from the natives. When I woke up, it was on my wrist."

"There must be more to it than that," said Bootie. "There's something you aren't telling me."

"There is, but I'm not sure I believe it myself."

His friend said nothing, so Hartley told him about the Pleiades. Bootie looked thoughtful. "I can see why you would want to remove this band."

The two friends made several attempts to remove the wristband, but it was as tough as steel.

"This is like no metal I've ever seen," said Bootie. "There's no join where the band is connected."

"I am stuck with this until I die, aren't I?"

"Don't give up yet. The armourer hides some tools in the longboat," said Bootie. "Let's see if they can break it."

After removing the sheet covering the longboat, they saw that shipworm had entirely eaten out the bottom. "Damn worms have gotten into the boat," said Bootie. "If it gets into the ship, we'll be marooned here."

The naval shipworm, a type of mollusc called teredo navalis, was a voracious ship-eating monster that could destroy a vessel in weeks. They ranged from a few centimetres to a metre in length. Once they bore into the wood, it was impossible to get rid of them.

With all thoughts of the wristband gone, the two midshipmen rushed to report the problem to the captain. Cook ordered the Endeavour to head for the nearest island to be careened, tipped over on one side, and the bottom inspected. It was in good order, and despite their good fortune, the captain ordered pitch and brimstone applied.

The ship continued to explore the region. After three and a half months of circumnavigating New Zealand, the Endeavour left to search for the lost continent. When they anchored in Botany Bay four weeks later, Cook and his crew became the first Europeans to reach Australia.

Cook, Banks, Hartley, and two marines set out in the pinnace. As they approached the land, they saw several natives and two huts. The majority of the locals ran away, but two stayed. Tupaia tried to communicate with them but couldn't understand their language.

As the boat got nearer, one of the natives threw a rock at them. Cook fired a musket, and although some of the shot struck the man, his only reaction was to pick up a shield. Eventually, the sailors drove off the two natives, and then pillaged the huts, removing all of the weapons. After filling casks of freshwater, they headed back to the ship.

After a few days of exploring the region, the Endeavour left Botany Bay and explored the coastline to the north. The ship came across an area where the sea depth changed rapidly. Twenty-one fathoms became twelve, then eight before increasing in depth. Believing the danger had passed, the day crew and the civilians went to bed.

The lead line recorded a safe depth of seventeen fathoms, but the ship ran aground almost immediately after. The coral rocks of the Great Barrier Reef had cut through the hull. Seawater flooded the vessel, pouring in through the hole. If they didn't raise the ship quickly, there was a real danger that most of the crew would drown. Any survivors would most likely die at the hands of hostile natives.

Cook, who had been sound asleep, was on the deck in his drawers, shouting, "Shorten the sails." The crew leapt into action. The captain then commanded Hicks to throw heavy objects overboard. They needed to lighten the ship or risk further damage to the hull.

"Bootie, Hartley," ordered Cook. "Take a kedging anchor each and drop them ahead of the ship." The Endeavour might be pulled from the coral bed and into deeper water by embedding the anchors into the seabed and heaving when the tide rose.

An old sail was shoved into the hole in the hull to plug it. The men were sent to the pumps, although only three were working. They would be doomed if they didn't expel the water as fast as it poured in.

Hartley ordered six men to load a kedging anchor onto the pinnace. He positioned himself at the bow while the six men rowed. After a short distance, Hartley shouted for them to stop. He tapped the nearest man on the shoulder and said, "Help me lift the anchor onto the side of the boat."

The man who turned around was Samuel Moody, the would-be poisoner and shanghaied sailor. He leered at Hartley before slowly getting to his feet. "Yes, Sir," he spat.

Moody grabbed one side of the heavy metal weight, Hartley the other, and they rested it on the side of the boat. While Hartley checked that the cable was firmly tied, Moody looped a shackle around the midshipman's wrist. He shoved the anchor into the ocean, pulling Hartley overboard with a loud splash.

As Hartley dropped rapidly, he desperately tried to free himself from the shackles. Even if it were possible to break free, he would drown before reaching the surface. This was how he would die—at the hands of a cutthroat who had outmanoeuvred him.

The metal wristband started to glow, which focused Hartley's attention and fought off the panic. The metal expanded and drifted apart into tiny metal bubbles. They reformed into a blade and floated. Hartley grabbed at the knife, which vibrated in his hand. He touched it to the chain, and it moved through the iron with little resistance.

Hartley might be free, but his carbon dioxide levels were rising, and he was running out of oxygen. His chest started to burn, and his diaphragm began convulsing. He desperately wanted to breathe in deeply. Ignoring the pain, he pushed hard off the seabed.

He was moving too slowly and would never get to the surface in time, but the knife seemed to pull him upwards. Darkness formed on the edge of his vision, and Hartley blacked out just as he reached the surface. His hand relaxed, and the knife fell from his grasp. Two seamen jumped into the sea and dragged him into the boat.

When Hartley awoke, the surgeon, William Monkhouse, was stood over him. "You're a lucky chap," he said in his thick Cumbrian accent.

"I don't feel lucky," said Hartley. "I must have swallowed a gallon of seawater."

"You didn't swallow much water at all," said Monkhouse. "I can't believe you let yourself get tangled in the anchor. Bloody stupid, if you ask me."

"I didn't—" started Hartley but stopped himself. He had no proof Moody had shackled him to the anchor. The other seaman had their backs to him. Besides, if he explained what Moody had done, how had he escaped? That could wait. It was more important to free the ship from the coral rock.

Hartley got up. "I'm needed on deck," he said. He half-expected Monkhouse to tell him to take it easy, but he didn't argue.

Hartley headed back on deck to see what was happening. The teams of sailors were working without complaint. He had heard that crews had stolen longboats in similar situations and saved themselves. It was Cook's leadership that was holding it together. He was barking orders to the other officers, who were urgently carrying them out.

Bootie, and several sailors, stood with both arms on the poles protruding from the capstan. They were ready to pull on the anchor using the drum-shaped device as a lever. Sailors would push, and the cables would wrap around the drum pulling great weights. The plan was to move the ship towards the embedded kedging anchor.

"Relax," commanded Cook. They stopped pushing and waited for the next command.

"Get ready," shouted Cook, pausing for the waves to lift the ship slightly. "Push. Give it everything, men."

Bootie and the sailors pushed with all their might but made no ground. The drum refused to turn. Hartley joined in alongside his friend, who moved across to make room.

"Glad to see you are well," said Bootie, puffing from exertion. "I thought you were a goner."

"Me too! I'll tell you about it once we're free of these damn coral rocks." Hartley tried to sound more confident than he felt. If they didn't get free soon, the ship would go down. Even if they got the vessel moving, that might rip a large hole in the hull.

Hours passed with the crew operating the pumps, throwing tons of weights overboard, and manning the capstan. As exhaustion set in, Cook set up a rota to allow the men to recover. He worked the pumps himself, and this act brought him tremendous support. He even let the men open the casks and drink beer and spirits.

Privately, Hartley agreed with Cook's sentiment. Why not let the men drink themselves stupid? Soon, they may be dead, and the casks would only be thrown overboard to lighten the ship. Even in their drunken state, the men followed orders. They admired the officers, and if they were to die, they would die as heroes.

When all appeared lost, the ship moved. Only a little at first, but men at the capstan were no longer stationary. The momentum increased, and they burst free of the coral. Hartley's relief was short-lived because the ship was taking on more water. They needed to patch the hole in the hull. Cook ordered Midshipman Monkhouse, the surgeon's brother, to fother the leak.

Monkhouse, who was slightly senior, asked Hartley to help. He was seen as a good luck charm because he had repeatedly avoided death. Standing at the stove, Hartley boiled the tar and turpentine to make the pitch. The two midshipmen mixed in rope fibres, wool, and sheep dung before covering a sail with this concoction.

They pressed the sail over the hole and prayed it would be sucked into the leak and get stuck there. Fifteen minutes later, the ship had been pumped dry and no more water leaked into the hull. They needed to find a harbour close to the shore to make more permanent repairs. The boats found the mouth of a river, and the Endeavour made its way through the narrow channel.

Twice they ran ashore, but the captain guided the ship to a point six metres from land. The next day they examined the hole. A coral rock the size of a man's fist had broken off and partially plugged the hole. The carpenter made temporary repairs to the hull, but the crew had to wait ten days for favourable tides.

Hartley told Bootie what Moody had done, and his friend was livid. "The captain will have him shot for trying to kill an officer," he said.

"But I have no proof," said Hartley. "Let me think about it, John."

Ciara woke to find Zixin sitting on her bed. "Finally! Do you know what time it is?"

"Haven't you heard of personal space?"

Scottie, Hana, and Chan came running into the bedroom. They had been waiting in the living area for Ciara to wake.

"11 am," said Zixin. "Now tell us about your dream."

"Get out. All of you," said Ciara. "I will shower first and then tell you where the key is."

Ciara found the excitement amusing. "Yes! Fighting!" exclaimed Scottie doing a double fist pump. The Korean phrase was a firm favourite to fire up a teammate.

"At least, tell us if it's close," said Zixin.

"It's off the coast of Australia. Let me shower, and then I will tell you everything."

Ciara ate her breakfast and, between mouthfuls, told the story. When the anchor pulled Hartley into the sea, Chan gasped, and Zixin placed her hand on his arm in a comforting gesture.

"This should be a movie," said Chan.

"And Ciara experiences it for real," said Zixin.

"For real?" said Chan. "As in, it feels like it's happening to you."

"Yes!" said Ciara solemnly. "I feel his pain and emotions. I thought I was going to die."

When Ciara had finished the story, Scottie asked, "Do you think that will be the last of the dreams? I want to know what happens in the rest of the voyage."

Ciara laughed. "I have no idea. I only have dreams when I need information."

Then she remembered the bottle and the note from Fernley.

Hana had remained quiet throughout the story but finally spoke up. "I will get the bottle analysed. It would be useful to know what you drank."

Hana's father was at the cave entrance, so they headed there. It had changed from the previous day. The team had installed a range of electronic equipment with several monitors showing the inside of the cave. There was a tent with medical equipment and men in white coats analysing samples.

Dr Kim had purchased several robotic quadrupeds from Boston Dynamics, the Hyundai-owned company, and deployed a dozen of the four-legged mechanoids. The quadrupeds were fitted with cameras and carried equipment to and from the central cavern.

A team of researchers tried to figure out what was putting people to sleep. Even general anaesthetics took several seconds before they worked. But in the cave, sleep and recovery were instantaneous.

Soil and air samples were typical for the region. Sound and light frequencies were within the expected frequencies. There was no evidence of any phenomenon.

One disproved theory was that gravitational forces depleted brain oxygen. Astronauts exposed to extreme g-forces lose consciousness because of oxygen depletion. But the effect isn't instantaneous. It takes four or five seconds to deplete the brain's oxygen reserves. Besides, continued oxygen depletion causes brain damage and death. A dog had been left unconscious for an hour but woke up perfectly healthy.

They hadn't made any real progress, and Dr Kim was growing impatient. He was shouting at one of the scientists when Hana called out to him. He stopped and then walked over to them.

"We have some news, Appa," said Hana.

"Go on," said Dr Kim.

"Ciara had another vision. She knows the location of the key that opens the spacecraft," said Hana.

Dr Kim's eyebrows raised slightly, but there was no discernible change in his expression.

"William Hartley had it with him but lost it when the Endeavour ran aground on a coral reef off the coast of Australia. We want to go there and get it. We're all qualified divers."

"I don't think that is a good idea," said Dr Kim slowly. "Even if you know exactly where the ship ran aground, there is no chance of finding the key after 200 years. At least not without specialist equipment."

"But Ciara saw where it went, and besides, the scientists are doing all the work now. You don't need us hanging around."

"Ciara is the only person who can enter the cavern. I need her here."

Without another word, Dr Kim turned and walked back to the scientist.

"You should have mentioned the prophecy—the sun and the moon sounded for the key," said Scottie.

"I should have," snapped Hana. "You could have said something."

Zixin walked over to Dr Kim. After a brief exchange, Dr Kim beckoned to his assistant, Yuna. They talked for a few more minutes, and then Zixin came back. "Yuna has arranged for the private yacht to go to Cairns. We will fly there in two days."

"What did you say?" asked Hana.

"I did what Scottie suggested. I told him about the prophecy."

"And he's just letting us go?" asked Hana.

"He insisted his personal bodyguard accompany us," said Zixin.

Scottie puffed his chest out and widened his arms, trying to impersonate the hulking man. "I can just picture Oddjob bulging out of a wetsuit."

"His name is Dongwoo," said Hana. "If he hears you are calling him Oddjob, I will need a new boyfriend." She paused before adding thoughtfully, "Although, I do look good in black."

Hana spent the next two days working with Yuna to organise everything. They arranged scuba gear, stinger suits, and permits. Scottie said it was better to avoid Hana when she was in business mode, so he caught up with some friends while Ciara, Zixin, and Chan went shopping.

The results from the lab showed that the bottle had contained water. There were trace amounts of oil, alcohol, aldehyde, musk, oud, and coumarin. The lab suggested they were only there because the water had been placed in an old perfume bottle. Had Fernley left it as a placebo?

Before they knew it, they'd boarded the Gulfstream and headed to Cairns. The yacht was waiting at the Port of Cape Flattery, 200km north of Cairns. They had gone from cave explorers to scouring shipwrecks.

Chapter 11
Venomous Reef

Dr Kim suspected his superyacht might be needed, so he ordered the captain to sail south. The Aleumdaun Kkoch, which translates to Beautiful Flower, set sail from Busan, South Korea, long before the Gulfstream left for New Zealand. The vessel was designed and built in the Netherlands, but the interior fittings were Italian. It had cost $200 million to construct, was 100 metres long, and had six decks. There were eight guest cabins, so Ciara had one to herself.

They had 24 hours to spend on the yacht before scuba diving, or they'd risk decompression sickness. Ciara had put on her bikini and swam a few lengths in the glass-bottomed swimming pool. Now she was stretched out on a sun lounger drinking sparkling water. The temperature was in the early thirties, and despite the factor 50 sunscreen, she was turning pink.

Ciara was cloud-watching, although there were few of them in the bright blue sky. This scene matched her vision perfectly, except the handsome man hadn't arrived yet. When she had been shopping for clothes and saw the bikini, she knew it was the one. Ciara briefly considered buying a different one to see what would happen but was worried it would jinx the event.

Right on cue, the tall, handsome second officer walked over. He was in his late 20s and had the air of one who knew his uniform appealed to the opposite sex. Despite his good looks, he was too cocksure for Ciara's liking.

"You have clearly been on many ships," he said.

"Why do you say that?" asked Ciara.

"When you walk about the deck, you move like an experienced sailor. Your stance is wider than normal, and when the ship sways, you move into it."

Ciara smiled, knowing that she must have subconsciously adopted Hartley's gait. She wasn't sure how to respond. Yes, and he might ask more questions. No, and he would think she was lying.

"You can tell that while I am lying down?"

"I saw you walk over here," said the man smiling.

"So, you were watching me?" Ciara looked straight up into his eyes and, after a momentary pause, added, "Like a stalker."

The overconfident smile vanished. "Um. No. Not in that way, miss," he said formally.

The arrogant slouch was replaced by an upright bearing with shoulders pulled back. The second officer looked relieved when Hana walked over and asked him to set up a sun lounger alongside Ciara's. He gave a short bow and retreated in haste when he was done.

Ciara felt a little uncomfortable being alone with Hana. Even though nothing had happened between her and Scottie, she was worried Hana would ask her about him. She was relieved when she asked about the second officer. "Was he bothering you? He is nice to look at but loves himself a little too much."

"He was trying a little too hard, but it was harmless," said Ciara.

This was the first time Ciara had been alone with Hana. They had developed a kind of friendship these past few days but not a close one. Was she distant because of the differences in their social status? Maybe it was cultural, although Hana had spent more time in the United States than Korea.

"Where are the others?" asked Ciara.

"Chan and Zixin are doing something together." Then her voice changed, and she sounded slightly conspiratorial. "I never pictured those two as a couple. Has she told you they are dating?"

"No, she didn't. I saw her rest her hand on Chan's arm, and I wondered."

"I think listening to him sing Ava Maria did it. Even I feel emotional when I hear him sing."

"Why even you? Are you not emotional?"

"Not really. I wish I was, though. I think that's why I like Chan's company. He reminds me that there is beauty in life. Same with Scottie."

Ciara felt a little uncomfortable talking about Scottie, so she changed the subject. "It must have been difficult to get permission to dive at Endeavour reef."

Hana barked a laugh. "Nothing could have been easier."

"But Australia is notoriously strict. You can't bring anything into the country or take anything with you."

"Those rules don't apply to people like my father. If he asked their prime minister to jump like a kangaroo, he'd do it." There was bitterness in Hana's voice. The kind you hear from someone who has suffered a lifetime of hardships.

"Do you know why I hate him so much?"

"I'm sure you don't hate him. At least, not deep down."

Hana ignored Ciara's response. "He is evil. Obsessed with power and influence."

"If he wants power, why doesn't he become Korea's president?"

Hana swung her legs off the sun lounger and sat upright. "Do you think presidents and prime ministers have any real power? They're puppets, doing the bidding of the hectobillionaires."

Ciara had never heard that word before. She knew hecto meant 100, so she guessed it meant people with 100 billion dollars. Hana explained that there were only eleven hectobillionaires—nine American, one French, and one Korean. They'd formed a kind of club to gain even more wealth and power.

"It pains him to be ranked eleventh," said Hana. "Even though he helps run the world. And before you suggest this is a conspiracy theory, let me remove all misapprehensions. I have seen, first hand, my father meet with the other billionaires and talk about the next premier for just about every major country."

A waiter wearing a bright white uniform came over. "Would you care for anything, Miss Hana, Miss Ciara?" he said.

"Bring some frozen grapes and watermelon juice," said Hana. "What would you like, Ciara?"

"The same as Hana, thank you."

Hana waited until the waiter was out of earshot and continued. "They identify young politicians early and brainwash them on a Global Economic Federation training program. Those who think the approved way are given power, and then they do what they're told."

Ciara said nothing. It all sounded a little too like a Hollywood movie.

Hana changed tact, taking Ciara's silence as disagreement. "The rich have always controlled politicians. Take the Roman republic, for example."

Ciara nodded, not knowing what else to do.

"It was a republic in name only. Marcus Crassus, Gnaeus Pompeius Magnus, and Julius Caesar formed a triumvirate to run the empire. They bribed voters and officials to ensure their representatives were elected as the two consuls. Of course, they had to do it annually because consuls could only serve for one year. It's easier now because most premiers serve for four years."

Hana's point about the Roman Empire was valid, and this was a first-hand report from the controlling elite. Could the world's foremost leaders all be puppets? Ciara still had her doubts.

The waiter came back, and Ciara sat up. She tried a frozen grape. "Oh my God. These are amazing. So refreshing."

"I know," said Hana. "They were served at a health spa on Koh Samui, and now I can't stop eating them in hot weather."

The respite from Hana's rant didn't last long. "The super-rich want more power and influence."

"Not everyone is driven by money and power," said Ciara. "I'm not."

Hana laughed. "Only someone who has never had real money would say that. You can't begin to imagine how seductive it is."

"But many billionaires give money to charity," asked Ciara. "Some even have their own foundations."

"Charitable donations are tax-deductible, and donating money buys influence," said Hana. "Creating your own foundation is not altruism. It ensures you aren't giving away money. You are merely moving it. You still control how it is spent."

"What do you mean?"

"Suppose you invest in the development of a new drug," said Hana. "Your charity offers free vaccines to poorer countries. That way, you can conduct your clinic drug trials. Your drug gets FDA approval and gives you 20% returns on investment."

"But that is criminal. Surely, Governments wouldn't allow such unethical practice," said Ciara.

"Politicians rely on donations. Quid pro quo."

Ciara knew that Latin expression meant a favour for a favour. Something in her expression must have convinced Hana that she wasn't making any headway with her argument.

"Okay," said Hana. "Think of it this way. Korea's president earns around $200,000 a year. Your prime minister earns a fraction more. My father has annual returns of 12% on 100,000 billion dollars. That is twelve billion per year, so one billion dollars a month, over thirty-three million dollars per day. Can you see why he has so much influence? Politicians are merely pawns in a chess game."

"Is that what I am? A pawn to be manipulated."

Hana sighed. "Actually, I don't think you are. I think you have your own reasons for finding the Pleiades. They just happen to coincide with what my father wants."

"So why does your father want to contact the Pleiades?"

"He doesn't want to contact the Pleiades. He just wants their technology. The ability to travel hundreds of light-years, manipulate DNA to live forever, communicate telepathically, put anyone to sleep, and who knows what else."

"I never thought about that. I just wanted to uncover the mystery."

"If he gains access to their technology, he could control the world."

"So, is that why you hate him?"

"It is part of it. The real reason is that my father could do so much good. End world hunger, cruelty to animals, and implement environmental changes."

"So you don't think the world leaders are doing enough for climate change?"

"Do you? Instead of telling the public to stop using plastic bags, why not prevent manufacturers from producing them. Cut it off at the source. But they won't do that because plastic is made from crude oil, and the wealthy make too much money from the industry."

"Does he know you hate him?"

"I doubt it. I stay the obedient daughter because I will inherit his money one day, and then I will make a difference."

Ciara was shocked by Hana's monologue, but some of it resonated with her. She wasn't quite sure what to say. Could she stop Dr Kim from exploiting the Pleiades?

"Do you think the Pleiades are still alive?" asked Ciara.

"I suppose they could be," said Hana. "They could be in stasis. Waiting for you to arrive with a way to stop the European diseases from killing them."

"Yeah, that's what I assumed. I hope we're right."

Hana reached over and hugged Ciara. "Thanks for listening to my tirade. We better go and find the divemaster my father hired."

Dr Kim had insisted that an experienced deep-sea diver accompany his daughter and their friends. John McAlpine, a 38-year-old Australian shipwreck explorer, would be joining them on the descent. The Great Barrier Reef is home to some of the world's deadliest creatures, and McAlpine's local knowledge would be helpful.

He had shown them photographs of creatures to avoid. First among them was the Australian box jellyfish, the world's most venomous animal.

"The fifteen tentacles are covered in tiny darts loaded with poison," said McAlpine. "The slightest brush will tear the skin, and when the venom enters the bloodstream, it is pumped to the heart. Paralysis occurs mid-contraction, and you die two to four minutes later."

"Don't they just float around following the sea currents?" said Zixin.

"Not this monster. It can reach 4 knots, over 7 km/h, and is agile," said McAlpine. "Plus, it has 24 eyes that it uses for navigation."

"But the stinger suits will protect us," asked Hana nervously.

The full-body stinger suit was engineered to prevent jellyfish tentacles from piercing the skin. They were one of many precautions McAlpine had insisted upon.

"The suits will protect you, but you must be completely covered at all times, so never take your gloves off. Do you understand me?"

The friends all nodded, so McAlpine continued his lecture.

"The Australian box jelly is just one of many dangers. The Irukandji jellyfish is just 2 cm and almost impossible to see. They're less likely to kill you, but the pain is unbearable. I was stung once, and it was the worst experience of my life."

Seeing that Hana was nervous, Scottie joked, "Don't worry—the Chinese eat jellyfish, so one look at Zixin, and they'll swim the other way."

"There's always a smart-mouthed Kiwi making light of the dangers," shouted McAlpine. "One more smart-arsed comment from you, and we'll be turning this boat around. I don't care who your bloody father is."

Keen to defuse the situation, Ciara asked, "Is there any danger from sharks?"

"We'd be lucky to see one," said McAlpine. "Shark attacks are rare. If they bite you, it's probably because they mistook you for something else."

Then McAlpine ran through the ascension safety protocols to avoid decompression sickness. This was because they expected to dive up 30 metres, the kind of depth that makes nitrogen absorption a consideration.

It was agreed that Dr Kim's bodyguard, Dongwoo, would be suited up and ready to dive if they didn't return within 45 minutes. Having support on the yacht may prove helpful.

The Beautiful Flower came equipped with a diving platform. Ciara expected to do a back roll, which is how she had learned to scuba dive. Instead, all they had to do was take one giant step. Ciara plunged into the sea and took an involuntary deep breath, her body reacting to the temperature change. Not that 23°C was cold.

They descended quickly and were fortunate because the water clarity was excellent. Ciara had almost forgotten why they were there. It was too easy to watch the clownfish dart between the zooxanthellate corals. The vibrancy of the colours was incredible. She had even spotted a bright blue starfish crawling slowly over hard corals.

McAlpine started making rapid movements with his hand and pointing behind Ciara. She felt a momentary sense of panic, thinking a shark was right behind her. She turned her head rapidly, and a leatherback turtle swam past. It was almost as long as her. Ciara exhaled relief flooding her body.

This was a wonderful experience, but Ciara couldn't help but feel uneasy. The stinger suit was so tight that it restricted her movements slightly. As someone who suffered from claustrophobia, it made her feel on edge. She repeatedly looked around for dangerous creatures. What was the point of having so much venom that a single jellyfish could kill sixty people?

To the right and below, a blueish glow caught Ciara's eye. She couldn't have spotted the key so quickly. Without notifying McAlpine, she excitedly swam towards the faint light. As she got closer, the excitement turned to panic. She was heading straight for a box jellyfish, and behind it were several more.

She completed a tumble turn and headed back towards McAlpine. There was no signal for box jellyfish, so she simply pointed at the jellyfish. He gave her the okay sign, pointed to the other divers, and then indicated upwards. He must want to let the others know and then head back to the ship.

Before they could do anything, a large grey shape appeared behind McAlpine. Ciara's eyes widened. This couldn't be what she thought it was. She pointed frantically to her eyes, then gestured behind McAlpine. He turned to see the apex predator, Carcharodon Carcharias, more commonly known as the great white shark.

McAlpine pointed down towards the coral and signalled with the flat of his hand facing the seabed. She could almost hear him saying, stay low and move slowly. She did as directed and moved slowly, practically touching the coral floor. McAlpine turned around and swam slowly upwards. Ciara guessed he was going to help the others.

The shark must have noticed her movement because it abruptly changed direction and accelerated towards her. Ciara held her breath but then remembered the German dive instructor saying, never hold your breath underwater. She tried to relax and breathe evenly. Fortunately, it was a reconnaissance mission, and it swam just above and to the side of her. The beast was huge, maybe four or five metres in length, and cast a huge shadow. It was close enough for Ciara to see its many scars and look into one dead eye.

There was a dark patch up ahead amid the corals' bright colours. Ciara swam towards it to hide the outline of her body. It turned out to be a tunnel, so she squeezed through. She felt a sharp pain in her right thigh. The razer-sharp spiky spicules had parted the stinger suit and ripped into her muscle. Blood oozed out of the deep cut. She slammed her hand over the injury, trying to stop the bleeding. She knew sharks could smell blood from hundreds of metres away, and this one was closer than her diving buddy.

Ciara's breathing had become irregular, faster and shallower, like a panting dog. There was pressure on her chest. The stinger suit must be too tight. She fumbled for the zipper at the back of her neck. Her hands were shaking, and her vision started to blur. She felt a large shape moving closer and closer. She wanted to scream, but the mouthpiece was in her mouth. She bit down on the rubber.

It was then she felt it. Pressure on her arm. Would the shark rip it away like a band-aid? She waited for the pain and the gush of blood. It didn't come. Instead, someone was gently shaking her arm. She looked and saw it was another diver. The mask obscured their face. Who was it? It wasn't McAlpine, Scottie, or Chan. The shape was too big for Hana or Zixin.

The shadow of the shark circling above them distracted her. She pointed to it, and her new dive buddy looked up. He calmly raised a speargun. Ciara grabbed the arm holding the gun. What was he doing? Shooting the shark would make matters worse.

The man held up his other hand and gave the universal diving gesture of its all right. He turned the speargun away from the shark and fired. His spear went straight through the body of a metre-long giant grouper. The fish thrashed, pulling the weapon from the diver's hand.

With a thrust of its tail, the shark launched itself at the giant grouper, tearing chunks of flesh from its side. A second great white appeared, at least as large as the first. It swam at terrific speeds towards the injured creature. A frenzy ensued, with small pieces of flesh floating in all directions. Smaller fish dashed in to join the feast.

It was then that Ciara noticed a bluish glow in a hollow below them. She started to head towards it, but the diver grabbed her legs, slowing her momentum. He pulled himself alongside her and pointed to Zixin, Chan, Scottie and Hana, who had been watching. Ciara signalled for them to swim to her, which they did. Not wanting to be left alone, Hana reluctantly trailed at the back.

Ciara pointed to the glowing object, and they swam towards it moving as closely together as possible. Six bodies in one mass presented too big a target for a shark. A trail of blood oozed from Ciara's wound. It must have attracted another shark. This one was a tiger shark, just as long as the great white but easily identifiable from the faint stripes on its greenish-blue body.

The unknown diver grabbed Ciara's arm. He pointed at her, then at the glowing object. He placed his hand on his chest, waved his arm to indicate the others and then pointed at the shark. His meaning was clear—you get the key, and we'll frighten off the predator. Ciara made her way towards the faintly glowing light while the other five divers had formed a large mass and headed straight at the tiger shark.

Despite their ferocious reputation, a large object heading towards a shark is not prey. Apart from humans, orcas are their only natural predators. The tiger shark turned and swam away from them. Their bluff had worked.

As Ciara got closer, she could see the light filtered through a mound of beige-coloured hard coral that looked like a tiny tree bereft of its leaves. Small orange fish darted away from her between the coral's branches. This part of the reef must have grown over and around the alien artefact. Ciara couldn't bring herself to damage this living organism, but how else could she reach the light.

She tried to squeeze her hand through a small gap, but the glove was too bulky. If she took it off, but no, that was the first rule McAlpine had stated—do not remove any of your equipment. Besides, who knew what was inside. She had been warned that the venomous 2 cm Irukandji jellyfish was nearly impossible to see. The last thing she needed was a more severe injury. That thought prompted her thigh to throb painfully.

Damn it! She removed the glove from her right hand and carefully pushed it inside the gap. No sudden movements, or she'd rip her hand to shreds on the spiky barbs. Unable to see clearly, the respirator bubbles obscuring her vision, Ciara stretched her arm further into the reef. Suddenly, she felt something warm ooze over her hand and towards her wrist.

She visualised a blue dragon sea slug sliding over her skin. The brightly coloured marine gastropod was one of the poisonous creatures potentially fatal to humans. Unable to move, Ciara felt the creature move up to her arm and wrap itself around her wrist. That was weird. Why would it do that? Moving as slowly as possible, she pulled back her arm. On her wrist was a metallic blue band.

Ciara relaxed! This experience had been awful, but she felt better with her glove back on. It was time to begin the ascent protocol and get out of there. *I will never scuba dive again,* she told herself.

As soon as they were back on the yacht, Hana ran up to McAlpine and shouted, "Where the hell did you go?"

"I signalled for you all to head up," said McAlpine. "You should have followed my orders."

"You coward!" screamed Hana. "I will see you ruined for this."

"Don't threaten me, little girl." McAlpine's face was red, and spittle sprayed from his mouth. He was towering over Hana, threateningly.

Scottie stepped forward and shoved McAlpine backwards. The Aussie was about to punch the boy, but Dongwoo gripped one large paw around the man's throat. The diver master's shoulders slumped. All the fight had left him.

"Get off this yacht," said Hana. "You will be hearing from our lawyers."

"You're losing your touch, Zixin," said Ciara. "You're normally the first to a fight."

Before Zixin could respond, the ship's doctor intervened. "Dongwoo, help me take Ciara to the medical centre. I need to clean her wound."

The large Korean picked up Ciara and carried her off the deck. Once inside the surgery, Ciara was placed on an operating table, and the doctor cut her stinger suit away.

"This will hurt a little. I need to clean the wound and check there are no coral fragments."

It hurt a lot. The hydrogen peroxide bubbled up, removing crusty blood and tiny pieces of coral. "Not too deep. You should be fine. I will give you a broad-spectrum antibiotic, just in case."

The doctor opened the door to the medical centre and called, "You can come in now."

Ciara's friends piled through the door. "Show us the key," said Zixin.

Ciara helped up her wrist, and the others crowded around, touching it. "I can't believe we found it," said Chan.

"We wouldn't have done it if Dongwoo hadn't saved me," said Ciara.

"That wasn't Dongwoo, down there," said Scottie. "I think it was Mr Fernley."

Chapter 12
The Lake

When they arrived back in New Zealand, Dr Kim insisted they meet him at the cave entrance. He wanted to see if the key opened the spacecraft. The robot quadruped would broadcast events inside the cave now that cameras were attached. More importantly, he could give Ciara instructions via the microphone system he had installed.

When Ciara walked into the main cavern, it looked completely different. The robots had installed lights and cameras, and for the first time, she could see the vessel in detail. The fascia was an exact match to the band she wore on her wrist.

For whatever reason, this time, it felt different. Maybe it was what Ciara had been through, but she was confident the spacecraft would open. Although, she wasn't sure where the key would go. Dr Kim's voice came through the speaker system, "Touch the key to the spacecraft, Ciara."

Ciara did, and the wristband melted into the ship. Nothing happened for several minutes. Then the shape seemed to split open up. The lights shut down, and the robot quadrupeds collapsed to the ground, their strings cut.

Ciara was very much alone. When she turned back to the ship, a tall slim blonde-haired boy was framed in the doorway, unchanged for 250 years.

"Welcome, Ciara," he said. "Did you bring a sample of the diseases that killed us?"

After everything she had been through, she'd expected a little gratitude. She had an entire speech planned, but the direct question unbalanced her. "Yes! I brought a sample of the viruses with me. Are you sure you can use them to protect yourself?" She gestured to the bag she had left three days ago.

"We have a device that will determine what frequencies will kill the viruses. When we know that our immune system will be programmed to resonate at that frequency, none of these viruses will affect us again."

One of the boys picked up the bag and took it into the ship. While they waited for the samples to be analysed, Ciara told the Pleiades about Dr Kim. She said he was helping them because he wanted their technology, but he would prove very useful to them.

"You don't seem surprised by anything I've told you," said Ciara.

"Why would we," said the boy who seemed to be the leader. "One of our people saw this in a vision. He explained what we would need to do."

"You said he rather than we," said Ciara. "Was he not part of your collective mind?"

"He was not one of us," said the boy.

"Am I one of you?" asked Ciara. "I mean, am I descended from you?"

"No!" said one of the girls, "we would not breed with an inferior species."

First contact with an alien species wasn't going how Ciara imagined it. These aliens were jerks. Only they didn't seem to realise it.

"Then how was I selected?" asked Ciara.

"We can alter DNA. We reprogrammed William Hartley's telomeres to ensure he passed on memories to his descendants."

"So my dreams about William Hartley were programmed into my DNA by you?"

"Yes."

Ciara felt used. When Fernley told her about the unknown DNA, it was exciting. If the Pleiades hadn't saved William Hartley, she wouldn't be alive now. In reality, she was a pawn for them. To think she was worried about being used by Dr Kim.

"So what happens now," asked Ciara.

"Bring Dr Kim to us, and we will talk with him."

Ciara walked the three kilometres back to the entrance. Her leg throbbed, but the exercise might help. She had fulfilled the prophecy and was ordinary again, and her life was pretty good before all this started. She felt bitter about being used, but no doubt the Pleiades would be exploited by Dr Kim, and it would serve them right.

Dr Kim was ecstatic that the Pleiades wanted to meet with him. As expected, he was able to enter the cave. Ciara didn't bother accompanying him and told him about the totem guides. Dr Kim said he knew the route from watching the quadrupeds move back and forth.

Two weeks had passed since Dr Kim's meeting with the Pleiades. They agreed to enrol at Sanjung Academy, and the empty boarding house became Pleiades house. The principal had called an assembly to introduce the new students. Ciara and her friends agreed to keep their background secret. As far as the students and teachers knew, the new arrivals were human.

There were no rumours on the Internet. Ciara couldn't believe how easily Dr Kim had arranged New Zealand passports and residency in Korea. Maybe Hana hadn't exaggerated about the hectobillionaires controlling politicians.

It was strange going to lessons and seeing one of the Pleiades sitting in the classroom. Ciara knew that when one of them learned something, they all knew it. Their knowledge would be growing at an exponential rate, and she wondered how long they would stay.

Ciara saw one of the Pleiades girls walking alone. She jogged to catch up with her. The girl was drinking E-neo-Ji, a sports energy drink that was an unnatural blue colour. For some reason, the Pleiades were addicted to the stuff. Ciara guessed that their mental abilities required a great deal of energy, and the high glucose content probably provided it.

"Why did you come to Sanjung Academy?" asked Ciara.

The girl continued to walk, forcing Ciara to keep pace. "We came here to learn."

"But your technologies are far more advanced than ours. What can we teach you?"

"There is much we need to know."

It was like getting blood out of a stone. The Pleiades only seemed to answer in single sentences. "Like what?" asked Ciara.

"If you found yourself in the Amazon jungle with no technology, would your advanced knowledge help you?"

Ciara shrugged. "I guess not."

"So, what would you learn?"

Thinking of her experiences as William Hartley, Ciara said, "I'd learn how to survive in the jungle."

The girl took a swig of her energy drink. "Now you understand why we are here."

"You're here to learn how to survive in our world?"

"Yes! We are here to survive."

"What will you do afterwards?"

She finished her E-neo-Ji drink and dropped the empty bottle in a recycle bin. "We will lead."

And without waiting for a reply, the girl entered a classroom, leaving Ciara alone in the corridor.

Lead what? Lead their people?

Despite their disposition, the Pleiades settled in quite well at Sanjung Academy. Although, they didn't mix with other students and refused to participate in the house competition because many events were physical. The aliens' home world had lower gravity than Earth, so they were more fragile than humans.

Life at school was much less exciting than it had been before. There was no mystery to uncover, and Ciara rarely saw her friends. Zixin spent most of her free time with Chan, and loneliness resulted. Ciara couldn't even focus on her sprint training because her leg was still healing. She wondered whether James Fernley had returned to England now that she wasn't extraordinary.

Ciara had just left her English lesson and was walking to the cafeteria. A boy called Sewang Yun ran past her, probably trying to get to the front of the lunch queue. He rounded a corner and went out of sight. An unearthly high-pitched yell rang out. Ciara hurried to see what had happened and saw one of the Pleiades boys lying on the ground grimacing in pain. Standing next to him was a Pleiades girl. Instead of helping her friend, she was staring at the boy who had caused the accident.

Sewang stopped, turned around and ran as fast as he could straight into a brick wall. He didn't even try to put his arms up to protect himself. His face hit the wall with incredible force, and a sickening crack of broken bone rang out. Blood sprayed in all directions before Sewang slumped to the ground. The three witnesses didn't move, transfixed on the Pleiades girl.

Ciara ran over to Sewang and checked he was breathing. She yelled out to the onlookers to call the medical centre, but none reacted. Once she had moved Sewang into the recovery position, she called the nurse's office. Angry at the spectators, she yelled, "What the hell is wrong with you people."

Her anger broke the spell, and the three students rushed over to Sewang. The female Pleiades helped her male friend to his feet. She picked up his energy drink bottle and handed it to him. They walked away silently and didn't look back.

Ciara turned to a girl whose name was Eunju. "Did you see what happened?"

"I'm not sure," said Eunju.

"What about you?" said Ciara to the other girl.

"Same as her," she said, indicating Eunju.

"What is wrong with you people?" shouted Ciara. "What do you think happened?"

"Sewang ran into one of them," said Eunju. "Then he ran into the wall."

"You were nearer than I was," said Ciara. "Why didn't you try to help him?"

"I was too frightened to move," said Eunju.

Sewang made a groaning noise, so Ciara helped him sit up. His breathing laboured because blood was dripping from a broken nose. Ciara took out a tissue and held it under his nostrils. The boy wasn't in a fit state to answer questions, so Ciara sat quietly with him.

The medical centre was close by, so the nurse arrived quickly. She took one look at Sewang and said, "We need to take him to the hospital. Run to the medical centre and get a wheelchair for me."

"I'll go," said Eunju and ran to fetch it.

In the following few days, students talked of nothing else. Sewang had suffered a fractured cheekbone and a broken nose and hadn't returned to school. A few of his friends visited him and spread a rumour the Pleiades girl made him run into the wall.

Eunju and the onlookers said they tried to run to Sewang, but their legs wouldn't move. This excuse didn't convince Ciara since she had felt no such compulsion. She told Zixin and the others as much. Still, it was enough for the students to avoid the Pleiades even more than before.

If a student saw one of the Pleiades walking down the corridor, they would give them a wide berth. Some students would even turn around and go in the opposite direction. The bad feeling towards the Pleiades continued until two grade 11 boys decided to get some revenge.

One evening, two eleventh graders, Kihoon and Jiwon, sneaked up on one of the Pleiades boys. Kihoon hit him from behind with a baseball bat, breaking the boy's arm. The Pleiades boy fell to the ground holding his arm and the two Korean boys proceeded to kick him into unconsciousness.

The nurse took the Pleiades boy to the medical centre but surprisingly didn't send him to the hospital. Instead, a doctor visited the school and treated the boy there. The two Korean boys were considered heroes because they broke the veil of fear that gripped the school.

The following morning, Kihoon and Jiwon didn't go for breakfast. They hadn't slept in their beds, and no one had seen them. The police arrived, and an inspector interviewed the Pleiades.

Days passed with the inspector interviewing staff and students. Police searched the forest, then trawled the lake, where they found the bodies of the two boys. An autopsy showed the cause of death was drowning. The boys had no injuries or contusions, so the police recorded their deaths as suicide.

The principal resigned and shouldered the blame. A fence was erected around the lake, making it impractical to gain access. The boys' parents had tried to sue the school for negligence, but Dr Kim's lawyers got it thrown out by a judge. The defence argued that the boys felt so guilty for attacking an innocent that no precautions could have stopped what happened.

Ciara walked into the cafeteria a few days later. She spotted Zixin, Chan, Scottie, and Hana sitting together and went over to join them. They had been whispering and looked worried when Ciara sat down.

"What's happened?" asked Ciara.

"Not so loud," hissed Hana. "A couple of students have tried to leave the school, but the Pleiades won't let them go."

"What do you mean?" said Ciara.

"Sewang packed all of his things and waited for a taxi at the main entrance," said Zixin. "One of the Pleiades was sitting on a bench watching him. Then, for no apparent reason—"

"—he carried his luggage back inside and unpacked it," said Chan.

"Oh no!" thought Ciara. "They've started finishing each other's sentences." Out loud, she said, "So he changed his mind."

"No, he didn't," said Scottie. "When the taxi arrived to collect him, he left his stuff and went to the taxi anyway. He opened the car door, then closed it again without getting in."

"The taxi driver got very angry, insisted Sewang pay for the fare and drove off," said Zixin. "He still wants to leave, but the Pleiades won't let him."

"What do you mean, won't let him?" said Ciara. "How are they making him stay?"

"He says the Pleiades are controlling his body," said Chan. "And he's not the only one. Mina Park, one of the Grade 10 students, had the same experience."

"And on both occasions, one of the Pleiades was present?" asked Ciara.

"Yes," they all said in unison.

"But Ms Hamilton went to the supermarket this morning," said Ciara. "She was allowed to leave."

"She probably agreed to buy them some bottles of E-neo-Ji," said Zixin.

"That can't be it," said Sophie. "They get E-neo-Ji delivered directly from the manufacturer. I saw a truck last night, and the driver unloaded several boxes outside Pleiades House."

"Doesn't your father own E-neo-Ji?" asked Zixin.

Hana seemed irritated by the question. Maybe it was the assumption that her dad owned everything. "No, he doesn't. He is friends with the CEO and helped him get planning permission to build his factory in Jeju City."

"I think we're getting off-topic," said Scottie. "They probably aren't stopping teachers because they don't want to draw attention."

Ciara asked Hana, "Have you told your father any of this?"

Hana didn't reply for a few seconds, then said, "He didn't believe me and said I should be ashamed for being so childish."

"I'm not surprised he'd think that," said Ciara.

A moment later, Ciara realised that might be taken as an insult. She'd meant that their story sounded far-fetched. Hana was scarlet with rage. "How dare you?" The cafeteria went silent. Hana said, "There are—"

"I'm sorry. I'm sorry," interrupted Ciara, then quickly said, "I didn't mean it like that. I just meant there's no proof. Anyone not living here wouldn't understand."

"Everyone is staring at us," said Zixin. "We discussed this earlier today, and we think you should talk to one of them, Ciara."

"Why me?"

"Because you rescued them," said Zixin. "They might listen to you."

Ciara stood up angrily, shoving the chair back. The legs scraped, and the chair clattered to the floor. "So it's my fault two students died. Is that what you're saying?"

Zixin said nothing.

"I thought as much," screamed Ciara. "Ever since we've gotten back, you four have avoided me. Now I know why." And she stormed off.

Ciara needed to clear her head, so she walked outside despite the rain lashing down. Without realising it, she had arrived at the lake. An ugly wire mesh fence about three metres high encircled the lake. Pinned to it were photographs of Kihoon and Jiwon and dozens of bouquets. There was also a bronze plaque embedded in a wooden frame with a message in Hangul. Ciara guessed it was a commemoration.

Ciara was still angry, mainly with Zixin. Her relationship with the others was more to do with circumstance than genuine friendship. Not only had she been abandoned by her friends, even Mr Fernley hadn't contacted her, and he was supposed to be watching out for her. In fairness, he'd done exactly that at Endeavour Reef.

Sitting down on the wet bench, Ciara put her hands to her face and tried to fight back the tears. It was her fault. Her selfishness. Her desire to find an alien race. The two boys would still be alive if she hadn't come to Sanjung Academy.

Eight weeks ago, she lived in Oxford, and her life was great. She was sure of one thing—she didn't fit in here. Maybe she should talk to her aunt about returning to England. She could go to a boarding school if her aunt and uncle stayed in Korea. Yes, that's what she'd do.

Ciara sensed somebody walking towards her. Thinking it was Zixin, she turned around and shouted. "What…"

"Hi," said a quiet voice.

"Hi, Sophie," said Ciara. "What are you doing out in this rain?"

Ciara had forgotten all about Sophie since they'd returned from New Zealand. She felt a little guilty for ignoring a friend who had helped her several times.

"The lake doesn't look very nice with this fence around it," said Sophie.

"No, I suppose not," said Ciara, knowing her friend's lack of empathy was unintentional.

"I want to show you something," said Sophie.

"I was just about to…" Ciara stopped herself from finishing the sentence. Maybe this would be a good distraction. "It doesn't matter. What do you want to show me?"

"We need to go to my room. I don't want anyone else to see it."

As the two girls walked back to the boarding house, Ciara asked, "Can you give me a clue about what you want to show me?"

"I could tell you how I came across it."

Despite knowing this would be a long story, Ciara said, "Sure."

"I was curious about the school network, so I wrote a packet sniffer program to track data traffic. By reading the IP headers, I could work out the network's physical structure."

"Sounds fun, Sophie," said Ciara, annoyed at herself for the sarcasm.

Her friend didn't notice. "It was! They don't even lock the rooms that house the switches, so I was able to enter and connect to them directly."

Ciara didn't know what switches did but knew they were part of a network infrastructure. She had seen a photo of one with lots of cables plugged in.

"So you want to show me the room with the switches?"

"Oh no! I am just explaining how I came across what I will show you."

In the distance, Ciara could see Zixin and Chan walking towards the boarding houses. If they carried on walking at the same pace, they would arrive simultaneously. Ciara stopped walking and tried to add some excitement to her voice. "Why don't you show me the switches now?"

Sophie sounded a little disappointed. "I could, I suppose. Are you sure you want to see them? The video is much more interesting."

"What video?"

"The video I need to show you."

Zixin and Chan had hurried up to avoid the rain. They would arrive before them, so Ciara said, "Show me the video first. We can look at the switches another time."

They continued walking towards the boarding houses.

"So, when I went into the switch room, I found that there were twice as many as I expected. The school uses a second network for video surveillance."

It was starting to make sense. "You hacked into the surveillance system and went through the video footage."

"Yes," beamed Sophie. "They have around a hundred cameras all around the campus."

"And what did you find?"

"That's what I want to show you."

The video clip showed Kihoon holding hands with a blonde-haired girl and walking towards the lake. Just behind them was Jiwon, holding hands with another blonde-haired girl. The two girls sat down on the bench while the boys went over to the lava stone wall and each picked up a large rock. Then they calmly walked into the lake carrying the rock. The girls did nothing for several minutes, then got up and headed towards their boarding house.

It was one of the eeriest things Ciara had ever seen, and the lack of sound made it even stranger. The police must have seen this video and assumed that the boys had committed suicide. It was why the inspector had interviewed the Pleiades. They wanted to know why the girls didn't report the incident.

140

"I don't suppose there are cameras in Pleiades house?" asked Ciara.

"I thought the same thing." And Sophie opened a new video.

This video showed two girls sitting opposite two police officers. One of them was showing the girls a video clip on a computer.

"Are you the two girls in the video?" asked the senior inspector.

"Yes!"

"Do you know why the boys drowned themselves?"

The two Pleiades sat there impassively. Bolt upright, with no fear of police authority. "To punish themselves for attacking our friend."

The inspector looked shocked and leaned forward. "Did they say that?"

"No, but they knew it."

"Did you know that the boys were going to drown themselves?"

The Pleiades continued to answer without any emotion in their voices. "We knew the boys were going into the lake."

"Is that why you walked there?"

"Yes," said one of the girls.

"Why didn't you call for help?"

"It would have been too late to help them."

The senior inspector seemed to be getting angry. He shouted, "You don't seem very upset by this. Two boys have died. Why didn't you report it."

"We just want to be left alone."

Dr Lockley interjected at this point. "You don't understand how much trouble you are in."

One of the girls turned her head to look at the principal. Her expression was one of irritation, like an adult who gets impatient with a child. "For what? Being present when the two boys drowned themselves?"

A radio crackled into life, and the speaker transmitted a distorted Korean voice. The senior inspector said something back in Korean and got up. The police and the principal walked out of the room. The two girls looked directly up at the camera as soon as the adults left. Ciara could feel their eyes boring into her.

"Have you shown anybody else this?" said Ciara.

"No," said Sophie. "I would get into serious trouble if a teacher knew I hacked into the surveillance system."

"Would you send me a copy of this video?"

"I have already put it on a USB," said Sophie handing Ciara a pen drive. "Much safer than sending it to you."

141

Chapter 13
The Bunker

The house competition resumed in the afternoon with a swimming gala. Although Ciara was a strong swimmer, she rejected the invitation to compete. She told Ms Hamilton that her leg injury hadn't recovered. The truth was her heart wasn't in it.

Ciara sat in the crowd when the first race started. The gun fired, and the swimmers leapt from the starting block, breaking the water with minimal splash. An almighty cheer rang out from the spectators, who continued to shout encouragement. Ciara stood up and walked out of the swimming complex, intending to talk to the Pleiades. They would be in their boarding house during the gala.

As she approached the boarding entrance, her stomach knotted. What might they do to her? When Ciara reached the lobby, a boy said, "What do you want? You're not welcome here!"

"I fly halfway around the world and dive into a shark-infested ocean to bring you virus samples to stop you from dying," said Ciara. "And you thank me by saying I'm not welcome."

"Why would we thank you? We programmed you to do those things."

"I have questions, and I'm not going to stand out here to ask them." Ciara pushed past the boy and headed into the main study area. She felt his mind willing her to turn around but shrugged it off.

The boy followed her in. "It seems that we cannot make you leave. We will tell you what you want to know if you leave us alone."

Ciara took a deep breath. She might as well be blunt. "I saw a video of the boys walking into the water carrying heavy rocks to weigh them down. Two of you sat on the bench and watched. Did you make them kill themselves?"

"Yes."

The shock hit Ciara like a slap across the face. "Why would you do such a thing?"

"To prevent other students from attacking us. They fear us now."

"You should have let the teachers deal with them."

"That would not have stopped others. Our way made certain that we are left alone."

Ciara felt sick. "If you want to be left alone, why stop students from leaving the school?"

"When humans realise that we will replace them as the dominant lifeform on Earth, they will seek to eradicate us. We know you have weapons that could destroy this school and everyone inside it, but you will not use them if there are children here."

"So we are hostages then?"

"Not you, Ciara. You are free to leave. The others must stay."

"If you keep killing people, the police will arrest you, and if that doesn't work, the military will come."

"Any that oppose us will turn on their own people."

This conversation was not going the way Ciara had hoped. She thought she'd give it one more try. "Couldn't you try to live peacefully with humans?"

"We considered that when we first came here. We studied your history and concluded that you will try to destroy us when you learn of our abilities. It is better if we attack first."

"Attack first? How do you plan to do that?"

Another boy walked into the room and sat down next to the first. "Why should we tell you?"

"Are you frightened that I will stop you?"

"You cannot stop us!" They said this in unison.

"So tell me how you plan to conquer over seven billion people."

"We already have Sanjung Kim, the most powerful man in Asia. With his influence, we control the South Korean president. We will travel to the United States in seven days to enlist nine other billionaires. Earth's most influential humans will do our bidding."

The plan was so simple. Ciara hadn't noticed that one of the Pleiades was missing, but it made perfect sense for them to control Dr Kim. Naturally, he would meet up with the other hectobillionaires, who would be just as easy to handle.

"What will you do when you have the most powerful men on earth?"

"We will denuclearise the world."

That didn't sound too bad. It reminded Ciara of Albert Einstein's prophetic words, "I know not with what weapons World War III will be fought, but World War IV will be fought with sticks and stones."

"We will detonate them. Fewer humans will be easier to enslave."

These beings would treat people as humans treat livestock. The frightening thing was that Ciara could see no way to stop them. She replayed the conversation in her mind and, despite their argument, decided to talk to her friends.

When Ciara arrived at the gala, it had just finished, and the students were pouring out of the swimming centre. Someone said that Odae had won thanks to a national swimming champion on their team. He'd won four of the events single-handed. Halla finished second, Jiri third, and Seorak last. That meant Seorak and Halla were level on points, but Seorak still led by virtual of the event victories, two to one.

Ciara spotted Zixin in the crowd. For once, she wasn't with Chan. She jogged over. "Can we talk?"

Zixin put her hands on her hips and pursed her lips. "We could have done with you tonight. We came last."

"I heard!"

"You seem to be moving pretty well for someone too injured to compete."

Ciara ignored the rebuke. "I went to see 'you know who'. Oh God, I sound like Harry Potter."

"Actually, Harry never had any difficulty saying Voldemort. It was the other wizards who called him, you know who." Zixin paused, realising what Ciara had said. "Did the Pleiades talk to you?"

"Let's move away from here," said Ciara. "I don't want anyone to overhear." She grabbed Zixin's arm and steered her to one side.

As they moved away from the crowds, Ciara said, "I'm sorry for shouting at you."

"I'm sorry for ignoring you. I wasn't trying to. It's just that…"

"It's fine." The two girls hugged, and then Ciara said, "A friend of ours hacked into the video surveillance system."

Zixin had a confused look before it changed to understanding. "What did she see?"

Ciara had copied the two videos to her phone, so she played them and watched her friend's reaction. Zixin's face hardened, and sparks flared in her eyes. "They can get into our heads and control us. Deep down, I didn't really believe it."

Ciara then told Zixin about her conversation with the Pleiades. "They want to take over the world and have the power to do so. By keeping students here, they are protecting themselves from military attacks."

"So what do we do?" said Zixin. "Dr Kim must be aware of this."

"Dr Kim is being controlled by one of them," said Ciara. "The puppet master has become the puppet."

"We have to do something," said Zixin. "Find a way to get out of here."

Ciara didn't answer. She was thinking about Hana saying her father was evil, driven by a lust for power. With all of his connections and resources, the Pleiades could do whatever they liked.

She came out of her reverie when Zixin broke the silence, "What do we do next?"

"Meet with the others to develop a plan," said Ciara. "I think that we should invite Sophie to join us."

An hour later they were sat by the wall in the cafeteria, as far away from other students as possible. Ciara showed her friends the videos and saw them react as Zixin had done. She followed this by telling them about her conversation with the Pleiades.

"I think we should run through everything we know about them," said Hana. "If we do that, we may find a weakness."

Ciara balled her hand into a fist and extended her thumb to indicate the first thing they knew. "They have a hive mind that can communicate over great distances."

Ciara extended her index finger to signify the second point. "When one of them learns something, they all know it."

"We don't know how they communicate though," said Hana. "My father ran hundreds of tests at the cave, and they couldn't detect what was causing the sleep paralysis."

"It is probably communication on a subatomic level," said Sophie.

"They like E-neo-Ji," said Scottie. "Have you ever noticed that when one drinks, they all do? I think that when one of them gets a sugar hit, the others crave it. They drink so much, their pee must be bright blue."

Zixin's eyes rolled. "Really? That's what you focus on?"

Scottie looked a little dejected. "It might be important."

Ignoring Scottie's point, Ciara extended her middle finger. "We also know they can control several people simultaneously, although I think I'm resistant to their influence."

"You've missed the most important point," said Hana. "They have to be present to control others."

"Regardless," said Ciara irritably. "We can't confront the Pleiades directly. We have to get outside help or find a way to get everybody out of the school."

"What about your father, Hana?" said Scottie. "If we show him the video, he's bound to help us."

"My father is locked away in his research centre on Geumdo Island. He doesn't communicate with me. His assistant told me that one of them is with him at all times."

"So they're controlling him," said Scottie. "But they can't control him all of the time. If there's only one of them, surely he can escape when they aren't watching."

Hana looked directly at her boyfriend. "Thank goodness your hot. They'll lock him up when they don't need him. Control him when they do."

Scottie looked dejected, "Oh yeah! I didn't think it through." Hana reached under the table and gave his hand a slight squeeze.

"Do we go to the authorities?" said Chan.

"And say what?" said Ciara. "There are aliens in our school, and they're controlling everybody with their minds."

"And they were just interviewed by the police," said Zixin.

"With no outside help, how do you get hundreds of students out of the school?" asked Scottie.

Hana suddenly perked up. "There is an underground bunker with a secret exit. It takes you into the Gotjawal forest. I saw it in the plans."

"Of course, there is," said Chan. "All of the schools in the GEC have reinforced underground bunkers in case of a North Korean attack."

The mood changed noticeably, with everyone sitting upright. "Why don't we check it out?" said Ciara. "If we got everyone to leave in the middle of the night, it might work."

"Do you know where the bunker entrance is?" said Scottie.

"Not from looking at a blueprint when I was 11 years old," said Hana.

"We could check the CCTV footage," said Sophie. "One of them is bound to show the bunker entrance."

The cafeteria was almost empty now, and the last stragglers were leaving. "Sophie and I will search through the video files to see if we can spot any places we don't recognise," said Ciara. "When we think we've found it, we'll let you know."

Ciara left her last lesson of the day and was excitedly heading back to the boarding house to meet Sophie. Some men in blue-grey coveralls were mending the elevators at the main entrance. As she walked past, sparks from the oxyacetylene torches flew towards her. They fizzled out just before hitting her.

One of the men was welding two pieces of metal together, but something about the scene seemed wrong. Then it hit her. There were no safety barriers around the work zone.

Ciara dismissed it as incompetence, but then she passed some more workmen in the blue-grey coveralls. One of them was standing on a ladder, changing a light.

She realised what had bothered her about the workmen. Their uniforms were different. They must be outside contractors. Repairing an elevator might be a specialist job, but changing a lightbulb wasn't. Ciara put it out of her mind. She was keen to look through the video footage.

Sophie connected to the server and opened the drive. The list view showed thousands of folders. The school had 100 CCTV video recording devices, each with its own folder. Data privacy laws meant that video footage was kept for a month, so there were 31 folders, one for each day. Inside the 31 folders were eight video files, each with three hours of footage.

Feeling overwhelmed by the task in front of them, Ciara said, "Oh my God. There are so many files."

"Yes, but we only need to look at one video file for each camera," said Sophie. Ciara kicked herself for being so stupid.

After going through 40 video files, Sophie opened an empty folder. "That's odd."

"Try the folder for the day before," said Ciara.

That folder was also empty, and so were several more. "The camera must be faulty," said Sophie.

Eventually, they found one with files inside and opened it. The video showed a long corridor with a door at the end. "Where is that?" asked Ciara.

"No idea," said Sophie. "It could be what we're looking for."

"Can we see if the folder sequence relates to the camera positions," said Ciara.

"Good idea," said Sophie, grabbing her tablet and pencil and sketching a map of the school.

The 100 folders each had a name that matched the camera's serial number. Sophie systematically went through all of the folders opening the video file and recording the location on the map. After several minutes, she'd worked out the video camera with the missing files was near the sports centre.

"There's nothing in that location," said Ciara.

"Nothing above ground," said Sophie.

"That must be where the entrance to the bunker is," said Ciara. "It makes sense for it to be near the boarding houses."

"So when do you want to look for it?"

"No time like the present," said Ciara getting up.

They headed to the sports centre. "I think I know where it might be," said Ciara. "At the back of the weights room is a maintenance area. It's out of bounds for students, but the door is always ajar."

Ciara used her pass to open the door to the gym. It was pretty late, so only a teacher and a student were there. The teacher was running on the treadmill while a blonde-haired girl was lying on a mat reading.

"Hello again," said the girl sitting up. She looked about 12 years old, had a few freckles on her nose and was almost certainly the teacher's daughter. Ciara remembered asking her about the books she was checking out, although she couldn't remember the title.

"Hi Eve. Still reading, I see," said Ciara.

"Yes, I'm on the second book now." The girl turned the book to show Ciara the book cover. She was reading The Hunger Games trilogy.

"Is it good?"

"Yep!"

The teacher hadn't even noticed them come in. She was wearing earpods and running hard.

"Well, Eve," said Ciara. "We'll let you get back to your book. We're going to look for one of the maintenance staff through here." She pointed to the emergency exit door at the back of the gym.

"Okay. Have a good evening," said Eve, lying back down on the mat.

Ciara and Sophie moved through the gym. Sophie whispered, "You handled that so well. I wouldn't have known what to say."

Ciara gave Sophie a smile and shoved hard on the mechanism to open the emergency door. She half expected an alarm to go off, but it didn't.

"Grab one of those dumbbells, Sophie," said Ciara. There was a row of dumbbells on a frame. Sophie picked up a 4kg weight and carried it over.

"When we go through the door, wedge the dumbbell inside it so it doesn't close completely," said Ciara.

They made their way along a corridor and down some stairs. There was a room on the ground floor. Ciara could hear a conversation in Korean. They tiptoed past the door and came across some more stairs. Heading down, they spied a video camera high up on a wall.

Ciara pointed. "That must be the one."

Sophie moved directly under the camera and looked up. "The two cables have been disconnected."

Ciara saw wires dangling down. The metal connectors had been deliberately unscrewed. "That explains why there were no video files for the last few days."

The two girls walked along the corridor to the door at the end. The padlock was hanging open. Ciara put her finger to her lips to signify that they should stop talking. She pushed the door open and walked through.

The air was heavy and smelled of mould. All of the walls, ceilings, and stairs were concrete. A fluorescent light strip cast shadows on the ground. The two friends made their way slowly down the stairs. At the bottom was a corridor heading left and right.

Ciara whispered to Sophie, "Which way?"

Her friend shrugged and pointed left. They walked along the concrete floor until they reached an open door on the right. Inside was a toilet. They continued along the corridor, passing by a kitchen area and a storage room. The dusty shelves contained hundreds of tinned food.

"What are you doing down here," shouted a man from behind them.

Startled, Ciara whipped around, ready to fight. The man smiled at them, but it took a moment before she recognised him. Without his beard, James Fernley looked much younger.

"Hello, Mr Fernley," said Sophie. "I miss our weekly chats."

"I miss them too, So Yon."

Ciara was puzzled for a brief moment, then remembered that Sophie's Korean name was So Yon. The momentary confusion delayed the overwhelming feeling of relief. She ran to Fernley and hugged the startled man. "Thank you for saving me."

"I'm sure you would have gotten out of that mess without me," said Fernley. "Shark attacks are rare."

"How long have you been living down here?" asked Ciara.

"I moved in as soon as I resigned from my job. Then I followed you to New Zealand and Australia."

Ciara was surprised. "Why didn't you talk to me when we were in New Zealand?"

"I didn't want anyone to know I was there. I was going to talk to you in the forest on Mount Pirongia, but you managed to evade me despite my infra-red binos."

"We thought it was Chan following us. He went missing on the same day. When we found out he was somewhere else, we never thought about the person tracking us."

"I have a great deal to tell you," said Fernley. "Let's chat over a cup of tea."

He led them to a kitchen stocked with all kinds of food. Ciara asked for honey and ginger herbal tea. When the drinks were ready, they sat down at a cheap plastic table. It looked more like garden furniture, but Jeju's summers were very humid, and wood would go mouldy.

"So why are you down here?" asked Fernley. "Were you looking for me?"

Ciara took a sip of her tea. "No. We had no idea where you were. We were looking for the secret exit to the Gotjawal forest."

Fernley's eyebrows raised. "Are you and So Yon trying to sneak out of the school?"

"No," said Sophie. "We are planning to sneak all of the students out of the school."

"What? Why would you do that?"

"You're a secret agent. I thought you would know what was going on."

"I think you'd better tell me everything."

As Ciara recounted the story, it was apparent Fernley knew nothing about the Pleaides' clashes with students. When he was told about the death of Kihoon and Jiwon, he shook his head sadly. "This is my fault."

When Ciara told Fernley she'd gone to talk to the Pleiades, he was astonished they let her in the boarding house. "Tell me what happened exactly," he said. "Word for word."

Ciara tried to remember as best she could. "I walked past the boy, and he said something like, it seems we cannot make you leave. If we tell you what you want, will you leave us alone."

Fernley stood up excitedly. "Are you sure, Ciara?"

"Yes! Why is it important?"

"Perhaps they can't control you," said Fernley. "Did you feel their mind connecting to yours—trying to take over?"

"I felt that they desperately wanted me to leave. Actually, it was more like trying to make me leave. But, I shrugged it off."

"This is wonderful news," said Fernley clapping his hands together excitedly.

"Why can't they control, Ciara?" asked Sophie.

Fernley looked directly at Ciara, his eyes flashing. "Do you mind if I talk about you?"

"Of course not," said Ciara smiling. "I'm my favourite subject."

Fernley blew on his tea and sipped it. The steam swirled upwards. "I'm afraid I haven't been completely candid with you. I've told you half-truths."

He looked at Ciara to see her reaction but she merely looked at him expectantly, so he carried on. "I told you that I worked for an intelligence division of the Ministry of Defence. One that specifically looked into alien sightings. While that is true, I didn't tell you that I am 300 years old."

Both Ciara and Sophie frowned and took a step back. "You're one of them!" said Ciara.

"I'm not. The Pleiades massacred my people, enslaved the survivors, and used us for their gene manipulation experiments. We experienced decades of abuse before they learned to extend life."

"So, can they control you?" Ciara sat back down and shuffled uncomfortably, embarrassed that she didn't trust this man who'd saved her life.

"I don't think so," said Fernley. "At least..." His voice trailed away as if he was trying to remember something but couldn't quite grasp it. "Not without specialist equipment. I was useful to them as I am."

"How were you useful?"

"I have visions of the future. I saw Ciara diving for the key, and inside a cave with a cure for the diseases that killed so many. They knew Ciara was descended from William Hartley. With that information, the Pleiades formulated a plan."

Sophie tilted her head slightly as she thought. "Why did you tell them about your vision? Surely you didn't want to save them?"

Fernley's head dropped, and tears welled in his eyes. "They already had most of the information. I was only filling in the blanks or confirming what they knew. Besides, they held my wife captive and promised they would let us both go afterwards."

"Did they keep their word?" asked Ciara softly.

"No. My wife and I got tuberculosis when the HMS Dolphin arrived. I survived after months of suffering, but my wife was not so fortunate."

"I'm sorry," said Ciara.

There was an uncomfortable silence before Ciara asked, "When did you leave Tahiti?"

Once again, Hartley looked confused. "It was so long ago. I remember sailing with an officer called William Bligh."

Once again, Sophie demonstrated unexpected knowledge. "Oh—he was captain of the HMS Bounty and that ship left Tahiti in 1789."

"The HMS Bounty?" said Ciara. Her voice went up an octave. "The mutiny on the bounty. I remembered reading about that. Were you one of the mutineers?"

Before Fernley had a chance to respond, Sophie interjected. "Are you saying the Pleiades reprogrammed William Hartley's DNA to pass it on to Ciara, whose genetically altered genes enable the visions she used to free them?"

Fernley chuckled. "Sounds farfetched, doesn't it. But you're absolutely right, Sophie. I couldn't have put it more succinctly myself."

"So are the Pleiades the reason I have visions?" asked Ciara.

Fernley shook his head. "Yes, but yours are not visions of the future. They are your ancestors' memories stored in their DNA and passed on to you."

Ciara chewed on her thumbnail, then said, "I have visions of the future too."

Fernley's eyebrows raised. "You never told me this!"

He frowned, then barked a laugh. "The fools. When they rewrote your DNA, they must have cloned some of mine to trigger the dreams. Except your gift seems to transcend the past and future."

Ciara had tried not to think about her abilities. Now there was someone with answers she needed to ask the questions that had been troubling her. "Will I see events from any of William Hartley's descendants?"

"Hartley—" said Fernley, then changed what he was going to say. "Theoretically, that seems reasonable. But you won't see any ancestors' actions that occur after you were born. The DNA is passed on once and doesn't update."

"I have a question," said Sophie. "Have you seen many future events?"

Fernley looked slightly anxious—like he was afraid of Ciara's answer.

"Not many. The visions are just glimpses and only last for a few seconds."

"Have any come true?" asked Fernley.

"Yes. I saw myself sunbathing on a superyacht. I didn't even know it was a vision until it happened."

"Anything else?" asked Fernley.

Ciara wondered why he was pressing her about this. He seemed concerned about something. "I saw myself as a prisoner in a neuroscience lab. That hasn't happened yet, so it might be nothing."

Bizarrely, Fernley looked relieved. "Visions are the most likely version of events, but we can change them."

"Are we more likely to have a vision of something important, or are they just random?" asked Ciara.

"Usually, it is something significant," said Fernley. "Although the vision of you sunbathing wasn't."

"The day when we stopped the intruders, I was right in thinking they were there for you," said Ciara. "Why didn't you have a vision warning you?"

"I don't know. It might have been important for you and Zixin to save me."

"You make it sound like everything is preordained."

"Sometimes I think everything is."

Sophie had been contentedly sipping her tea while listening intently. She finally spoke. "Who were the men trying to kidnap you?"

"They were Chinese MSS operatives. I'd gone undercover at a level 4 biosafety lab in Harbin on the north-eastern coast of China. The UK Government suspected that bioweapons were being developed there. I was captured, given psychoactive drugs and interrogated. They realised I wasn't human, but I escaped before revealing anything."

Ciara's thoughts went to the first time she saw Mr Fernley. He'd looked awful. Now she wondered if he'd been tortured.

Sophie focused on something else entirely. "Did you know the Mongols were one of the first civilisations to use biological warfare? They catapulted plague-infested bodies over the walls of forts. A similar strategy was used by European sailors who sent sick people to infect pacific islanders. They became too weak to defend themselves and were imprisoned as slaves."

Ciara interjected before Sophie could continue her narrative. "Did you find any evidence of bioweapons?"

"I'm not sure you'd call it a bioweapon," said Fernley. "They developed an antidote to ricin, which could be used as a bioweapon if your troops are immune to its effects."

"What's ricin?" asked Ciara.

"It's an odourless, tasteless poison extracted from castor beans," said Sophie. "Nobody has ever been able to create an antidote. Are you sure they have one?"

Fernley nodded. "They infected me with ricin. I assumed it was to kill me, but then they gave me the antidote, and after a couple of days, I was well enough to escape."

"That's not really bioweaponry," said Ciara. "That's vital research."

"I agree," said Sophie. "Was there anything else being developed there?"

"Not that I could find," said Fernley. "There were plenty of hazardous pathogens. They store the smallpox virus at Harbin. One of only two places in the world. The other is in—"

"Russia," said Sophie.

Fernley looked surprised that Sophie knew the second lab was Russian. "How do you know that?"

"I read an article questioning whether we should be storing the smallpox virus," said Sophie. "There was a fire in the Russian lab and concerns that the virus might have been released."

The thought of smallpox breaking out sent shivers down Ciara's back. She'd seen photographs of the survivors with their disfiguring scars. Had the virus been released, the devastation would have been catastrophic. Smallpox had killed more than 300 million people in the twentieth century until a global vaccination campaign eradicated the virus in the late 1970s.

"I assume you came directly to Korea after escaping from China," said Ciara.

"Yes. How did you know that?"

"When I first saw you, you looked dishevelled and underweight." Ciara could picture Mr Fernley in his office. It was only six weeks ago, yet it felt like a lifetime.

"Escaping from the lab was difficult. Perhaps I'll tell you about it one day. But for now, we have more pressing matters. I believe you were looking for a secret exit to the Gotjawal forest. I think I might know where to look."

With that, he took off. Ciara drank the last part of her herbal tea and put the cup down. "Come on, Sophie," she said.

They found the exit quite quickly. When you knew one existed, a small storage room at the back of a large open area was the only logical place. The room contained very little apart from a pile of neatly arranged cardboard boxes.

"I suspect the exit will be behind there," said Fernley indicating the boxes. "I assumed they had been used to carry the food down here, but that doesn't make sense. They're too large for food tins and would be heavy to carry."

The boxes were empty, and after moving them, they saw the faint outline of a doorway. It was hard to spot in the gloom and shadows cast by the light and had no handle or discernible difference to the walls on either side.

"It isn't much of a secret door," said Sophie. "We found it straight away."

"Yeah, but how do we open it?" asked Ciara.

Fernley tapped the door with a metal torch, and a hollow sound rang out. The adjacent walls produced a heavy, muffled sound.

"There's definitely a passage behind here," said Fernley.

They spent 15 minutes looking for levers, buttons, or anything that might trigger the opening mechanism. Ciara shoved the door in frustration, and it swung open after a brief moment of resistance.

"You're kidding me," said Ciara. "We just needed to push harder."

A quick inspection of the exit revealed it was a spring-loaded fire door. While it was heavy and difficult to move, it wasn't secret.

Sophie looked very excited. "Shall we follow the passage to see where it comes out?"

Ciara nodded but felt awful. The passageway narrowed after the entrance, and she would have to stoop to move along it. She imagined the walls and ceiling closing around her and visualised thousands of tons of soil and rocks collapsing.

She must have looked pale because Fernley said, "Are you okay, Ciara?"

"Fine!" she replied quickly. "Let's go!"

The sports centre was only 50 metres from the boundary fence. They travelled along the passage for 100 metres and came to some stairs. They were definitely out of school now. Ciara climbed the steps, and at the top was a wooden panel with a large metal bolt.

Ciara tried to slide the bolt, but it was rusty and wouldn't budge. She needed some WD40. The maintenance guys would have some. Suddenly, she realised that the men repairing the lift and changing the lights were Chinese MSS operatives. One of them was familiar—he'd tried to kidnap Mr Fernley.

Ciara wiggled the bolt handle from side to side with as much force as possible, and it slid. Pushing open the trap door, she climbed out into the dark forest. As soon as Sophie and Mr Fernley had joined her, she said, "The MSS operatives that tried to kidnap you. They're in the school!"

Almost immediately, a cry pierced the late-night sky, followed by two more. The sound came from within the school grounds. It was difficult to pinpoint where, but it sounded like an animal in pain.

Ciara looked to Fernley for guidance. "We need to get back," he said. "Hurry."

Fernley took off for the tunnel with Ciara and Sophie right behind him. Before they exited the bunker, Fernley suggested that Sophie go to the boarding houses and start taking students through the bunker. She must avoid the Pleiades, or the plan would fail, and her life would be at risk.

Ciara pictured Sophie running room to room, banging on their doors and trying to rouse them. Then she remembered burning the pasta. "Set off the fire alarm. That will wake the students and get them outside quickly."

Sophie nodded and set off to the west. Ciara watched her go, worrying about her friend.

"Hurry up," said Fernley. "We're the only ones that can stop them."

Chapter 14
The Hidden Assault

As they exited the bunker, they could hear screams of pain coming from the direction of the boarding houses. Fernley and Ciara ran towards the commotion. As the distance shortened, they could see a mass brawl, with students hitting each other. On the far side, one of the Pleiades was sitting on a bench with a smile on her face.

A young boy went down heavily from a blow to the head. His attacker looked around for his next victim. Spotting Ciara and Fernley, he ran towards them. They decided to avoid him because they didn't want to hurt an innocent person in self-defence.

"This way," said Ciara. "We can't get through that way."

They ran away from the battle and around the side of Halla House. The boy gave up the pursuit and headed back into the melee. When they were far enough away, Ciara stopped.

"We need a plan," she said, panting.

"If we can distract the Pleiades, the fighting will stop," said Fernley.

Ciara frowned. "Are you suggesting we sneak up to them and hit them over the head with a bat?"

"Of course not!" said Fernley. "We need a more sophisticated approach."

Ciara thought for a moment. "If we can get close enough to one of the Pleiades, perhaps we can convince them to stop or threaten to hurt them if they don't."

"So we need intel and a weapon," said Fernley. "Where do we get that?"

"Let's go to Seorak House," said Ciara. "Perhaps someone there knows what's going on."

When they got to Seorak House, they saw Sophie in the kitchen. She was yelling at some Grade 7 students who were frightened. Fernley spoke to them, and his authority was enough to get them to move.

"We got most of them to head for the bunker," said Sophie. "Zixin is downstairs chasing the remaining few out. I'm going to head over to Odae House now."

"Why don't you find Zixin? I'll go with Sophie," said Mr Fernley, and he dashed off before she could argue.

Instead of looking for Zixin, Ciara headed along the corridor to her room. She went inside and then opened the drawer to her bedside table. The only items in it were a penknife and the two sodium bicarbonate tablets taken from the escape room. She pocketed the knife. Then, after a moment of reflection, she picked up the tablets.

She was about to leave but was overcome by a bout of dizziness. Before she knew it, Ciara was William Hartley sitting opposite John Bootie. They were eating turtle soup and drinking watered-down beer. The master had caught three green turtles, one weighing 300 pounds.

"Listen to me, William. You have to tell the captain that Moody tried to drown you," said Bootie.

"I've thought it through, John," said Hartley. "I have no proof, and even if the captain believes me, it looks like I can't control the crew. It will go on my record, and I'll never get promoted."

Bootie shook his head in frustration. "Moody will succeed one day. I've met his type before—it is a matter of honour that he takes revenge on you."

"I know you're right, but I can't kill the man in cold blood. All I can do is be prepared the next time he tries something."

"I think you're making a mistake, William, but it's your life. I'll keep an eye on Moody for you, but I can't watch him all the time."

Bootie was true to his word and watched Moody like a hawk as the Endeavour sailed north around the east coast of Australia. They continued to find shoals, so they looked for channels where the ship could pass between them. Progress was slow, with the rowing boats leading the way. Eventually, they reached the shores of Pulau Habeeke in Papua New Guinea.

Cook struggled to find a suitable spot to land because the coast was as muddy as the Thames at Gravesend, as he put it. When they did find a sandy beach, they spied a handful of natives. Cook ordered a double landing party so that the marines could provide protection. They took the pinnace and yawl to shore, accompanied by the two Tahitian translators, Tupaia and Tua.

The ship was running low on drinkable water, so there was a need to replenish the stocks. Cook, Banks, and four marines walked along the beach but had barely travelled 200 yards when they were attacked by four natives, who emerged from the woods throwing rocks and waving spears. The marines fired upon their assailants, who quickly scattered, frightened by the noise of the muskets.

Banks was still keen to collect plant specimens, so the two search parties were ordered to gather anything unusual. Hicks led one search party, Hartley the other. While the beach extended a great distance in both directions, it was only 30 metres from the forest.

Hartley ordered his team into the thick of the heavy, dense foliage, the men cutting their way through using their cutlasses. They headed uphill, hoping that if they got high enough, they would be able to spot freshwater from their vantage point.

The bush cleared a little at the top of a hill, but the only view was straight down a steep cliff face to jagged rocks below. Hartley ordered the men to fan out and search the surrounding areas. They were to meet back in the clearing after 30 minutes. Hartley sat down on a large rock that faced the sea while he waited for the scouts to return.

Moody watched as the men disappeared into the surrounding forest. He emerged from his hiding place and crept slowly towards the midshipman. The loud squawk of a native bird rang out, and Hartley's head turned to look at it. Moody stayed motionless until it was safe to continue without being seen.

When Hartley sensed the presence of another, it was too late. Moody had pulled his sword from the scabbard. Hartley jumped to his feet and turned to face the sneering seaman.

"This is mutiny, Moody. They'll crucify you for this."

"That's as maybe. But only if the captain finds out what happened here. And I don't think the captain will be checking your body when it's lying on the rocks below."

Instinctively, Hartley looked down. Moody was right. It would be impossible to retrieve a body if he was forced off the edge. Moody could cut him down and dispose of him.

"I see you've thought it through and agree with me," said Moody. "Once I'm done with you, I'll take care of your damn friend. The one who's been watching me day and night."

Hartley racked his brain for an escape. Behind him was a sheer drop and any movement left or right would easily be cut off. There was only one option left. He ran straight at Moody, who responded by swinging the sword. He should have stabbed but was unaccustomed to a gentleman's weapon with its long thin blade.

By the time the sword struck, it was behind Hartley, whose forehead smashed into his opponent's nose. Blood splattered in all directions, and Moody reeled backwards, tripping over a root to land heavily on his back. The wind was knocked from his lungs, and the sword was jolted from his hand.

Hartley's brain raced. Should he run down the hill calling for his men or try to reach his sword before the mutineer got to his feet? The first act was cowardly, and he would lose face. The second was risky but an officer's behaviour.

It was a close race to the sword. Hartley grasped the handle and ducked away as Moody swung with the cutlass he'd pulled from his belt. It had been two years since the confrontation in the Minerva Inn, and the Midshipman had changed from a gangly youth into a wiry man. Finally, there would be a conclusion to this ongoing battle.

Moody was all aggression as he ran at Hartley, swinging the cutlass frantically back and forth. Hartley dodged back nimbly, looking for weaknesses. Moody was a broader, more muscular man with iron muscles and a savage disposition. His fighting style was crude, relying on strength and fitness.

Hartley's weapon had the edge in length, but he was concerned that a heavy blow from the cutlass might break the blade. He briefly considered letting Moody tire himself out, but the sailor was supremely fit. Time was Hartley's friend because his men would return in 20 minutes. But he doubted he could defend himself for that long.

Moody gave an animalistic snarl and launched his second assault. Hartley blocked one of the blows with his sword, and the sound rang out like a bell. All the while, he could feel himself being guided towards the cliff face. A place where he wouldn't be able to dance away.

Both men were breathing heavily, more from the stress than the exertion. Moody's third attack was predictable. Hartley blocked, and the cutlass slid along his blade's length, thundering into the crossguard. The sudden stop threw Moody off balance, and he stumbled forward. Quick as a flash, Hartley brought his weapon down.

A cry of pain passed Moody's lips, and although the cut was deep, it seemed to energise him. He pulled a knife from a sheath and now had a weapon in both hands. He charged forward again, swinging the cutlass back and forth, driving Hartley back towards the cliff's edge.

The heel of Hartley's boot caught a rock, and he tripped, barely catching himself. The cutlass sliced through the air, but Hartley blocked it. Moody stepped in close and, with his left hand, drove the knife into Hartley's side.

Paralysed from pain and unable to breathe, Hartley fell to his knees. The strength had left his body, and his sword arm fell limply. Kneeing like a man at the guillotine, there was only one outcome. Hartley waited for the blow to land and hoped it would end quickly.

With his cutlass raised and poised to deliver the death blow, a hand-sized rock struck Moody on the right side of his face. The impact would have felled most men, but Moody slowly turned his head to see a nervous Tua looking panicked.

Blood trickled down the side of Moody's face, but his arm was still raised, ready to strike the final blow. Instead, he threw his cutlass over the cliffside. Tua let out a gasp and collapsed to his knees, exhaustion etched over his face.

Moody reacted quickly and raised the dagger to end the matter. That moment of respite allowed Hartley to recover, and he drove his sword through the seaman's gut. Blood bubbled from Moody's mouth like water from a faucet. He pitched forward, pinning the weakened midshipman to the ground.

Hartley lay unable to move for several moments before the muscular sailor was dragged off him. He looked up to see the young blonde-haired youth, his hands covered in Moody's blood.

"Is he dead?" asked Hartley wearily.

"Yes, Sir! He won't be bothering you again, Mr Hartley."

When Ciara snapped back from the vision, she panicked. How long had she been out? Only ten minutes, but it felt like hours. She ran downstairs and found her friend hustling students down the stairs and barking orders. When Zixin saw Ciara, her face went ashen, and she looked away.

Once the students were out of earshot, Ciara asked, "Are the MSS operatives here for the Pleiades or Mr Fernley?"

Zixin looked guiltily down at her feet. "The Pleiades."

"How did they know about them?"

"I told my dad what was going on here. I didn't think he'd send in a team. I'm sorry, Ciara. I just—"

"Acted alone," said Ciara coldly. "Didn't think it through! Didn't discuss it with your friends." Each sentence was said with greater emphasis until she shouted, "Your actions might have gotten people killed."

Ciara wanted Zixin to get angry—to shout back. Instead, her friend did something completely unexpected. She put her head in her hands and started to sob.

In an instant, Ciara's anger was gone. "I'm sorry, Zixin. This might not be a bad thing. While they're distracted, we can get the students out of the school."

Ciara moved forward and hugged Zixin. She was annoyed at herself for not realising who the maintenance men were earlier. She had been distracted and hadn't thought it through.

Zixin seemed to pull herself together. "There's one more thing. Mr Fernley is one of them. My dad captured Mr Fernley in a bio lab a couple of months ago. He found out that he wasn't human, but he escaped. He sent men to get him back, and we stopped them."

"You're right about Mr Fernley not being human, but he isn't one of the Pleiades. He and his people were enslaved by them."

"Are you sure? How do you know?"

"Because he's helping us get the children out. I'll tell you everything later. What I really need to know is what weapons did the MSS operatives bring?"

"They have tasers and anaesthetics. I think they planned to sneak into the Pleiades dorm while they slept."

"If I can get hold of a taser, I might be able to use it on them," said Ciara. "I'm resistant to their mind control, and stopping them would free any students under their influence."

"Do you want me to come with you?" asked Zixin.

"I have an idea about how we might stop them."

"How?"

"One of Sophie's interesting facts reminded me of something the Pleiades said to William Hartley. It reminded me of their main weakness." She beckoned Zixin to come closer, then whispered in her ear.

After a minute or so, Zixin pulled away and said, "That's too dangerous, Ciara. It could go horribly wrong."

"I admit it's drastic, but the Pleiades plan to start a nuclear war. Billions will die, and the rest will be enslaved. Trust me, Zixin, this is the only way. Help Sophie get the students out of the Odae House, and we can implement the plan afterwards."

Zixin looked like she was about to argue. Instead, she reluctantly wished Ciara good luck and headed off to find Sophie.

Ciara decided to go to the Pleiades boarding house. If the MSS agents tried to catch the Pleiades sleeping, that was the most likely place to find a taser and syringe. When Ciara exited Seorak House, she could see several students lying on the ground, either hurt or unconscious. The odd student was looking around for new opponents to fight.

A large boy spotted Ciara and hobbled towards her. She decided to run around the back of Seorak House to lose him. When she emerged, he was nowhere to be seen.

When Ciara entered the Pleiades building, it was deserted. She ran from room to room on the first floor and found several Pleiades unconscious. Unfortunately, the syringes were empty, and there were no signs of any tasers.

Ciara ran up the stairs to the second floor. There was an unconscious man in the first room with a needle sticking out of his hand. On the floor lay a dropped taser, and attached to a belt were its spare firing cartridges. Ciara removed the man's taser belt and strapped it on before picking up the taser.

Indecision clouded Ciara's mind. Should she keep searching for a syringe or use the taser on the first Pleiades she came across? She decided on the latter. Her priority was to stop the fighting and get the students out of the school.

She ran outside and headed towards the sound of fighting. A maintenance man was crouched over a student whose hands and feet were bound together by a thick cord. He stood up, blood dripping from his nose. There was a glassy-eyed look in his eyes as he looked directly at Ciara. A little way behind him stood one of the Pleiades with a quizzical look on his face.

The man ran at Ciara. He was athletically built and very quick. Not surprising, given that he was a Chinese intelligence operative. Ciara waited calmly with the taser in her hand. A worrying thought crossed her mind. She assumed that it hadn't fired, but there wouldn't have been any charge if it had. She resisted the urge to look at the light on the side of the weapon.

The man would charge directly into Ciara as she had to the other Chinese intelligence operative. She waited until he was close enough that she couldn't miss him. The similarity between this and the Māori warriors charging at William Hartley struck her suddenly. He'd panicked the first time before redeeming himself.

The man was upon her when she pulled the trigger. He hit her, but the force had gone out of his body, and he collapsed face-first on the ground. At the last moment, she had wondered if touching him while he was tasered would electrocute her. It hadn't!

She had to move now. She strode purposefully towards the Pleiades, pulled out a firing cartridge from her belt and reloaded the taser. She glanced over her shoulder at the Chinese operative stirring. It seemed that he had been released.

She felt something touch her mind, trying to push her away. She shrugged it off and marched forward. The Pleiades didn't try to run. Instead, he stood there looking at her. She fired the taser straight at him, and he collapsed in a heap. She ran over to the tied-up student and removed the cord binding him.

"Go to the weights room and through the door at the back," said Ciara. "Head down the stairs. There is an underground bunker that leads out of the school."

The boy had a dark bruise over one eye. He looked at her blankly. "Go now!" she yelled.

The Pleiades groaned and tried to get up. Ciara shoved his face into the ground. She whipped the cord around his ankles and pulled his arms back roughly. After tying all of his limbs together, Ciara reloaded the taser and fired again. She'd heard that being tasered was incredibly painful and briefly wondered if they all felt the pain when one of them was hurt.

Ciara went to reload the taser but had none left. Stupid of her to have wasted the last cartridge. She paused and listened intently. There were faint sounds near the sports centre. She hoped it was students heading towards the bunker. Instead, a Chinese MSS operative was blocking the building entrance as she approached. In his hands was a wooden hockey stick, and he was brandishing it aggressively towards Zixin.

The man swung the weapon, but Zixin ducked and darted in, throwing a one-two punch that seemed to have no impact. He struck with the stick again. Zixin leapt back out before it hit her. He had at least 20 kilos on his opponent, but she was light on her feet and very fast.

Why was he stopping Zixin from leaving? It made no sense. He reported to her father, so he must know who she was. Nobody was in sight, so the students must have left already. No doubt Zixin would be able to explain after dealing with their opponent.

"Zixin," yelled Ciara. "Step back."

Ciara pulled out the taser from the holster. She covered the flashing red light with her finger. When Ciara pointed the taser at him, he backed away slightly. Getting tasered was painful, and she was counting on him wanting to avoid that fate. If he called her bluff and swung, she planned to duck under. Of course, he might not aim for her head.

"I've heard getting tasered is excruciatingly painful," said Ciara slowly. "Drop the hockey stick, or I will drop you."

Ciara took a step closer. The man's back was at the door. With nowhere to go, he had two choices. Attack or surrender. "Last chance," said Ciara.

She could see the indecision in the man's eyes. They blazed for a moment, and she was sure he would swing, but then the fire died resignedly, and he dropped the hockey stick.

"Kick it over here."

He did as he was told. Zixin walked over and picked up the hockey stick. She stepped behind Ciara and hit her firmly on the side of the neck, compressing the vagus nerve. A blow to this region causes immediate unconsciousness.

The man took out a syringe and removed the plastic top. He crouched over Ciara's inert body and lifted her hand. She didn't regain consciousness before the needle slid into a vein on the back of her hand. He bent down and picked her up. Then he and Zixin walked away from the sports centre.

Chapter 15
Bio Lab

When Ciara came around, she felt groggy and nauseous. She didn't know where she was or understand why she couldn't move. Her arms ached, and her wrists were sore. She could feel the small movements of an aircraft yawing and pitching as it pushed through the air currents. She was cold, and it was dark. Eventually, she drifted back into sleep.

The second time Ciara awoke, she was much more alert, but her predicament wasn't any better. She was in a chair with both arms strapped down and couldn't move. She looked around, and a dozen electrodes pulled at her hair. The low hum of an EEG machine echoed around the room. This was her vision from a few weeks before. When her life had been normal.

In the vision, she'd ripped the fabric straps apart. She gave them a slight tug and could feel the material stretch slightly. Craning her head to the left, she could see the EEG screen. Rows of jagged green lines ran from left to right, changing as the screen refreshed. There was a kidney-shaped tray on the countertop, and within it was a scalpel. She might escape if she could reach it, but that was impossible.

A short, frail, grey-haired Chinese man wearing a white lab coat entered the room. His skin was leathery with the craggy texture of someone in their seventies. The lanyard around his neck was attached to a plastic card with his photograph and name—Dr Feng Wang.

"Ah, you're awake. Good, good!"

Dr Wang walked over to the EEG machine and pressed a button. A dot matrix printer leapt into life, and its scratchy whirring noise echoed around the room. It was loud and hurt Ciara's head which was hazy from the drugs. When the printer had done its job, the doctor ripped the paper from it.

"Completely normal," he said, nonplussed. "Tell me, Ciara. Can you control your visions?"

Ciara thought about refusing to answer for a moment, but what did it matter if she told him the truth. Besides, she wanted to learn to control her visions. If she worked with him, they might uncover something worthwhile.

"No! They're completely random."

"Pity! We're going to be here for a while then."

"My name is Ciara. What should I call you?"

The man laughed. "Such confidence in a prisoner." He shrugged his shoulders as if deciding it didn't matter and said, "Dr Wang."

"My aunt is a neuroscientist, so I am familiar with your equipment." Ciara nodded towards the EEG, MEG, and fMRI scanners. "Have you checked the magnetic fields generated by my neural activity?"

Dr Wang raised an eyebrow. "No, I've only looked at the electrical activity. Everything is normal."

Dr Wang walked across the room and picked up a notebook and a pencil from his desk. He placed the pencil in Ciara's hand and put the notepad on her leg. She could move her wrist just enough to write.

"Solve these problems," said Dr Wang.

Ciara wondered if he deliberately avoided using her name. Was he desensitising himself by referring to her as a prisoner and not thinking of her as a person? She wanted to create a connection, and the best way to do so was through conversation.

"Of course, Dr Wang. I think you'll find that my brain waves switch from beta to gamma as soon as I start thinking about these problems."

Dr Wang said nothing and continued to stare at the EEG screen. Ciara started to solve the problems. The gaps between the wave frequencies shortened as was typical when subjects concentrated. It was classic gamma activity and completely normal.

Ciara wrote the answer to the final problem and closed the notebook. She glanced at the EEG monitor and saw the wavelengths widening as the brain returned to beta frequencies. "Completely normal, Dr Wang?"

"Yes, they are." He took the notepad and pencil off Ciara and placed them on his desk.

"Aren't you going to mark my answers? It would be nice to know how I've done."

Dr Wang scowled, and Ciara realised her flippancy was a mistake. She must appear arrogant and disrespectful. "I'm sorry, Dr Wang. I'd like to help you figure out what is different about my brain."

Dr Wang's face morphed into a grotesque smile. One that said, I will hurt you and enjoy doing so. Creepily he leaned over Ciara and gently caressed her cheek. Then in a soft voice, he said, "You won't feel that way after I cut open your pretty little head."

His breath smelled of fish, but Ciara resisted the urge to pull her head back. Did he intend to kill her once he had the information they needed? There was a scalpel on the side, so maybe he did. She swallowed hard and said, "Is the girl who captured me here?"

"Are you hoping your little friend will change her mind and rescue you?"

That was precisely what Ciara was hoping. "No! I want her to see me like this—to see the extent of her betrayal."

Dr Wang laughed—a high pitched girlish laugh. He seemed to be enjoying Ciara's discomfort. "Like this? Sat comfortably in a chair."

His mouth parted, and a pink tongue emerged to move slowly around his lips. "When I have what I want from you, we will get to know each other much better. Would you like me to record that? Then your friend can see the full extent of her betrayal."

Dr Wang walked over to his desk and picked up a syringe with a red label. "This is succinylcholine—a muscle paralytic. You will be awake but unable to move."

He pulled a smartphone from his pocket, turned on the video and placed it on the side with the camera pointing at Ciara. Dr Wang smiled again. The same creepy grotesque smile from before. He pulled the plastic lid from the syringe and ambled towards his prisoner.

Ciara felt sick to her stomach at what this pervy old man intended. She felt an intense rage course through her body. Her knuckles went white as her hands gripped the chair's arms. She must have had an out-of-body experience because she could see herself sitting in the chair. Then a hand picked up the scalpel and cut the straps holding her arms.

Simultaneously, the wavelength on the EEG monitor started oscillating at a faster frequency, a value close to 200 Hz. Approximately 120 Hz higher than expected when a subject is concentrating on a task.

Ciara's arms burst out of the fabric straps, and she leapt upright. Bending down, she unhooked her legs. Dr Wang staggered back in shock and dropped the syringe. He steadied himself by leaning against the MRI machine.

Ciara bounded across the room. She towered over the cowering researcher, who seemed to age abruptly. "I…I was joking," he stammered. "I'm too old for such things. It was just part of the experiment. I wanted to see if it would have an effect. And it did, Ciara. Look at the readings." His shaking arm pointed to the EEG machine.

"What happened to you calling me a prisoner?"

Ciara grabbed the old man by his striped necktie and pulled him upwards, choking him. "Tell me what I want to know, and I won't hurt you."

Dr Wang tried to pull away, but Ciara was far too strong. His shoulders slumped. "Of course! Of course! Anything you like."

"What is this lab called?"

"Harbin Vetney Research Institute." In his haste, Dr Wang stumbled over the word veterinary.

Ciara frowned. "They sent me to an animal lab?"

"All experimental research is tested on animals initially. It's safer that way."

"So, is this a level 4 biosafety lab?"

"Yes! Yes! One of only two in China. The other is in Wuhan."

"Was a man called James Fernley a prisoner here?" She thought he was, but she'd better double-check. Her plan counted on being in the same place Mr Fernley had been.

Dr Wang made a strange ummmm sound like he was playing for time. This was a question he didn't want to answer. He seemed to realise that he should have played dumb immediately and reluctantly said, "Yes! But he escaped before we could test him properly."

"You used him as a human guinea pig. Where is the substance you gave him stored?"

Dr Wang's jaw dropped in shock. Thick strands of saliva dangled from the sides of his mouth. To think this man wanted to…Ciara pushed the thought out of her mind.

When no answer came, Ciara loosened her grip on his tie. Dr Wang had been pulling away from her but, with the sudden release, flew backwards across the lab. He crashed into the desk, shunting it back a few centimetres.

Ciara strode forward and stopped just in front of him. "Please don't make me repeat myself."

Finally, Dr Wang said, "In the freezer that stores the level 4 viruses." He hurriedly took off his ID card and shoved it into Ciara's hand. "This pass will open the door to all of the labs. Go now, and I won't raise the alarm until you are far away from here."

Ciara placed the plastic ID card around her neck. It might open the doors, but no one would be fooled by the photograph. "Where is the freezer that stores the level 4 viruses?"

"Along the corridor outside of this room. It is the last lab on the right."

Ciara held up Dr Wang's ID card. "Will this pass get me in?"

"Yes! But you won't be able to get into the freezer."

Ciara bent down and picked up the syringe. "Why won't I be able to get into it?"

"It can only be unlocked by the retina scanner."

Dr Wang looked pitiful now. Gone was the malevolence. "Will your eye open the freezer?"

Dr Wang cowered away from Ciara. "I'm not going to scoop out your eye." She visualised that action and winced at the thought.

"No! Only the Institute Director can open that freezer."

Ciara grabbed Dr Wang by his necktie and tightened it. "You better not be lying to me!"

"I'm not! I'm not! I swear."

Dr Wang looked shaken. Ciara could tell he was telling the truth, so she released him. "Where do I find the Director?"

"His office is down the corridor. Next to the lab with the deadly viruses."

Ciara plunged the syringe into Dr Wang's thigh. The needle went straight through the fabric and into the muscle. It would take around three minutes for the paralysis to take effect. He would be unable to move for the next two hours. She would be gone by then.

Ciara riffled through his desk, hoping to find a pistol. She picked up a letter opener, held it in her hand for a moment, and then put it back down again. Turning, Ciara picked up the scalpel lying on the floor by the EEG machine and slid it up her sleeve. Realising that Dr Wang's phone was still recording, she collected it and headed out of the lab.

The Harbin Institute of Veterinary Research is a vast complex with multiple large grey buildings, each five stories high. Walkways are lined with trees separating the buildings, and the place is styled much like a university campus. With 566 staff members, the research centre was not the kind of place an English girl could sneak around.

As soon as Ciara left the neuroscience lab, she knew it would be difficult to find her way around. The corridor was blandly uniform with a cream-tiled floor, white walls and fluorescent lights set into the ceiling every few feet. Several white fireproof doors lined the passage, but there were no windows, and the signs were written in Chinese.

Ciara should have asked Dr Wang more questions. She had no idea which building she was in or what floor. She didn't even know if it was the middle of the day or night. The clomp of heavy-soled shoes on a tiled floor rang out. Although it was difficult to pinpoint the source due to an echo, it could only have come from a corridor to the right.

Ciara retreated back into the neuroscience lab. After a great deal of effort, she managed to pull Dr Wang's white lab coat from his inert body. In the process, she noticed his watch said 20:05 hours. Would the Director still be in his office working at this late hour? She imagined most people would have gone home.

Walking over to a closet, Ciara opened the door. On its back hung Dr Wang's coat and a grey cashmere scarf. Ciara carefully fashioned the scarf into a hijab to hide her blonde hair. Then she put on the white lab coat.

Feeling more confident in her disguise, Ciara left the lab for the second time. She followed it, passing several doors and a couple of empty corridors. When she reached the Director's office, she tried the handle. The door was locked. She tapped the ID card against the plastic card reader, but it turned red.

She knocked on the door and waited. She heard a female voice call out in Mandarin. Not knowing what to do, she said nothing. The door automatically unlocked, and the light on the card reader turned green. She pushed open the door and walked in.

The room looked like any other anteroom. It had a thick, plush grey carpet and expensive dark wood furniture. A large painting of a Chinese man in a suit and wearing a red tie filled one wall. A beautiful woman in her late twenties was sitting at a desk and looking at Ciara expectantly.

"你是谁. (Nǐ shì shéi)."

"I'm sorry! Do you speak English?"

The woman seemed irritated. "Who are you?"

Ciara walked over to the desk. "I'm the new intern on exchange from the UK. I was due to meet the Director earlier, but my flight was delayed."

The woman pressed the intercom button and said something in Chinese. Her eyes never left Ciara's. A male voice, deep and rich, replied in English. "Send her in."

Ciara walked into the sizable office. An enormous television screen dominated the room. A man wearing a white shirt and a red tie stood on the far side. A Type 11/QSZ 11 semi-automatic handgun was in his hand, and it was pointed at Ciara.

"Please come and sit down, Ms Alinac." Then he noticed the ID card around her neck. "Or should I say, Dr Wang? I hope you haven't hurt our resident neuroscientist."

Ciara's mind raced—desperately trying to find a way out of this mess. She put her hands in her pockets and felt the two sodium bicarbonate tablets. "Of course not. What kind of girl do you take me for?"

Ciara popped the tablets in her mouth and felt them start to fizz. As soon as she sat down, she rolled her eyes into her head and faked convulsions. Her body jerked while foam leaked from the sides of her mouth, and she shook uncontrollably.

The Institute Director's calm composure disappeared like the pea in a three-shell magic trick. He rushed over to Ciara, fearful his prize was going to die. He shook Ciara's shoulders, one hand still holding the pistol. "Are you having a vision?"

The scalpel slid down from her wrist and into her hand. Ciara felt the cold steel handle reach her fingers and plunged the weapon into the Director's upper arm. He screamed and reeled back, dropping the gun. By the time he had recovered, Ciara was pointing the pistol at this chest.

"Tell your secretary to go home immediately. If you say anything else, I will shoot you, then shoot her."

The Director leaned over and pressed the intercom button on his desk. "现在回家 (Xiànzài huí jiā)."

Ciara put her finger to her lips and walked over to the door, where she listened intently. All the while, she pointed the gun at the Director's chest. When she was satisfied that the secretary had left, she beckoned the man over.

Ciara opened the door and gestured for him to go out first. All the while, he kept his left hand over his wound. Blood dripped through his splayed fingers, staining his white shirt in red. He moaned softly as he walked past Ciara.

"Head to the lab with the ultra-low temperature freezer. If you try anything, I will shoot you in the head."

The lab was brightly lit and smelt of ammonia. Fortunately, the staff had gone home for the evening, so it was quiet. There was a row of five vertical freezers. Each had a large grey metal box with a vent at the bottom and a retina scanner on the front.

Ciara shoved the Director in the back, and he staggered towards the freezer. "Open each one, now!"

The Director pressed his eye to the camera and turned a large lever. He repeated this several times, and each freezer door swung open. "Sit over there," said Ciara indicating a stool at one of the countertops.

The man's misery was obvious. "Are you going to kill me?"

"Shut up!" Ciara headed over to the first freezer and looked inside at the rows of small bottles covered in plastic. Each one had a sticker with the black and yellow skull and crossbones symbol. After picking up each bottle in turn, Ciara moved on to the next freezer. It wasn't until the fourth one that she found what she was looking for.

Ciara took out Dr Wang's phone and recorded the lab and the Director. Then she took a vial from the freezer and showed it to the Director. "Where is the machine that prints these labels?"

The man looked shocked when he read what virus it contained. "W-why?" he stammered.

"I want to change the label. If I get searched at customs, I want it to say something else." Ciara's tone was full of impatience. "Where is the label machine?"

"Over there in the corner."

Ciara levelled the pistol at him. "Come over here so I can keep an eye on you. If you make any sudden movements, I will kill you."

Ciara removed several bottles from the freezer and replaced the labels. Some she put back, and some she pocketed. Then Ciara searched through the cupboards until one revealed some empty vials. Carefully, she filled them with water before turning her gaze back to the Director.

"What is the best way out of here?"

"There's no way out of here. You're two levels below ground, and armed security men are positioned at every stairwell."

Ciara couldn't have a shootout with armed security men. A pistol against machine guns was not a fair fight. She took the still-recording phone out of her pocket and carefully entered a phone number. Nothing happened! She looked at the phone and saw that there was no signal.

Ciara swore under her breath. "Where are the stairs?"

"Take the corridor on the left. Go all the way to the end and turn right. It's along that passage. But as I said, there are two armed security guards—"

"If you're lying to me—"

"I'm not!"

Ciara had to get past security, but only after getting rid of the Director. "Head down the corridor to the neuroscience lab."

When they got to the lab, Dr Wang was still lying motionless where she had left him. Ciara picked up the broken fabric straps. They'd been partially cut. She'd only had a few fibres to snap when she'd ripped herself free. She smiled to herself—maybe she wasn't alone.

After tying up the Director, Ciara picked up the phone handset on the desk and pressed 9 to get an outside line. It didn't work. She considered questioning the Director, forcing him to tell her, but a better idea popped into her head. When Dr Wang had leered at her, she'd noticed his yellow teeth and smelled his stale breath. He was a smoker, and where there's a smoker, there's a lighter.

Ciara picked up the notebook she'd used before and tore out some pages. Using the lighter she found on Dr Wang's desk, she lit them under the sprinkler in the ceiling. An alarm rang out, breaking the silence. Water cascaded down from the ceiling putting out the small fire. Ciara ran for the door and down the corridor on her right.

Despite the deafening alarm, she heard footsteps and ducked into a room. She knew it would be empty. Anyone still working would be making their way to the exit. She listened as a man's boots thundered past the door. It was then she noticed a fire extinguisher.

Ciara took out Dr Wang's phone, opened the web browser and typed in, "Translate, help me! The fire is out of control in Chinese." The website translated the message into simplified Chinese. She clicked on the listen to icon, and the phone pronounced the message. Several attempts later, she could pronounce the Chinese almost perfectly.

Ciara picked up the fire extinguisher and headed out of the room. She ran towards the stairs and saw a man holding a QCQ-171 submachine gun. Keeping the fire extinguisher in front of her face to hide her nationality, she repeatedly shouted, "帮我. 火势已经失控 (Bāng wǒ. Huǒshì yǐjīng shīkòng)."

She shoved the fire extinguisher at the man and ran up the stairs once he'd taken it from her. She never saw his face, which meant he never saw hers. The stairs led to a deserted corridor, which meant no one was working late or they had all evacuated.

It took several minutes to find the stairway. Ciara turned a corner and nearly walked in front of the two guards. She quickly backed away and out of their sight. They were busy talking to the fire crew who had just arrived. The trick with the fire extinguisher wasn't going to work. If she hid her face from one, the other would see her.

Now they'd been given instructions, the fire crew started moving in Ciara's direction. Would they call out to the guards when they saw her? She'd gotten past Dr Wang, the Director, and distracted the guards on the previous floor. Had she'd come so far to fall at the last hurdle?

Ciara pulled the phone out of her pocket and put it to her ear. Turning her back on the oncoming fire crew, she pretended to be deep in conversation. She repeated the Chinese word for yes, several times, and the fire crew ran right past her. The last person called out, "立即离开大楼 (Lìjí líkāi dàlóu)."

Ciara had no idea what it meant but guessed he was telling her to leave. "是的先生 (Shì de xiānshēng)," she called out. Turning Dr Wang's scarf into a hijab had been a lifesaver.

As Ciara put the phone back in her pocket, she noticed that the signal strength had one bar. She dialled the number she had tried previously. This time she heard it ring.

A female voice was emitted from the phone's speaker. "Are you alright, Ciara?"

"Fine, I'm one floor below ground level, but I have two guards with submachine guns to get past."

"Send me your GPS location."

In less than five seconds, Ciara had opened the map app and shared her GPS coordinates. "I've sent it. I assume you're nearby?"

"I'm just outside your building. Give me three minutes."

Ciara waited in the corridor, feeling very conspicuous. She didn't like relying on someone else to get her out of this fix but didn't know what else to do.

It wasn't long before voices drifted from the stairway, and then light footsteps moved towards her. She turned her back and pretended to be on the phone again.

"I see you've converted to Islam," said Zixin.

Ciara enveloped her friend in a great hug as tears rolled down her cheeks. She'd never be so relieved to see someone in her entire life.

Zixin shoved a khaki bag at Ciara. "Put this on quickly."

Inside the bag was a dark blue uniform and helmet, identical to Zixin's. She was about to protest that she didn't look Chinese when she spotted an ID card like the one pinned on her friend's jacket. The name read, 'Anya Svetlana'.

"Russians from Vladivostok join us occasionally. It's on the border with China, and the people have a similar ideology." Zixin straightened Ciara's uniform and hat. "Head up and shoulders back. Walk behind me and look straight ahead."

Ciara shoved the lab coat and the scarf into the canvas bag. "Thank you, Zixin."

Her friend nodded and turned on her heel. As they approached the two security guards, Zixin barked something at them, and they straightened up. They didn't even look at Ciara as she passed them and headed up the stairs.

When they emerged into the main reception area, Ciara could see the entrance. There was a black limousine waiting for them on the road at the front. The first stage of her plan had worked.

Chapter 16
True Colours

Even as they taxied to the runway at Harbin Taiping International Airport, Ciara half expected them to be detained. She needn't have worried. Few people would stop Dr Kim's Gulfstream jet.

Hana sat opposite her on one seat. Next to her was Scottie, whose face looked like a victim's mugshot in a police report. He'd obviously been caught in a fight while they escaped from the school.

Ciara winced when she looked at Scottie's face. "That looks painful."

"Nah! It's worse than it looks," said Scottie.

Ciara looked from Hana to Scottie to Zixin. "Did Sophie, Chan and Mr Fernley get out okay?"

"They're fine," said Hana. "We got nearly all of the students from Halla, Seorak, and Odae out of the school. But not Jiri House."

Ciara didn't want to ask, but she had to know. "Was anybody badly hurt?"

"The odd broken bone but nothing worse than that," said Hana. "I think the Pleiades just wanted some revenge."

The stewardess entered the cabin and checked that they were all strapped in. She told them the plane had just received clearance and was about to take off. The conversation stopped while the engines revved, and the noise became deafening.

When they levelled off, Scottie asked, "Do you think these Pleiades are the Patupaiarehe?"

Scottie seemed worried. The Māori legends had portrayed these supernatural beings as having mana, yet the Pleiades were inhumane. In his place, she'd feel like part of her culture had been taken away. "I don't know," said Ciara. "There are a few things that don't add up."

Scottie seemed to brighten. "Like what?"

"The Pleiades coexisted with the natives in Tahiti," said Ciara. "They tended to avoid the Māori but didn't try to subjugate them."

"Then they caught the European diseases and started to die," said Scottie. "Do you think that affected them?"

"It's possible," said Ciara. "Henry VIII was supposed to be a charming man until a blow to the head from a horse-riding accident caused brain damage. After that, his personality changed."

"That's interesting, Sophie," said Zixin, emphasising the word Sophie. "Please tell us some more facts."

Ciara was about to say something back, but Hana interrupted them. "Enough myths and legends. Are you going to tell us what happened in the lab?"

"Yeah!" said Zixin. "How did you escape?"

Ciara looked quizzically at her friend. "What do you mean? You came in and smuggled me out."

"I meant before that. You were already free and had the virus."

"That's because you weakened the straps holding my arms down. I could never have pulled my arms free if they hadn't been cut."

Zixin looked confused. "What are you talking about? I didn't even know which building you were in."

Ciara thought back to when Dr Wang had removed the lid from the syringe and leered at her. She'd almost blacked out and saw the scalpel cutting the fabric.

"I think I made the neuroscientist who held me captive cut the straps."

"How?" said Zixin. "Please stop making statements you don't explain."

"I think I controlled him with my mind."

Her friends stared at her intently—worried expressions on their faces. Were they frightened of her now?

"Don't look at me like that," said Ciara. "I'm not one of them. I don't know how it happened, and I couldn't do it again."

Nobody said anything for several seconds. Ciara felt like an outsider again. A misfit not to be trusted.

"That's awesome," said Zixin. "Once this mess is over, we'll have so much fun. Imagine the pranks we can pull."

Ciara could have kissed Zixin for saying that. Nobody said anything else, so she continued her story. When she told them about stabbing the Institute Director, Zixin interrupted. "When did you become so badass?"

"Hartley killed two of the Māori and ran his sword through Moody. I guess it's changed me."

After the story was finished, Ciara said, "I know it's not important, but I have to know what you did with 200 students after exiting the bunker."

"I phoned the bus company and told them to send four buses," said Hana. "We walked the ollie trail that comes out of the bottom of snake road. They picked us up from there."

Once again, Ciara marvelled at Dr Kim's influence in Korea. Who else could phone a bus company in the middle of the night and get four drivers out of bed without notice?

"Zixin told us you wanted to be captured and taken to Harbin," said Scottie. "Isn't it about time you explained why?"

"Yeah, that reminds me, Zixin," said Ciara. "Why did you have to wallop me? Couldn't you have just injected me with an anaesthetic?"

"I didn't have to hit you," said Zixin, "but I wanted to." She laughed at her own joke. "It was necessary to make the MSS agent believe I was one of them. Besides, I've been knocked out a dozen times that way. It's part of unarmed combat training."

Interrupting before the conversation turned ugly, Hana asked, "How did you know you'd be taken to Harbin? They might have taken you anywhere."

"It was a calculated risk. I couldn't think of anywhere else I'd be sent," said Ciara. "Neuroscience equipment is specialised and expensive. Plus, Fernley had been a prisoner there."

Scottie looked irritated. "You still haven't explained why you wanted to go to the Harbin lab."

"Let's see whether you can figure it out," said Ciara. "What are the Pleiades scared of?"

"Ciara's cooking," said Zixin, referring to the burnt pasta incident in their first week.

Zixin glanced at Scottie and, when she saw his irritated expression, burst out laughing. She put her fist in her mouth to stop herself, but that didn't prevent her body from shaking in amusement. That set Ciara off, and she started giggling uncontrollably. It was probably a reaction to the stress more than the quality of the humour. The more they laughed, the angrier Scottie became.

"Will you two be serious," said Scottie.

Ciara managed to get herself under control. "Can't you guess?"

"I don't know!" said Scottie. "Just tell us already."

"They were frightened of the European diseases," said Hana. "But they are immune now. We gave them the viruses."

"Exactly!" said Ciara. "They had no immunity to it. When one of them got sick, they got disconnected from the collective. It's probably an immune response but getting disconnected from the collective terrifies them."

"But how does that information do us any good?" said Scottie. "As Hana said, they are immune now."

"We didn't give them the smallpox virus because it was eradicated in the late 1970s," said Ciara.

Hana looked horrified and said, "Please don't tell me that's why you went to the lab. You stole the smallpox virus!" She looked at Ciara, who didn't react. "Oh my God. Do you know how deadly that is? And you have it here on the plane?"

Scottie was desperately trying to catch up. "Are you saying Ciara got captured so she could steal smallpox and use it against them?"

Hana turned to Zixin. "Did you know that's why she was going to Harbin?"

Zixin nodded. "But that wasn't the only reason."

Hana put her hands over her face and shook her head back and forth. "And now I'm smuggling the world's deadliest virus into Korea after helping you steal it." She paused, trying to come to terms with what she'd learned.

Suddenly, Hana shouted, "No! Absolutely not. This plane is going straight back to Harbin, where you will return the virus."

She marched towards the pilot's cockpit, but Zixin blocked her way. "Stop! Hear what Ciara has to say first."

Hana tried to shove past Zixin but ended up on her backside. She screamed long and hard, stamped her feet and flailed her arms. It was the first time Ciara had ever seen anyone over the age of five have a tantrum. It would have been comical in other circumstances. Scottie bent down and tried to put his arm around Hana's shoulders. She pushed him, yelling to get off her.

Ciara expected the stewardess to come running, but she didn't. Perhaps this wasn't the first tantrum on this plane.

"Hana," said Ciara. "I need your help to stop a nuclear war. One that will happen soon after your father meets up with the other billionaires."

Ciara waited for Hana to respond, but she just sat on the floor sulking. "Do you think I risked my life for nothing?" said Ciara. I have a plan. "There won't be a smallpox outbreak."

Scottie was crouched beside Hana being careful not to touch her. "I think that you should listen to Ciara. I don't want to live through a nuclear war."

Hana looked up at him. Her eyes were wet, and her cheeks streaked with tears. She sniffed and wiped her face with her sleeve. "Have you seen pictures of smallpox survivors? Their faces are so badly scarred that I can barely look at them. If you can guarantee that smallpox won't get out, I'll help you."

"I give you my word, Hana," said Ciara. "Let me tell you my plan."

Ciara explained why she wanted to be taken to the Harbin bio lab. At first, she'd thought her vision was the lab in Dr Kim's research facility, but that seemed unlikely. When she found out that Dr Kim had used a Chinese company to build the lab, it was clear the vision was the Harbin lab.

Ciara spent ten minutes explaining her plan before saying, "The first step is to leak information about the stolen virus to the press. They'll want proof that we have it, so I videoed the freezer's contents in the Harbin lab. Send them some stills from that footage."

"What are we going to say to them?" asked Zixin.

"I'll write everything down, then whoever makes the call can read it out," said Ciara. "Is everything clear?"

The others nodded their assent.

Ciara stood up. "Before I do anything else, I need to phone my aunt. Is there a phone on this jet?"

"Near the cockpit," said Hana. "The air hostess will show you."

Ciara phoned her aunt and told her everything that had happened. Her aunt confirmed that Dr Kim and a blonde-haired boy were at the research centre but locked away in his office. Ciara explained everything that had happened but wasn't believed, so Hana confirmed the story. Aunt Jean was sceptical but reluctantly agreed to do as she was asked.

The flight time from Harbin to Jeju International Airport was a little over an hour. Before they had even landed, news reports had flooded news channels and social media. The Korean Chronicle ran a story that outlined the main points.

British spy steals smallpox virus from Harbin Veterinary Research Institute.

By Kim Younah

Earlier today, a British intelligence agent broke into a level 4 biosafety lab in Harbin, China and stole three vials of the smallpox virus. Sources suggest that the operative has fled to Jeju Island, South Korea, increasing tensions between the two Asian countries.

Yang Wenqing, Director of the Department of Justice, issued a statement, "This espionage is an act of war. We suspect the United States, South Korea, and the United Kingdom collaborate to undermine our great nation. An investigation is underway, and as soon as it is concluded, we will take swift and decisive action."

Sir Simon Moore, Chief of the UK's Secret Intelligence Service, was asked to respond to Mr Yang's statement. He said, "We wish to assure China that if a British operative was involved in the theft, he did so without our authorisation. We will do all we can to ensure this individual is found and the virus returned." When asked if there was an intelligence agent in Harbin, Sir Simon said, "We can confirm that an operative disappeared in Harbin several weeks ago. We have not heard from him since."

Smallpox killed 300 million people in the twentieth century before it was eradicated in 1978. An outbreak of this deadly disease would be catastrophic in densely populated areas. A stockpile of vaccines is stored at the World Health Organisation headquarters.

The break-in occurred at 20:00 China Standard Time. The Institute Director and a researcher were injured. Both are being treated in a local hospital and are expected to fully recover. Although there was a small fire in a lab, it is believed that this was used as a diversion.

Stock markets have dropped by 5% in the last hour. Global economist, Lee Youngjae, has said that a smallpox outbreak would cause a stock market crash even more significant than Black Monday in 1987.

More on this story as the news breaks…

When they touched down, Chan and Sophie were at the airport to greet them. Ciara reminded the others that they couldn't tell their friends the entire plan. The Pleiades would force them to reveal everything if they went with her to school and got caught.

As soon as they walked out of customs, Chan ran forward and hugged Zixin so tightly that a grunt emitted from her lips.

"Do you know where Mr Fernley is?" asked Ciara.

"He's in the car," said Sophie. "He doesn't want to be seen in public."

Ciara addressed Chan and Sophie directly. "Let me quickly explain our plan. You will be risking your lives, so you will need to decide whether you want to participate." She felt terrible for not telling her friends the whole truth, but it was risky for them to know.

Chan had gone a little pale but looked earnest. "I'm in! This seems to be the only way to stop the Pleiades."

"Me too!" said Sophie. "It's this or nuclear war."

The plan required Scottie, Hana, and Zixin to travel separately. They had a stop-off to make, and then they would go to Geumdo Island. Ciara would travel with Chan and Sophie back to school.

They wished each other good luck. Zixin hugged her boyfriend. "Don't go taking any stupid risks. If anything happened to you…" Then she turned on Ciara. "Keep him safe, or you'll wish you were never born."

"If anything happens to him, it will happen to me too, so I won't be around for your retribution."

Despite the harsh words, Ciara gave her friend a hug. "Everything depends on you, Zixin. You've trained for this your entire life."

Ciara turned to Hana and Scottie. "Don't act until you receive a text message from me, or you've waited 48 hours."

Hana, Scottie, and Zixin headed for one of the black range rovers waiting for them. It would take them to a location unknown to Chan and Sophie before going to Moseulpo harbour. A boat would take Hana and Scottie to Dr Kim's research centre on Geumdo Island.

Ciara, Sophie, and Chan walked over to one of the range rovers. A man wearing a baseball cap and sunglasses got out of the front passenger seat. Ciara ran towards him, the water in her open bottle sloshing from side to side and hugged him. Her water went everywhere, and they both got wet.

Mr Fernley stepped back, trying to brush the water from his clothes.

"Sorry, Sir," said Ciara looking sheepish. "It's been such a nightmare, and I never thought I'd see you again."

"I saw in the Korean Chronicle that you've been busy, Ciara." He was attempting to sound relaxed, but Ciara could hear the tension in his voice.

"Just what do you intend to do with a smallpox virus?"

Fernley sounded a little confrontational. Ciara gave a quick glance at Sophie and Chan. Subconsciously, she was looking to them for support. "When I was William Hartley, the Pleiades told me that their people died in Tahiti from diseases brought by the European sailors. The Pleiades are protected against those viruses apart from smallpox because it was eradicated. You told me that the lab in Harbin held the smallpox virus, so Zixin arranged for me to be captured and taken there."

Mr Fernley turned around in his seat to see Ciara clearly. The sense of unease she felt the first time she met him returned.

"You plan to release a virus that has killed hundreds of thousands of people. I'm beginning to think you're more of a danger to the world than they are."

"I'm not planning on releasing the virus anywhere except Pleiades House. The virus will disperse if I can release it into the ventilation system. As long as we stop anyone entering their boarding house, the virus won't spread."

"They've seen the news reports and will know you're planning something. To counter you, they'll take hostages into their boarding house."

"But we can free them once they're sick," said Ciara. "I think that when one of them gets ill, they get disconnected from the collective and lose their ability to control people."

"And those hostages will have smallpox," said Fernley. "They'll die too."

"I'll break into Pleiades House and take them to one of the other boarding houses," said Ciara. "If they get infected, we'll take them to a hospital."

"There is no treatment for smallpox," said Fernley. "Even those that survive will be disfigured for life."

Ciara was getting angry now. "Better that than living through a nuclear war. People are going to die one way or another."

Nothing was said for the next few miles. The range rover with Zixin, Hana, and Scottie pulled off the 1135 dual carriageway. Ciara had been expecting it, and was hoping nobody would notice.

"Where are they going?" asked Fernley.

"They're getting some pizza," said Ciara. "There's a great restaurant that Hana knows. She said they'll meet us in Seorak House."

The speed limit on the main road was 80 km/h, but the range rover exceeded that by some margin. They'd reach the school in 15 minutes.

"Mr Fernley! I think you and I should try to rescue the hostages," said Ciara. "We can use the element of surprise."

Fernley shook his head slowly. "The Pleiades expect us to do that. It really isn't much of a plan, Ciara."

"It doesn't have to be much of a plan," said Ciara. "They can't control us, and it will be too late when they realise."

"I admire your optimism, but we're dealing with a species who have successfully enslaved other races."

"With or without you, I'll rescue the hostages."

"I'll help you too," said Sophie.

"Me too," said Chan.

The car had just driven by the Osulloc Tea Museum and made the final turn before the school entrance.

"Pull over," said Fernley. The driver pulled into a layby. Fernley turned around and pointed a pistol at the three students. "I can't let you release a smallpox virus in the school."

"Mr Fernley, why are you pointing a gun at us?" asked Sophie.

"Give me your bag," said Fernley. "I assume the virus vials are in there."

Ciara grimaced. "Don't do this, Mr Fernley. If they start a nuclear war, it will be mass genocide."

Fernley turned the gun on Sophie. "Give me the bag, or I will shoot your friend."

Ciara looked in the rear-view mirror. The angle let her see straight into the driver's terrified eyes. She willed him to attack, but the feeling she'd had in the Harbin lab wouldn't come. Reluctantly, she shoved the bag at Fernley.

"Drive into the school and stop outside Seorak House," said Fernley.

A short while later, Ciara, Chan, and Sophie found themselves locked in the electronics room. This was where the younger students left their mobile phones, tablets and computers before bed. Prior to imprisoning them, they'd been searched to ensure they didn't have any more vials of the virus. Their phones had been confiscated, and Ciara felt naked without hers.

There wasn't much space in the electronics room. Just a kitchen table with four chairs and a series of pigeon holes for storing students' phones and computers. The three friends sat at the table. Although it was late and they were tired, they needed to discuss what had happened.

"I still don't understand why Mr Fernley is doing this," said Sophie.

"He's doing this because he is one of them," said Ciara.

"I thought you said he was enslaved by them when he was a boy," said Chan. "Why would he help them? It's not Stockholm syndrome, is it?"

"No, it isn't," said Ciara. "He lied to us, and I believed him."

"Hmmm!" Chan seemed doubtful. "He doesn't look like them."

"That's because they were in stasis, and he wasn't. He's at least 250 years older than they are," said Ciara.

"But he's ginger, and they're blonde," said Chan.

"He wasn't always ginger," said Ciara. "He called himself Tua and saved William Hartley's life in Papua New Guinea."

"But he told us he left Tahiti in 1789 on the HMS Bounty," said Sophie. "How could he save Hartley's life?"

"He lied," said Ciara. "He left on the Endeavour as Tupaia's servant."

"Zixin said Fernley helped get the students out of the school." Chan's face lit up slightly when he said his girlfriend's name. Ciara couldn't help but smile despite their predicament.

"I'm pretty sure he didn't help us," said Ciara. "Just after we travelled along the bunker tunnel, I realised that the maintenance men were MSS operatives. I blurted it out, and a few seconds later, we heard a cry because he'd alerted the Pleiades."

Ciara stood up and stretched. Her body was still stiff from being tied down in a chair. "When he left Seorak House with you, Sophie. What did he do?"

"I don't know, really," said Sophie. "He disappeared."

"I'm guessing that he went to stop the students of Jiri House from escaping," said Ciara.

"I suppose that makes sense," said Chan. "I never understood why he helped Ciara find them. If I was their slave, I would have left them in stasis forever."

"I thought he did it because he saw her as a great-granddaughter," said Sophie. "I don't think we could have released the Pleiades without his help."

"I suppose now we know he's one of them, it makes sense. But why didn't he travel to New Zealand to free them?" said Chan. "Why did he need you?"

"He told me that he got sick with tuberculosis, which meant he was disconnected from the collective. The Pleiades told me that everyone on Tahiti had died, so they thought he was dead. I'm guessing he sailed with the Endeavour to join them."

"That still doesn't explain why he didn't go to the cave once they had the virus samples," said Sophie.

"He didn't know where they were," said Ciara. "I don't think he knew about William Hartley until much later."

"Is Mr Fernley part of their collective now?" asked Chan.

"I don't know, but I think not," said Ciara. "They're clones, and over the past 250 years, his brain would have changed a lot. I am sure he can communicate with them, but he doesn't have the same ability to control people's minds."

"Why do you say that?" asked Chan.

"If he had the same abilities, he would never have been caught by the Chinese in Harbin," said Ciara. "I think that he can control people for a second or two. He did that when saving William Hartley, and I think he did the same to escape the bio lab."

"Maybe their mind control is directly proportional to the number of minds in the collective," said Sophie. "Fernley is on his own, so his abilities are limited."

"I think we better try and get some sleep," said Ciara. "Things are going to get interesting tomorrow."

Chapter 17
Return to Geumdo Island

It was 5:30 am when Ciara woke up. It had been an uncomfortable night because the room was tiny. They'd turned the table on its side, stacked the chairs and shoved them in the corner. She gave Sophie a gentle shake, and her friend stirred.

"What time is it?" asked Sophie.

The sound of Sophie's voice woke Chan, who looked up bleary-eyed. The room was pitch black, with no window to let through the light.

"Turn on the light, Chan," said Ciara. "You're nearest."

Chan staggered towards the light switch, and Ciara heard the sound of furniture being shunted. Chan swore under his breath. There was a click, and the room was bathed in artificial light, causing them all to squint.

"Why are you making us get up?" asked Sophie. "I've only had around four hours of sleep."

"We need to talk," said Ciara.

The three students dragged the chairs and righted the table. Once everything was back to normal, they sat down.

"When we met you at the airport, you asked where Mr Fernley was," said Sophie. "You knew he was one of them."

"I was 99% certain but hoped I was wrong. I realised Fernley lied to me when I saw him rescue William Hartley in Papua New Guinea. I also couldn't understand how he escaped from Harbin Institute without help. I know he's a secret agent, but they knew that too. He still has some mind control abilities, but they're limited. Still, it was enough for him to break free and avoid recapture."

"So why did you let him capture us?" asked Chan.

Ciara shook her head and then pointed to her ear. She was trying to convey that there might be a recording device in the room.

"Do either of you have fake phones?"

Both Chan and Sophie shook their heads. It was a stupid question because Grade 11s didn't need to hand in their electronics at night. "One of the Grade 10 students, Mina Kim, has one that doubles as a storage device. She hides her cigarettes in it then hands it in at night, so she's not tempted to smoke."

Ciara pulled out Mina's phone. It was incredibly realistic, and momentarily, she worried it was real. After several seconds of squeezing and twisting the phone, it opened. Inside were three cigarettes, two matches, and a card with a lighting strip. Ciara lit a match and cupped her hands around it until there was a decent flame before holding it under the sprinkler sensor.

The door unlocked with a satisfying click. "The building is on fire. Please make your way to the nearest exit," bellowed a female voice.

"Follow me," shouted Ciara, making sure she could be heard over the combination of siren and announcement.

They ran out of the boarding house and headed for the nearest forest. They needed to sit down and plan their next steps. As they ran across one of the paths that circumvent the school, they saw one of the teachers out jogging. He was a short, wiry man wearing a red tracksuit.

"It's Mr McGreggor," said Sophie.

They ducked into the forest but heard his booming voice, "You three! What do you think you're doing?"

Ciara called from the forest. "Mr McGreggor, it's us. Ciara, Sophie, and Chan. Could you please come and talk to us?"

The PE teacher jogged over. He wasn't even out of breath. "If they see you three, there'll be hell to pay."

"We've just escaped from them," said Chan. "That's why the alarm is sounding."

Mr McGreggor looked worried. "If you defy them, we will suffer." He paused for the briefest moment. Ciara opened her mouth to speak, but he interjected. "Come to think of it, I thought you three escaped."

"We did, but we've come back to stop them," said Ciara. "Would you please tell us what happened yesterday? You know, after the breakout."

Mr McGreggor went as white as a sheet. "They hung the men in maintenance uniform and one of the teachers." His voice cracked when he said, teachers. It was like he couldn't bring himself to say their name. "And they made us watch. The bastards!"

"I'm sorry, Sir," said Ciara.

"Sorry, Sir," mumbled Chan.

Then after a delay, Sophie echoed their sentiments. "Sorry, Sir."

Mr McGreggor seemed to have regained some composure. "They've taken three students into their boarding house as prisoners. One of them is a teacher's kid. If any teachers or students resist, they'll kill them, so you need to stop what you're doing."

"In that case, we'll leave immediately," said Ciara.

"No!" said McGreggor. "You need to go back to where you escaped from. They've taken over the surveillance cameras. If they spot you, they'll kill the children."

"It's too late for that," said Ciara. Mr Fernley and one of the Pleiades were walking towards Sereok House.

"Turn yourself in," said McGreggor. "Tell them the alarm went off, and you left the building because you were worried about a fire."

There was a pleading tone in the teacher's voice. He was clearly terrified, and Ciara was concerned he was about to turn them in.

"If we give ourselves up, they'll kill us," said Ciara. "Do you want our deaths on your conscience?"

Ciara pulled on Sophie's arm. "Come on! We need to get away from here."

The three friends headed deeper into the forest, leaving Mr McGreggor rooted to the spot. Once they'd moved out of sight, they sat down on a large volcanic rock.

"It was lucky that Fernley locked us in the electronics room," said Chan. "What are the chances of knowing Mina Kim stores her cigarettes and matches in a fake phone?"

"Fernley could have locked us in any room, and we would have escaped. I still have the lighter I took from Harbin lab."

"Then why didn't you use that?" asked Sophie.

"I was trying to impress you both. It was pretty cool when I found Mina's matches."

"You think this is a game?" yelled Chan unexpectedly. "We could have been killed. They've already murdered several people. We're lucky to be alive." His face had gone red and blotchy, caused by histamine release. Mr McGreggor's news they hanged one of the teachers may have tipped him over the edge.

"I'm sorry, Chan," said Ciara. "I spent so long formulating this plan that I've become detached from reality."

"Or you're just like them," said Chan vehemently. "You don't have any emotions."

Sophie looked at Chan appealingly. "You don't mean that. Ciara has risked her life several times to stop them. An unfeeling person wouldn't do that."

"Fine! But I want to know exactly what the plan is. You could have told us Fernley was one of them for a start."

"I couldn't tell you everything. The Pleiades might have forced you to say what we were doing. You have to understand that it was necessary."

Chan said nothing, but his shoulders relaxed. The alarm that had been sounded the entire time finally stopped.

"I never stole the smallpox virus because it is too dangerous. I took three empty vials and filled them with water." Chan opened his mouth to speak, but Ciara held up her hand. "I printed some smallpox labels and stuck them on, then relabelled the smallpox vials in the freezer to make it look they were missing."

"That's brilliant," said Sophie. "You should be a magician with your misdirection."

"I spilt water on Fernley yesterday to make him think there was smallpox in it," said Ciara. "It will throw him off-balance, and he might start doubting himself."

"We must assume they have someone watching the CCTV footage," said Ciara. "I need to sneak into their boarding house to rescue the students, but I don't want them to see me coming. Is there a way you can turn off the CCTV?"

Sophie scratched her chin. A clear sign she was thinking. "The server room is the only place to turn them all off, but that's locked. And before you suggest another fire alarm, the room is fireproofed, so it won't automatically open."

"Fernley unhooked the cable at the back of the camera, and that stopped the transmission," said Ciara. "Couldn't we do that?"

"There are a hundred cameras, so we'd almost certainly get spotted," said Sophie. "I could disconnect the switches. That would block out a dozen cameras in one go. Besides, we only need to turn off the cameras in and around the boarding houses."

"Do you know where the switches are for the boarding houses?" asked Chan. "Surely they're in a locked room?"

"Some of the switches are inside the boarding houses," said Sophie. "They connect directly to the internal cameras. A switch room for the external CCTV is located in the main building, and isn't locked. The cleaners leave it unlocked so they can sleep in there."

Both Ciara and Chan looked at Sophie as if she was mad. Noticing their reaction, Sophie said, "There's a kettle, blankets and a camping mat. They take a break or nap when they're supposed to be working. I woke one of the cleaners once. He swore at me, so I made a quick exit."

"Surely that isn't safe," said Chan.

Ciara shook her head in disbelief. "Really? We're about to risk our lives to stop an alien race from starting World War III, and you're concerned about electrical safety."

Chan looked sheepish. "When you put it like that…"

The three students walked alongside the forest and headed to the switch room. The place was utterly deserted. They'd gone into an office to grab a pair of scissors on the way. Sophie unplugged the cables from the switch and cut them so they couldn't be plugged back in.

"They'll figure out the cables have been unplugged when the monitors go blank," said Sophie. "We better get out of here quickly."

"I suggest you hide out in Seorak House," said Ciara. "It will be the last place they look."

Chan looked at Sophie questioningly, then said, "We didn't come back here to hide." Sophie nodded in agreement.

Ciara really didn't want an argument. They'd started the clock ticking by taking out the surveillance. She needed to act now. She said, "At the moment, the Pleiades still have their abilities. If they spot us, they can make you attack me. Wait until they get sick, then they'll be separated from the collective and lose their abilities."

Chan looked at Ciara unhappily, then shrugged. "Alright! We'll do as you ask, but only if you agree to tell us when they are vulnerable. Then we'll come and help."

Chan and Sophie headed towards Seorak House, leaving Ciara contemplating her approach. She knew that a large nutmeg grew at the back of the Pleiades House. The tree was over 600 years old, and its thick branches might provide a route to the second floor of the boarding house.

Ciara managed to make her way to her destination without being seen. Climbing the tree was straightforward, and one of its thick branches almost reached a balcony. She walked to the point of the branch closest to the building to assess whether it was feasible to jump the gap.

There was no point in coming this far and changing her mind. Ciara took two steps back, swallowed hard, and leapt. Her ankle rolled on a knot just as she took off, and she hit the rail with an almighty thunk. There was a sharp pain in her ribs, but Ciara climbed onto the balcony.

The door was double-glazed glass, so Ciara peered through to see an empty room. She turned the door handle and pulled. There was a little give suggesting it was locked but not bolted. The next balcony was close enough to leap across. Was it likely that the door would open?

The hell with stealth! Ciara turned both door handles and pulled the doors with all her might. They swung open, causing her to careen back into the railing. The rib pain intensified, but Ciara managed to stifle a cry. She was in and hadn't been too noisy. She had to disconnect the CCTV before trying to find the hostages?

Ciara moved silently through the bedroom and peered into the corridor. She could see a camera positioned to view the entire space. There was no way to get past without being seen. She might be mistaken for one of them with her tall stature and blonde hair.

Making sure that she kept her head down, Ciara strode purposefully along the corridor and towards the stairs. There was a utility room on the first floor, so she assumed that was where the switches were stored. The sound of a chair sliding on a tiled floor drifted up from below. She paused, listening intently for the sound of someone heading towards the stairs.

Hearing nothing, Ciara descended the stairs quietly. When she reached the foyer, she glanced around while her heart pounded. If anyone was close by, they must surely hear the boom, boom, boom. The boarding house was silent, almost too quiet.

Ciara began to wonder if they had left. Maybe they had decided to punish the others because of the escape. Was someone being hanged or tortured while she sneaked around accomplishing nothing? The self-doubt wasn't helping, so Ciara decided to push on towards the utility room.

She reached the room and tried the handle. It was locked, but Ciara knew the key was hanging from a nail in the office. To get there, she had to walk through the large common room. The place where they had meetings and gathered. It might be better to check the electronics room for the hostages instead of going to the office.

The electronics room door was open, so that wasn't where the prisoners were being kept. The most likely place was the office, so she headed there. As soon as she walked into the common room, she heard a voice.

"Please come in, Ciara," said Fernley. "We've been waiting for you."

A Korean girl stepped behind her, preventing a retreat into the corridor. Min was a Kendo Master and in her hand was a shinai, a Japanese sword made of bamboo. She was clearly under the Pleiades' control and would be a deadly adversary.

Warily, Ciara moved further into the room, trying to stay out of Min's reach. James Fernley was sitting on a sofa in the middle of the room. Next to him was Eve, the blonde-haired Australian girl whose parents were teachers. Two of the Pleiades were sitting at opposite corners of the room. Ciara could feel minds reaching out, touching hers like tendrils. She pushed them away, and they scowled.

Ciara's rucksack, the one taken from her, had been shoved into the corner of the room. It was half open, with the contents removed. Fernley saw her eyes fall on the bag, and he smiled.

"When did you figure out that we were on opposing sides?"

"I had a vision just after you'd run off to stop the Jiri House students from leaving the school. I saw you save William Hartley's life on the mountain top in Papua New Guinea."

"Ah, yes! That was so long ago I'd nearly forgotten." Fernley had a nostalgic look on his face. "It wasn't the only time I saved his life. That man was forever putting himself in harm's way."

Realisation dawned on her that, but for his intervention, she would never have been born. William Hartley didn't have any children until after the Endeavour returned to England.

"I thought you were infecting me with smallpox when you spilt water on me," said Fernley. Ciara wasn't sure what he meant for a moment, but then she remembered her attempt to rattle him.

Ciara's face must have expressed astonishment, but she said nothing.

Fernley laughed. "I thought it was odd that you split your water bottle over me, so I went straight to the biology lab and tested the liquid. The electron microscope showed no virus particles. I showered and disinfected myself, just in case."

"I have to admit I am extremely disappointed in you, Ciara," said Fernley. "Getting to Harbin was inspired, but your plan to spread smallpox inside the boarding house was very clumsy."

Min stepped forward, and the bamboo sword arced towards Ciara's head. She ducked, but the Kendo Master had been fainting and switched the move to a thrust. The blow struck her solar plexus causing her diaphragm to spasm. The wind was knocked out of Ciara's lungs, and she fell to her knees in pain. Half a second later, she was knocked unconscious by an unseen blow.

When Ciara came around, she had a throbbing in her head. Oh no, she was tied to another chair. What was it with people tying her to furniture? She opened her eyes. The room was exactly as she had left it, except Min was positioned like a terracotta statue at the door.

"What are you going to do with me?"

"We're going to keep you alive for your gifts, Ciara. You're too valuable to waste."

"As soon as you let your guard down, I'll escape again."

Fernley glanced left and right at the Pleiades. It was a look that Ciara couldn't read. One of the Pleiades drank from their blue energy drink, and immediately the other did the same. Fernley smiled at Ciara. "You won't escape because we are about to blind you. It's ironic, really. We'll remove your sight to acquire your second sight."

Fernley handed Eve a small knife, and the young girl walked robotically towards Ciara. Even when she raised the sharp implement to the older girl's eye, it was done with the ease of raising a glass. Ciara scrunched her eyes and braced herself for the excruciating pain that was to come.

Seconds passed—three, then four, and Ciara started to think that Fernley had changed his mind. If she opened her eyes, would the thrust come? A deafening yell of loss and despair filled the room, causing Ciara to jump in panic. Had she been blinded, and it was her making that noise?

As desperately sad as the first, a second cry came from the other side of the room. Ciara turned to see one of the Pleiades sitting on the floor, holding his knees to his chest. He was sobbing and rocking from side to side. The spell that captured Eve had gone, and the young girl moved behind the chair to cut through the cords.

Fernley jumped to his feet, but before Ciara could react, Min leapt forward and struck Fernley an almighty blow across his neck, poleaxing him. In less than ten seconds, the former social counsellor had been hog-tied. He lay unconscious on the floor with arms and legs bound together.

Eve looked to be in shock and was shaking uncontrollably. "I'm so sorry, Ciara," her voice quavered. "I nearly blinded you."

Ciara hugged Eve tightly, and the girl started to sob. "You didn't do anything wrong, and it's over now. We'll take you to your mum and dad."

Still holding on to the sobbing girl, Ciara turned to Min. "Will you take Eve to her parents? It is safe now, but I still need to do one thing."

Min nodded, so Ciara removed Eve's arms from around her and put her hand on the Korean girl's. The two were curled up in a foetal position, moaning softly. It would be some time before they got used to being alone with their own thoughts.

Min pointed to one of them and asked, "What did you do to them?"

Zixin walked into the room dressed in the uniform of the E-neo-Ji delivery person. "I poisoned their drinks with a substance called ricin that Ciara stole from a bio lab in China. Hana contacted the E-neo-Ji CEO, and we went to their factory just outside of Jeju City, and they helped us. We poisoned 96 bottles and had them resealed so they looked untouched. I drove their delivery van to the school and swapped their stores with the tainted drinks."

"What if somebody else drank the energy drinks?" asked Min.

"Yeah, right! Who in their right mind is going to steal their favourite drink? Besides, we have the newly developed antidote, and the poison doesn't kill immediately."

"It obviously acts quickly," said Min. "Look at them. They're curled up in agony.?"

Ciara said, "It's painful, but I think that is the effect of them being disconnected from their hive mind. It seems to be a defence mechanism, which we've seen before. For the first time in their lives, they are alone and can't think independently."

Min looked impressed. "I can't believe you managed to stop them. How did you make sure they were all poisoned simultaneously?" asked Min.

"Scottie noticed that when one drinks, they all do," said Ciara. "We counted on that to ensure they were all poisoned simultaneously. We couldn't get an E-neo-Ji drink to the one with Dr Kim, but he will be incapacitated by fear and loneliness."

"Do you think they've lost their powers permanently?" asked Zixin.

Ciara shrugged. "I'm not 100% sure. Fernley couldn't rejoin the hive mind, and their powers seem to come from applying their collective will. If we give them the ricin antidote, I think they will lose their ability to control others."

"So it's really over!" It was more of a statement than a question.

"Yes!" Ciara walked over to the rucksack Fernley had taken from her and pulled out her phone. "I just need to let Hana and Scottie know they can free Dr Kim."

Ciara sat down on the sofa, feeling exhausted. Fernley started to revive but said nothing. She sat in silence for ten minutes, and then her phone rang. When she looked at the screen, there was a photo of Hana on it.

"Did you free Dr Kim?" said Ciara.

Hana said they'd walked into the private office unopposed. The facial recognition database had an image of her. They found her father handcuffed to a cabinet and weakened because he hadn't eaten for days. The Pleiades boy was incapacitated and didn't even notice them.

Dr Kim took the phone from Hana and asked Ciara about the smallpox virus.

"I took one vial of smallpox from the lab but left it on his jet," said Ciara. "I never wanted to use it but needed a backup if our plan failed. The three vials Fernley took from me were water labelled as smallpox. They were used to misdirect Fernley, so he wouldn't suspect we had poisoned the energy drinks."

"What do we do with them now?" asked Dr Kim. "I assume you've thought this through."

"Ummm," stuttered Ciara. "It really depends on whether you agree."

"Spit it out," said Dr Kim. "You've just saved millions, maybe billions of lives. You can ask for anything you want."

"Take the Pleiades to your lab on Geumdo. Give them the ricin antidote. I don't think the Pleiades will be able to reconnect to their hive mind. Have ships patrol the island to ensure they don't try to leave. They could grow their own crops, and you could drop off supplies using parachutes."

"That might work. Turn Geumdo into Alcatraz but have no face-to-face contact. Yes, that could be the perfect solution. I could exchange supplies for knowledge, and maybe I could make something from this mess."

A security team arrived within 30 minutes and took the Pleiades from the school. They were transported to the harbour, where three small boats were waiting to take them to Geumdo island. Hana and Scottie had taken the ricin antidote with them, so they stayed at the laboratory.

That night there was a celebratory banquet at the school. Dr Kim's private chef and a catering team had been flown in from Seoul. The six friends and Dr Kim sat around a large oak table. A waitress brought a bottle of champagne and poured each of them a glass. Ciara looked at the menu, trying to decide what she should eat. Her thoughts were interrupted.

"A toast to all of you." Dr Kim raised his glass, and the others followed suit. "건배 (geonbae)."

"건배 (geonbae)," they echoed.

Ciara was sad at the loss of Fernley because she had cared for him despite his deceit. He'd saved William Hartley's life in Papua New Guinea, and without him, she would never have been born. He'd also saved her life at the Great Barrier Reef and supported her.

She looked around the table to see everybody was looking at her. It was as though they could read her thoughts. "What? Why are you all staring at me?"

"Fernley is gone," said Dr Kim. "He fell into the sea on the way to Geumdo. His hands and legs were tied together, so he must have drowned. The security team circled the area for ten minutes, but his body wasn't found."

Ciara wasn't sure how she felt about that news. What do you say when the person who tried to blind and enslave you dies? Everyone was staring, waiting for her to say something. She was saved by the sound of her phone ringing.

"Sorry!" said Ciara. "I'll turn it off." As soon as she pulled her phone from her pocket, the ringing stopped. A message said, "Missed call. Withheld Number."

The phone pinged and Ciara received a text message from an unknown person. It read:

"AGGTTTACGACGTACGTAGGTTTTACGACCGTACGTCCCCCGTA CACGTACGTAATTTACGTAACCGTACGTAGGTTTACGGGTACGTACA CCGTACGTGGTTTACGTGGTTACGTATTTACGTACACCGTACGTATT TTTTAC."

Author's Note

This story interweaves fact and fiction, so I will clarify what is real and fantasy out of respect to the various cultures and individuals.

The Global Education City (GEC) and the other locations on Jeju exist. The Gotjawal forest is beautiful, and there was one particular place where I visualised Sanjung Academy.

Marado Island is just off the coast of Jeju and was formally called Geumdo Island, which means Forbidden Island. With regard to Renoir's waterlilies, artists frequently painted over canvases because they often couldn't afford new ones. It seems likely that Renoir did so too.

The main characters are fictional, but I have included two of my students for fun. Dr Sanjung Kim is not based on anyone. There are ten hectobillionaires, but none of them is from Korea. Hicks and Bootie were naval officers, but their interactions with Hartley are fictitious. I used real names for Endeavour's crew and described their adventures as accurately as possible.

A boarding house competition is standard practice in private education. A team of researchers heated 4-methylpyridine, water, and a-cyclodextrin to form a solid. It is possible to bypass the login and password using safe mode with some computers.

Some people do have unknown DNA from an extinct hominid. Scientists are developing the ability to rewrite DNA to store information. Lucid dreamers can control their dreams, and neuroscientists have communicated with individuals while they are dreaming.

You can visit the Minerva Inn in Plymouth. It has a secret compartment under the stairs where former sailors were forced to enlist. The scene where Moody and his friends are shanghaied is fiction, but it might have happened that way. Cook lost 18 men before they set sail from Plymouth, and he shanghaied a replacement in Portugal. Hicks never had a bag of nails, but sailors on the HMS Dolphin did remove the ship's iron nails to trade with Tahitian women.

HMS Endeavour's route is accurate, as are the encounters with the Tahitians. Everything I have described in Tahiti is correct except Moody adding poison to the fish and Princess Aimata warning Hartley. Queen Purea was the ruler of Tahiti. A civil war occurred in the 18 months between Dolphin's departure and Endeavour's arrival. Apparently, there were blonde-haired people on Tahiti when the Dolphin arrived.

The interactions with the Māori were accurately described, except when Bootie and Thomas Dunster were captured. European diseases decimated populations in the pacific. Blackbirding, sending an infected person into a community to spread the disease, was developed to weaken islanders so they could be enslaved.

I have tried to describe the Māori welcome ceremony accurately. The scene with the penny divers was an experience I had when I went to a Māori village. Māori legends mention tall, blonde-haired supernatural beings called the Patupaiarehe. Polynesian navigators used the Pleiades star cluster to navigate their ocean journeys.

Cook's ship ran aground on Endeavour reef, and the scene is relatively accurate except for Hartley being pulled under the sea. The creatures described in the scuba scene all live around the Great Barrier Reef.

Harbin Veterinary Research Institute is one of a handful of level 4 bio labs. Harbin is in northeast China and close to the border of Russia. I have no idea what research they are doing there, but only level 4 labs can store smallpox. Ricin is a potent toxin extracted from castor beans, and there is no antidote. Famously, the Bulgarian defector, Georgi Markov, was assassinated on a street in London with ricin injected from an umbrella.

E-neo-Ji drink is made up, although it wouldn't surprise me if there was a drink called that. The Korean word for energy is 에너지 (eneoji), so I just added the hyphens.